PRAISE
CRAIG CLE

"I swear to god, this is the best book I have read in easily five years... Maybe ten."

Chuck Palahinuk, author of Fight Club

"Craig Clevenger has crafted an unforgettable antihero in John Dolan Vincent. This is an extraordinary debut."

Richard Kelly, director of Donnie Darko

"*The Contortionist's Handbook* gets under your skin like a bacterial infection that irritates raw nerve endings as you devour page after page until you collapse in a filthy heap screaming for more."

Lydia Lunch, singer, poet, and writer

"What sticks out about this remarkable debut are its pitch-perfect shock ending and John Vincent himself – his complex, conflicting mind, original voice and unnervingly self-defeating existence."

Time Out

"A very impressive debut. The reader sees it from the con-artist's perspective, delivered in a snappy, first-person voice that Clevenger writes with assured flair. This is a tightly controlled piece of work with an intriguingly original approach to the genre that marks the author out as one to watch."

Metro

"Clevenger has created a manic monologist whose paranoia-inducing world pulls you in completely."

Seattle Times

Craig Clevenger

THE CONTORTIONIST'S HANDBOOK

DATURA

DATURA BOOKS
An imprint of Watkins Media Ltd

Unit 11, Shepperton House
89 Shepperton Road
London N1 3DF
UK

daturabooks.com
twitter.com/daturabooks
Do you know who I think I am?

A Datura Books paperback original, 2025

Cover by Sarah O'Flaherty
Set in Meridien

ISBN 978 1 91552 336 5
Ebook ISBN 978 1 91552 337 2

Printed and bound in the United Kingdom by CPI Group (UK) Ltd, Croydon CR0 4YY.

9 8 7 6 5 4 3 2 1

"My cigar is not a symbol. It is only a cigar."
– Sigmund Freud

"I kissed her… It was like being in church."
– James M. Cain, The Postman Always Rings Twice

FORWARD

Jacque Lacan tells us that all knowledge is paranoiac. Everything you learn is distorted by your mind; everything you know just hints at everything behind it that is unsayable or unseeable.

All novels are paranoiac, too.

Novels create worlds that aren't real, but you can live there. These lies make the outside world go away and at the same time make everything around you feel more real, more graspable. You can become another person, or at least peek into their skulls in a way the physical world won't permit. The person whose head you are in isn't real – but who is?

If the novel is good, the fact that it's all lies won't stop you from learning the truth from it.

The Contortionist's Handbook is a very good novel. Let's get that out of the way right now. Its antecedents are clear – the noir of Jim Thompson, the literary underground from William Burroughs to Chuck Palahnuk – but it's much more than the sum of its influences. It feels new, even now twenty years later, new and special and so sure of itself. It has that most precious thing a novel can have – unity. Every choice made, from the language and metaphors, the characters, the structure and themes and pacing – all of it feels of a piece; all of it works together. The style is the character is the plot is the theme.

This is the good stuff.

Check the very first line: "I can count my overdoses on one

hand." A strong opening line, one that promises that story and conflict are coming, and that you're meeting a character you want to know more about. But as you read the list of overdoses on the first page don't miss the best bit. I don't want to spoil it. Just count along with the narrator. And keep reading.

Paranoid, yet?

John Dolan, or whatever you want to call the man you are about to meet, lives a life full of lies, lies made possible by an astounding amount of paranoid knowledge the character possesses. He knows how to age paper, how to lie to psychiatrists, the methods the system uses to entrap you, and how to spring those traps and pass through them unmarked. The novel seduces you from the jump with all this secret knowledge – it opens up this hidden world all around us; you feel smarter just being in the company of someone who could ever know all this.

Do I mean our protagonist, or our author?

Yes.

I have never asked Craig Clevenger how much of Dolan's knowledge is real. I don't know if the masterful and intricate details of building a false identity, or the deep insight into the worlds of psychiatry and law enforcement and the criminal underworld are the result of Craig's research and life, or if they are pure fantasy. And Craig, if you're reading this, I don't want to know. It doesn't matter – all that matters is that I believe every world of it while I'm reading.

It doesn't have to be real. It just has to be true.

One thing I learned about writing from reading this book – among many other things – is that you have to let the reader know right away that you know what the fuck you're talking about. Especially when you're making it all up. The secret to it is: don't blink when you're talking to the reader.

This novel doesn't blink. Not once.

I've been praised in my own work for my deep research and knowledge of the worlds I write about, with people granting me deep knowledge of skinhead gangs, criminal families, Hollywood sickos. Sometimes these people will give an example of my research by directly citing something I made up. I don't feel bad about this – it just means I'm doing my job.

I just thank Craig and keep moving.

This is a formative novel for me, as it is for many authors of my age and disposition. I read this book for the first time just as I was learning that I didn't want to be a music journalist, or any type of journalist, anymore. This book came to me at just the right moment – the slap that wakes you from your trance. Here was something new, something with words like muscles, like wires, like knives. Here was a book that showed me that a thing could be crime fiction and something else at the same time. Here was a narrator who was crazy and sane, stupid and smart, all at the same time. Here was a novel full of irony and cynicism and also deep love and romance. Here was a book that was *cool* – a thing I don't feel many novels like this try to be anymore.

I read it over and over again, and I told other people to read it, but I didn't tell enough, so I'm telling you now: read this book. Pass it along. Read Craig's other books too, *Dermaphoria* and his latest one, *Mother Howl*.

Read this novel and you will see the world through new eyes. The world will feel false, full of secrets you can barely see. People living lives you can't imagine, worlds of criminals and junkies and false identities, passwords and con jobs and lies. Maybe you'll even see the secrets in yourself that you can't face, the feelings that you haven't let yourself feel. This is what a good novel does, what this novel does – it wakes you up, it makes you doubt things. It gives you this beautiful paranoia. Lean it. Let it wash over you.

Because just because you're paranoid…

– Jordan Harper

DANIEL FLETCHER

ONE

I can count my overdoses on one hand:

August 1985. Percocet. The 5mg tablets were identical to the 325mg tablets which were identical to the generic laxatives. I was in no shape for fine print. ER, three ounces of ipecac and solid heaves of poisons and binder, thirty-seven hours of cramps and shitting blood.

February 1986. Methocarbamol. Yellow caplets, bright like a child's crayon sunscape. Those five pills stopped my heart and I saw the brain seizure tunnel of light before the EMTs shocked me back alive. They billed me $160 for that jolt.

June 1986. Demerol and thirty-two aspirin reopening the damage I did when I was fourteen.

November 1986. A busy year. Vicodin. Imagine waking up to your morning stomach knot and subsequent rituals:

Shower.

Coffee.

Traffic.

Talk radio.

Hell.

Home.

Drink.

But you remember that it's Sunday. That four-second blast of relief is what Vicodin feels like for six hours. But overdose and you're heaving blanks, a pair of fists wringing your stomach like a damp rag, trails of warm spit hanging from your mouth while you try to move your limbs but can't. Words hit your brain like garbage churning in a breakwater, no order, no connection. *Fingers. Name. Hear.*

February 1987. Darvocet. And a pint of bourbon.

Yesterday, August 17, 1987. Carisoprodol. Comes in a white tablet like a big-ass vitamin, 350 mg of muscle liquefier for those tense, recovering athletes and furniture movers. Too much, and those relaxed muscles include your diaphragm, then your heart. It feels like drowning or a sumo wrestler sitting on your chest. I'd done three rails of blow to keep my heart from stopping before the paralysis set in, but they hadn't been enough.

That's how Rasputin found me. Fourteen pounds of mottled fur, Molly had adopted him after his collision with the passenger-side Bridgestone of a speeding pickup. Rasputin was blind and near toothless from the accident, his remaining incisor jutting out ninety degrees from his mouth. He ate soft food. He would howl and stare at you with two transparent orbs of eye gel, the flaps of dislodged retina hovering inside. I used to shut off the lights and hold him while he purred. Put a flashlight to his face and look through his dead marble eyes and see his brain. Molly got mad when I did that.

I tried to sit up, lift the weight of my ribs from my lungs, but I couldn't. Couldn't curl my fingers or move my lips. Couldn't stop my tongue from sliding backward and clogging my neck. Wanted to sleep but forced myself to *breeeathe*, a mechanical wheeze that cut through my fog. I lay on my back, a lance of orange twilight stabbing me square in the face through a slice of curtain where the gaffer's tape had come loose.

Rasputin yowled for attention and licked my face until his sandpaper tongue burned through my stupor. A loud purring, the noise of a slow- motion wasp in my ear. He settled onto my sternum, sandbag-heavy. The walls of my lungs touched, stayed touching.

Sounds: Door. Handbag hitting the carpet. Rasputin's weight gone and a merciful rush of sweet, sweet air. Molly's voice, *Baby, oh God baby*.

I remember my eyes being peeled open, a blurry face, plaster ceiling over the shoulder. Words, chopped and scattered into a white noise seashell blast of static, shredded phonemes landing in and out of sequence. *President. Are. Much. Day. Name.* The electro-paddle-blast horse kick to my chest and I'm awake beneath nylon gurney straps, breathing into a plastic muzzle and being carried down the flight of stairs outside my front door.

Best I can, I repeat the drill in my head: My name is Daniel Fletcher. I was born November 6, 1961. I had a headache and it wouldn't stop. I had some painkillers. They weren't working and I took too many.

Open my eyes, *Where are you taking me* but my words are a numbed mumble of bloated syllables and spit-foam covered with an oxygen mask. Dream-coma blur: That's not a dark blue medic's jacket, it's a dark blue suit. Then there's Jimmy's face, right over mine. I've got it all wrong, must have lost some hours because they're not taking me down a flight of stairs, they're lowering me into the dirt. Eliminating my position, phasing me out. I'm thinking *At least I'll be asleep when they bury me*, so it could be worse. But then I wonder what they'll do with Molly, and it is worse. Too weak to panic, my eyes collapse into dark.

Here's what happened.

LOS ANGELES COUNTY DEPARTMENT
OF MENTAL HEALTH

Attn: Richard Carlisle, M.D., Ph.D.
Sub: Assessment Referral
August 18, 1987

Richard:

The following request for a patient assessment came late yesterday while you were still in conference. Overdose victim is a male in his mid-twenties. Queen of Angels Trauma Center personnel could not positively conclude whether OD was intentional or accidental and have requested evaluation of patient. You will find detailed history waiting for you at ER admission desk.

Q of A has scheduled a 10:00–11:00 interview today so as not to further delay discharge of patient. Patient's history summary is enclosed; please interview and evaluate for signs of Depression/Bipolar Disorder and possible Somatoform Disorder and overall threat/risk level; cc myself and Dr. Lomax at Q of A Trauma Center.

Rgds,

W.K./p.l.

QUEEN OF ANGELS HOLLYWOOD
PRESBYTERIAN HOSPITAL

To: Crisis Intervention Division,
LA County Department of Mental Health
From: Brian Lomax, M.D.
Director, Trauma Center
Re: Patient Assessment Referral
Date: 8/17/87

Please be advised that we are in need of a member of your staff to interview a patient currently detained as a possible suicide risk.

Summary:
Patient: Daniel John Fletcher
Chief Complaint: Barbiturate Overdose

Patient was found unresponsive at home following 911 call. Per significant other (Wheeler, Amelia) patient had been suffering from a severe migraine for several days. Had been taking unprescribed med. but did not specify (toxicology results pending).

Patient received a field saline pump followed by activated charcoal flush. Subsequently went into fibrillation; defibrillation x1 administered. Patient is currently intubated (respiratory difficulty) and stable.

Patient is chronic tobacco user, as well as showing signs of long-term amphetamine abuse. With no further history on file and no apparent cause for headache, and police background check yielding no prior criminal activity or suicide attempt, OD intent is indeterminate. Will discharge immediately, pending psychiatric recommendation.

Full medical history and LAPD background check/ report is available on site. Regarding patient's history, a) Patient identified himself by his middle name, 'Johnny' during delirium, though A. Wheeler insisted he goes by his first name, 'Danny.' b) Please review carefully details in file under 'Extremities.' Note that patient has a fully articulated, extra digit on his left hand (likely a ring finger, based on identical proportion to fourth metacarpus); both the hand and all the digits, including the aforementioned, appear otherwise normal.

Patient will remain overnight; intubation should be able to be removed during that time. On-site interview facility reserved tomorrow, 8/18 for 10:00 am for expedient processing of patient. Kindly provide someone to evaluate patient and submit referral summary to my attention ASAP.

    – B.L./b.r.

TWO

I need coffee. The nurse said *No, you're dehydrated*, handed me a carton of apple juice with a plastic cocktail straw puncturing the top. *Finish this and then you need to eat.* Apple juice holds a mnemonic effect for me like the smell of isopropanol holds for a child awaiting a vaccination. It rapid-fire replays my every trauma center wakeup and close call waltz with a straitjacket.

The woman in the bed next to mine looks maybe forty. Hard to tell. Two cops speak to her, writing what she says into a spiral notebook, but I can't hear anything. She's talking through clenched teeth, wired together to keep her jaw from falling apart. She's pretty, with metallic hair the color of wet rock past her shoulders and parted straight, the way Mom wore hers, but this woman's face is thinner, darker. A splint shrouds her septum, her left eye a protruding knob of mottled purple with a matching left cheekbone, a silver zipper of staples zigzags from her chin along the left side of her jawbone and a blue-black stain like an ink leak rings her throat, pronounced on the left side. Her husband must be right-handed. She pleads with the cops using her one, good eye – bloodshot and shiny-wet with the exit of shock and onset of reality – and gestures with her right hand (splints on her forefinger and middle finger, defensive splotches up and down her forearm). Her left arm is cast, so she's right-handed, as well. One of the cops, the shorter one, sees me staring and closes the curtain.

The orderlies have instructions not to give me my street clothes back. If I'm trying to kill myself, I'm a candidate for the State ward and they don't want me to bolt. Either way, I puked on my T-shirt and the paramedics sliced it open with surgical steel scissors before they smeared me with saline paste and shot three hundred volts through my heart. They meant well.

I make my case, that I don't want to meet a psychiatrist while I'm wearing hospital garb. They concede, keeping my wallet and keys, bring me a tropical print shirt they've fished from their clothing bins – a mixture of donations and unclaimed DOA threads – and assign me to an orderly named Wallace. With my jeans and leather coat, I look like some porn theater doorman. Not the best option when meeting an Evaluator, but much better than the alternative. First impressions count. If I look like I'm crazy – and a hospital gown will have this effect – I might as well fold.

So we're clear from the beginning, my name is Johnny. John Vincent. John Dolan Vincent. Today my name is Daniel. Or Danny or Dan. Whatever. As far as the paramedics are concerned, my name is Daniel Fletcher. Same for the nurses, doctors, EMTs, LAPD and anyone else responsible for getting me here and/or keeping me alive and/or keeping me here whether I like it or not. My boss knows me as Daniel Fletcher, says so on my job application, so does the dispatcher, my regular pickups and drop-offs and the company's insurance carrier.

The only person who calls me Johnny is Molly, and only during sex. Usually once. Sometimes she'll call me Johnny two or three times if I've got the stamina or the drugs. But since Molly's real name is Keara, we're even. I made her Molly. She asked me to. Wanted to learn the ropes.

Keara was naked. She returned to her bedroom with a glass of water, set it onto the empty wine crate beside her bed. She coiled against me, settling into the curve of me beneath the blankets, closed her eyes.

Yellow streetlight glow seeped through the curtains, a perfect crescent shadow below her cheekbone. I looked at her, watched the slumbering symmetry of her face, the simple lines. Even without makeup, her lips looked carved, set into her face and, in her sleep, she was a jewel. I could draw the contour of her profile from memory with a single line, my eyes shut. Sometimes I'd do that if I couldn't sleep. Two hundred face lines, evenly spaced on a blank sheet, Keara's profile repeated mantra-perfect, each line identical to the previous and the next.

I placed my forefinger against her face, faint as a landing moth. I've got a gentle touch, when it's called for. Ran a line down her nose, straight septum from bridge to tip, out to the peak of her cheekbone, corner of her lips, down to her chin. Counting the different angles, their degree, feeling the dips and peaks on the surface of her skin.

"Don't." She moved her face, took my hand, interlocked her fingers with mine, kept her eyes closed.

"You're beautiful," I said.

"No."

"Keara." Whispered, wanted her to open her eyes. "Hey."

"I don't like my face," she said, then opened her eyes, held my left hand to the faint light, looked at my fingers.

"What you told me today," she said, "You do that by hand? No rulers or anything?"

"Sometimes. Depends on what I'm doing."

"But you can draw a straight line, can't you? I've seen you do it."

I cleared my throat, reached for the water. I don't ever get to talk about it, what I do.

"Yeah, but I still need certain tools. Templates, stencils. Sometimes an official stamp or seal. Whatever I make has to look perfect."

She smiled, the only unsymmetrical thing about her face. Her mouth stretched more to her right side than her left when she smiled, but her teeth were a perfect white and even row, her eyes squinting into twin sparks.

"Show me," she said. "Make me someone, *Johnny*."

The glow was as close to a coke rush as I got while straight and sober – laying out my process and putting pieces together, ensconced inside my own brain and feeling it fire, functioning in a way that made *thought* feel primitive, slow.

"Okay," I said. "But not the real thing. I'm not going through the whole process if the risk isn't necessary." But I owed her. She'd let me slide on my biggest lie, regardless of my intent, and so I wanted to indulge her.

"Just give me a name." She traced the outside of my fingers with one of hers. "Jones or Smith or something."

"That's the first rule," I said. "No Jones. No Smith. No Anderson or anything too plain. Names like that stand out because they're too ordinary."

She sat up, took the glass from my hand, and I was caught up in the rush, showing somebody for the first time how I worked, unseen and unknown.

"You want a name that's common enough to bury you with other identical names in any kind of directory or list. But it can't be too common."

"Like...?"

"Like Scottish or Irish surnames. O'Fallon, McGuire. Or Anglo-occupational names. Wheeler or Taylor," I said. "Archer, Carpenter, Cooper, Mason. Something forgettable to anyone who hasn't met you twice."

"Fletcher?"

"You're quick," I said and she giggled, nudged me. "But that's if you're doing it on your own. If you're taking an existing name, you work with whatever you can get, minding nationality."

"What about my first name?"

"Same rules, common but forgettable. How 'bout *Molly*?"

She'd told me that a guy had been drunk at the bar that evening. Golf shirt yuppie with bleached teeth singing *Molly Malone* over and over, substituting baby-talk syllables for the words he didn't know, which were most of them. *She pushed her wheelbarrow, through streets broad and narrow* and *Molly Malone* were all, so he sang them over and over, out of tune.

"Molly Wheeler," Keara said.

"You're getting it. I'll make Molly Wheeler a birth certificate this weekend."

She set the glass down, leaned over and swung one knee over me, straddling me in the half-dark of the bedroom. I was waking up again.

"I want to watch," she whispered.

Daniel Fletcher has a saline IV and a sore throat from being force-fed a rubber tube smeared with lubricant for a stomach pump. Daniel Fletcher is refusing the aspirin for his swollen trachea because a previous aspirin overdose ulcered his stomach. But Daniel Fletcher didn't take too much aspirin. That was Paul Macintyre. So that overdose isn't in Daniel's file, nor is any other overdose, suicide attempt or history of mental illness.

Daniel Fletcher is from Corvallis, Oregon. I come from Oregon a lot, or Arizona, or sometimes a remote part of Texas or Washington, Massachusetts once, but mostly Oregon.

I added thirty-one months to my birth date, then ran the numbers for my new parents' age brackets, the minimum and maximum age for each: Range for *Father's* age equals *target birth date* minus forty-five minus twenty-one; range for *Mother's* age equals *target birth date* minus thirty-five minus seventeen. I'm good with numbers.

Nine cemeteries later, I found Mr. and Mrs. Karl Fletcher buried side by side beneath matching marble slabs engraved with their vitals and enough information – *Humanitarian and Philanthropist* – to tell me they'd warrant a larger-than-average obituary, so their biographies were waiting on library microfilm. Mrs. Fletcher survived her husband by seven years, smack in the middle of the widow's bell curve. The library archive gave me the specifics of their birth and marriage dates, birth dates of their surviving offspring and details of Karl Fletcher's brain aneurysm that I noted for future reference. Sometimes I find couples who died on the same day. Plane crash, car wreck, sometimes a fire, and there's a whole row of stones: mother, father and children with matching dates.

After years of hiking through cemeteries, I started scouring microfilm newspaper obituaries more and more. I can read quickly, combing through a decade's worth of the dead, a light-speed pinball ricochet through ten thousand pinhead tombstones.

I'd found many before the Fletchers, with perfect matching dates but with Spanish or Asian names that I couldn't pull off. A Polish tangle of consonants that I logged for possible later use, an Armenian couple that I ruled out. I bypassed every *Nguyen, Wong, Gonzales*, and *Rodriguez*. My red hair and blue eyes narrow my options. I need Anglo names. I can get by with a French name sometimes, but I've got too much riding on what I do.

Jail scares me. Involuntary electroconvulsive therapy scares me more. Or jackets made from military-grade canvas with D-rings on the wrists that cross-hook to your hips. There was a psych hospital near where I grew up. Stories went that the far-gone cases would wet themselves and the floor, then had to be restrained or sedated or both. The newspaper broke that patients were kept in their restraints so long they were forgotten, they had no choice. Other things happened there and they closed it down. A bunch of the orderlies went to prison.

The Fletchers were New World, Mayflower working stock, God-fearing European Protestants with over four hundred and fifty identical directory listings in Los Angeles alone.

I found parents, so I had a name. I needed a birth certificate so I could get a Social Security number so I could exist.

Sunlight or black tea will age paper. Some guys think the smell of coffee or tea on a document can give you away. I say if a DMV or Social Security clerk is sniffing your birth certificate, you botched some other detail before that. I'm thorough. It's why I've never been caught.

I found *A Pictorial History of the American Railroad*, copyrighted 1957, at an estate sale. Paid ten dollars for it. Oversized with blank end sheets, I can harvest four naturally aged, empty paper specimens if I cut with a steady, straight hand. And I always do. My birth certificates could pass a carbon dating test. Like I said, I'm thorough.

Guys screw up by using an incorrect birth number on their birth certificates – Oregon babies always begin with 1-36 – or putting zip codes and two-letter state abbreviations on pre-1970 documents. I don't. I own a 1955 Smith-Corona I use to fill them out, once I've stenciled the form and transferred the engraving. Ribbons are a bitch to track down, though. When I find them, I soak them in turpentine to lighten the ink.

I bought a vintage business permit from an antique dealer near the Fletchers' cemetery. Made a wax mold of the embossed civic seal, cast it in plaster, and transferred it to my new birth certificate with an ink roller. Birth Certificate, Social Security Number, California Driver's License, credit history and employment record. It took time, but I became Daniel Fletcher.

Six months of hope cost me three thousand dollars. Travel, antique and estate sale purchases, materials, new mail drop, secured credit card and deposits and fees – DMV, SSA, passport application, car registration, insurance, first, last, deposit.

Wallace escorts me to the hospital's evaluation room. Wallace is courteous and deferential. He stands six-four, pushing two-sixty. The top of his skull and his shoulders barely clear the doorframe. He can be as courteous and deferential as he wants to be, or not. Wallace isn't sold on the healing properties of apple juice so he lets me keep my smokes and five dollars, indulges me in a bathroom stop, then a detour through the cafeteria where I buy a large cup of coffee, palm the lighter sitting next to a respiratory nurse preoccupied with her minestrone soup. Wallace never noticed.

Where I am: A ten-foot by twelve-foot room, one hundred and twenty square feet with nine-foot ceilings, one thousand eighty cubic feet of county-issue recycled air. They want to disassociate you from your normal environment, the place where your destructive behavior began. You don't know what to look for, you see a stark room, table, chairs, fish-tank and strip mall landscape paintings. You do know what to look for, and you know they mean business.

A metal door designed to withstand two hours of inferno heat before buckling, so your foot or shoulder won't have much effect, and covered with an innocuous coat of eggshell white, no inside lock, eight by ten wire-glass portal with diagonal spider-threads of cross-hatching filament. Means you need a sledgehammer to get through, and they didn't leave one in here. Bare, steel sphere for a doorknob, no keyhole, no lock. I don't even try. No magazines. You can roll one up into a tight cone, punch through somebody's trachea with the sharp end.

Brushed steel tabletop curving all the way down the edge and under, one piece of welded smoothness. Guys will rip the aluminum or plastic edge off a table if there is one, cut someone's throat or their own wrists if they're certain the doctors are alien-funded drones out to swap their prostate for a tracking chip. I've met guys like that. No edge here to rip. A fish-tank is recessed into the wall. They look too big, so I'm guessing one-point-five-inch shatterproof acrylic, refracting the fish to double or triple their size. They say fish are soothing.

Watercolor seascapes and sunsets. No Van Gogh. No Picasso. No borderline disorders or schizophrenia leaking through a reproduction to set off any alarms with a new patient. No Magritte, and that's a shame. I like Magritte. Lots of pale blues and muted greens. Keeps you calm. Same reason doctors aren't wearing traffic-cone-orange scrubs when they're telling you to *Calm down, this won't hurt, everything's going to be all right.* The paintings are behind plastic sheeting, all four corners bolted into the wall. No nails, no hooks.

I miss Keara. I can close my eyes and see her. I can see her freckles, hairline wrinkles, fingernails, the shape of her walking to and from the shower, and it fills me with a sweet ache to see her. I like sitting and watching her put on her makeup in the morning, while she stays oblivious to me, like I'm part of her surroundings, part of her *normal.*

I love her, and it should scare me – the ease with which I can say that, but it doesn't. I should tell her so. Her sister was in town again. Keara was gone for half the day before she came back and found me. I hope she's okay, and I'm scared she's not.

I need to:

Focus, focus.

Finish my coffee.

Ask for a cigarette break as soon as I can.

Ask for more coffee, maybe tea. I hate sodas.

Here's how it works: A hospital is legally obligated to detain an overdose victim for a psychiatric evaluation if the reason for the overdose is suspect. This psychiatric evaluator has a set checklist that he or she runs through, a predictable maze of questions looking at a series of cause-and-effect answers to determine if you're depressed, manic, or both (manic-depressive or *bipolar*), paranoid or schizophrenic. Like a job interview, your appearance, demeanor and responses either fit into the check boxes or they don't. And like a job interview, whether or not you're qualified means next to nothing. You came from a rival company or weren't recommended by the right person. Your boss is white, and you're not. Or you're not showing enough cleavage. You either get the job, or you don't. You either end up in the custody of the state, or you don't.

The ideal Evaluator wears a cheap haircut, a pastel sweater, a wedding band, and a watch. If you have an Evaluator *expressing* himself, wearing his identity on his sleeve, you've got a problem. Long hair, chunks of turquoise jewelry, designer interpretations of aboriginal garments, or scarves from third-world flea markets means that you've got someone who resents working at County and wants to be a *healer*. Silk shirt, overpriced sunglasses, and he's going through the motions while he thinks about his screenplay. What they wear tells you what they want to show, and what they show tells you what they want to hide.

The combination to be on guard for is *young* and *bored*, or young and *resentful*. You can spot them at social gatherings, the grad students or interns who tell you about syndromes, conditions, deviances and disorders, and they love, love, love to talk. They speak in half-sentences with a knowing smile-squint, watch you falter at the pause, and then keep talking.

During an interview, if you make a remark like *you know what I mean?* they'll say, *No, why don't you tell me?* And they're looking for a story to tell, confidentiality be damned. They swear they can see the emperor's clothes. Nothing scares a young shrink like summing up a patient *just a little unhappy right now, recommend exercise and sunlight.* You tell them you kicked a vending machine that swallowed your dime, they'll tag you schizophrenic with an acute bipolar personality disorder and an Oedipal complex. So you tell them you don't sleep well. Tell them you still think about an old lover. Do not tell them everything's fine or that you hear voices. Tell them, *my boss is a jerk, I can't sleep, I just don't know what to do with my life.* Keep it common and hope for the best.

If they're older, see if they're hiding their age. Look for a wedding ring. Age and marriage are big. Beyond forty, being single eats away at them. There's a chance they're childless and going to stay that way. Your answers are likely to ricochet off some long-buried stigma and they'll send you down as thanks for the reminder. Look for too much makeup or hair coloring, comb-overs and toupees. Glasses are okay, tinted glasses are not. I've seen them. Hiding crow's feet or just hiding. If I can't read your eyes, I can't trust you.

Never forget, even for a second, that your Evaluator's black-and-white, *yes*-or-*no* list of checkboxes gets filtered through his morning fog, his repressed homosexuality, his hatred for his parents, or men, or women, or the fact that he's married or divorced, childless or fat. Or all of the above. From his ears to his notebook, his own litany of childhood trauma and denial baggage that propelled him into psychiatric medicine is filtering your answers. And his signature can have you locked up.

Yes, I've done this before. I've made mistakes that almost buried me in a place with no hard edges, my name a needle in the California Department of Mental Health Haystack. I'm looking for an Evaluator that doesn't have an identity problem.

I can hear the muffled hallway voices while I'm waiting for the half-second of doorknob lock-tumbler clicking before the Evaluator enters. At the doctor's when I was a kid, that sound always made my heart thrash like a hooked fish. Always, after ten minutes of sitting on a tissue- covered cushion, staring at Pyrex jars full of cotton swabs and tongue depressors, machines with hoses and cables spidering out of them and iso-propanol hanging in the air, the doorknob would rattle, the doctor would come in smiling with a needle. The doctors are different now, and the needle is a clipboard.

The door opens, closes.

My Evaluator is a weathered thirty-five, wearing a silver ponytail and thick spectacles that warp his eyes out of shape, ballooning their red edges and swollen lids. He bends to pull out a chair and I see an ankh dangling from his left earlobe. Notepad and file under his left arm, he carries a large paper cup in his hand, coffee beginning to seep through the seam like it's his fourth refill and he's been awake since before dawn. Dress shirt, no tie, wool trousers and jacket, his grudging nod to administrative regs. His ID badge hangs clipped to his breast pocket.

RICHARD CARLISLE, M.D., PH.D.
LOS ANGELES COUNTY DEPARTMENT OF MENTAL HEALTH.

Aging environmentalist and activist, he would have been somewhere near draft age during Vietnam. Something there, but I don't know what. I get a feeling in my chest and stomach when I'm scared, like my guts are melting and hot but my bones are turning to ice, and I have that feeling now.

"Mr. Daniel–" looks at his clipboard "Fletcher?" I nod. "I'm Dr. Carlisle. I'd like to ask you some questions."

THREE

Yellow pad, legal, one, blank. Manila file, one, "Fletcher, D." inked onto the tab. The Evaluator writes eight lines of preliminary notes while snapping hummingbird f-stop glances in my direction. The Evaluator is clocking me clocking him.

Do not:

Tap feet

Drum fingers

Shift sitting position

Scratch

Wipe forehead. Because he'll record it.

But do not:

Sit too still.

I'm allowed to be nervous. Act too calm and it's suspicious. It's taken me years of practice to learn how to *act natural*. Think of the middle-class family man walking out of a triple-X theater, looking around like a startled rodent, checking his zipper, think of the kid airing out his bedroom and gargling away his bong breath before his parents get home. I've changed my name six times in three years, my name, Social Security number, parents, employment history, school transcripts, and fingerprints. I still have to remember how to *act natural*. I lapse into mirror mode, approximating the Evaluator's posture – feet flat, hands exposed with a slight forward lean, *confidence, honesty*. The most important detail to remember here is frequency, frequency,

THE CONTORTIONIST'S HANDBOOK

frequency. Keep moving, shifting every five minutes. Guys get so locked into keeping their story straight, they forget to move, juggling so many details in their head that a rigor mortis stiffness seizes them, and it shows, throws a floodlight onto the flaws in their stories.

I've got to keep my hands moving. Need a line. I work a quarter from the cafeteria over my knuckles, tumbling from finger to finger across the back of my right hand. Keeps me nimble.

Three minutes pass, he reads my file, runs through five more lines on his pad. I pull two smokes from the pack, keep one in front of my eyes while I clip or palm the other. I practice a screen-and-cup drill, close-up maneuvers that make one cigarette appear to snap from one empty hand to another. This is clearly not the way to *act natural*, but I need a line right now, and this pulls my brain into a solid point where I can think for lack of a good hit.

"That's pretty good. You a magician?" he asks. He needs to establish a rapport. He wants me comfortable enough to confess every infectious corner of my Id. He makes small talk to say *Don't be afraid of me*, wants to appear casual but I know he's listening.

Palms up, I show both cigarettes to the Evaluator. "Nah. Dabbled a lot when I was younger. It's a nervous habit." I smile. He's got a basis for my Nervous Habit. I'll use that later when I want him to think I'm on edge, pull his attention from the subjects that spook me. It's called a misdirect.

"Are you nervous, now?"

"Well, yeah. A little." I slide the smokes back into the pack, brush my hair out of my eyes with my right hand. "Yeah."

The Evaluator writes, I can read the word *magic* annotated with *HN*. He opens my file again, shielding it from my view. No matter, I already know what's inside.

* * *

Raymond O'Donnell had a Nevada driver's license but has never driven. Raymond O'Donnell had never voted, been arrested, leased an apartment, or been otherwise visible. Raymond O'Donnell kept cash in a Clark County account because Nevada is tight with banking privacy. His name was on twenty-four mail drops throughout the Southwest – Chatsworth, Indio, Twenty-Nine Palms, Visalia, Needles, Bakersfield, Lordsburg, Holbrook. Mail drops didn't care. They saw the driver's license, matched my face, took my cash, and forgot me in minutes.

The DMV and Social Security offices always need an address, so I add my new name as an additional recipient on the mail drop for another name, one I don't use in public. Sometimes I'll pick another address, a house or apartment in a respectable neighborhood or an empty lot, give that to the DMV, then submit a mail forwarding request to the Post Office, and that mail goes straight to the designated mail drop. DMV never knows. It doesn't even have to be a real address. When I change names again, I submit another forwarding request to a nonexistent address in Alaska. Somewhere up North is a mountain of mail miles high, waiting for a throng of people who were never born and never died.

I was getting good by this point, really good. Jimmy and the business were starting to pay me more, depend on me more, trying to convince me to quit legit work altogether. I was regretting I'd ever met them.

I was in Las Vegas, rotating mail drops and bank accounts in advance of another change, setting up ghost addresses and credit histories for some of Jimmy's people. One ounce into a bourbon, the carnival slot machine noise had dimmed and I was scanning – eyes left, down, right, and back – out of habit, the casino floor and the lobby entrance in my line of sight. Five sorority girls bounced from a primer-smeared Jeep and waved down a bellhop. They checked in, passing me on their way to the elevators, one of them said *pool*. I found them twenty-eight minutes later, all in a bronze, buttery row, sunning on ribbed lounge chairs.

I spent the afternoon keeping my eyes on them, playing two hundred dollars among the low-stakes tables with a poolside view. I'd run a halves count on a six-deck Twenty One shoe, watching the ebb and flow of the cards and betting small to stay off the casino's scope. Winning is bad for anonymity. Being photographed and thrown out is even worse.

The girls ordered cheap drinks and tipped cheaper, keeping their arm's length giggle from the orbiting packs of men – fraternity hounds, lounge lizards and tanned and leathery minor royalty dripping strange accents, coconut oil and gold jewelry – simultaneously playing them and blowing them off. I tracked them to the bar that evening, sent them a round.

"I'm headed back to New York for a business function." I'm doing, *Nervous but Sincere*. "And my ex is going to be there. If I can ask a strange favor of you, I've got a hundred bucks and cab fare to wherever you want. I won't bother you after that." I fanned five twenties onto the bar.

Inside a Las Vegas Boulevard souvenir shop, *Cindi-with-an-i* sat on my lap in a photo booth. I pinched her, told her to smile at the camera. Four bucks later, the booth spat out two strips of black-and-white stills of Cindi and me laughing and snuggling. The rest wanted pictures with each other.

"You each take shots with me, first."

Cindi had black hair and soft, rounded bones in her face. Skinny, small breasts and a deep tan. But Cindi was still in Raymond O'Donnell's Nevada safe deposit box when the ambulance took me to Queen of Angels. Jen was in my wallet. Jen was also skinny, but with a sharper face, spiky blonde hair, grey eyes, and a neon smile. The back of her picture said *Danny, we'll always have Mardi Gras*.–Karen. Thrift store textbooks are rife with handwriting samples. I picked one that suited the photo – bloated letters with bold flourishes on the capitals –

and mimicked it with a pink ballpoint. When they left, I had twenty-four new romantic memories, and they never saw my hand.

Too many changers are too clean to withstand scrutiny. They carry brand-new wallets, empty but for a new driver's license with a spotless record, and a new Social Security card. That's when they start to blow it. Nobody carries their Social Security card.

My wallet: a DF monogram – three dollars from a swap meet vendor – mink oiled and left on my windowsill for a month, then run through the rinse cycle. Driver's license, video rental card (I rent documentaries I don't watch to go with the magazine subscriptions I don't read – I have to change hobbies a lot), credit card, ticket stub (*The Divine Horsemen w/fIREHOSE* at the Variety Arts Center), receipts (ATM, liquor store, strip club, gas station), work ID, Jen/Karen's picture, an unused codeine prescription and business cards (mechanic, used record store, dry cleaner). The cops went through it, forgot it.

My file: Paramedic's report, ER chart. They ran my driver's license, I know, because they want to know a criminal history to corroborate a diagnosis. John Vincent has been a ward of the state. My juvenile offender record is sealed, though they can still verify its existence. But Daniel Fletcher is a churchgoing taxpayer, minus the intentional parking tickets so I wouldn't be a complete stranger to the System (if you're too clean, they start digging deeper). And Daniel Fletcher has no medical or psychiatric history.

You present a birth certificate at the DMV, they want to know why you're getting your first driver's license at age twenty-whatever. *I've grown up Back East, never driven in my life.* Anyone good at placing accents would peg me for East Rutherford. Never been there. But the utility and phone bill with the Bronx address, the Columbia University picture ID all matching the name on my birth certificate, are painless to fake. Time, effort, patience and a sharp eye for typefaces are all that are needed, and I have every one of them. After the tedium of the written exam and road test, I'm Daniel Fletcher. No criminal history, no psychiatric record, nothing. Sounds good, but the downside is no credit history, which needs to be built (I have to put large cash deposits on new apartments), which means a separate drill for the Social Security Administration to procure a number, which has its own pitfalls.

No job history, so one has to be fabricated for a new employer. Most driving and courier jobs are less concerned with job history than with insurance, which makes them easier to obtain. All told, the process involves more than most people outside of the FBI ever know.

College kids propagate the folklore that gets them and other amateurs busted: You comb through a cemetery, find someone who died within a year of being born. One who's your own age plus a few years. Counties didn't used to cross-index birth and death records, so it was easy to fool the DMV. You write the state a request for a birth certificate, bring it to the DMV with a utility bill or picture ID, and you've got a driver's license that says you're twenty-one.

That might work, and I mean might, if all you want to do is buy kegs for some jack-off Monday Night Football party from a liquor store that's never had its license suspended. That might work if, in a given year, two dozen people don't all apply for driver's licenses that all happen to share the same first, middle and last name. If they do, it might work if the DMV doesn't notice the astronomical coincidence.

Keara, the sound of her showering in the morning, radio on – a half-second of being with her jumps into my brain, and all at once I miss her. I want out of here.

"It's okay to be nervous," the Evaluator says. "This is probably a little unusual for you. Now, what I need to do here is very straightforward. I'm going to ask you some questions in order to gather some background information from you. From there, I'll assess your psychological health, and the opinion that I draft regarding that is the only disclosure of our discussion that I will make. Anything else you tell me, barring the divulgence of a crime or risk to yourself, is strictly confidential.

"This interview is mainly for insurance purposes, so that the hospital doesn't release a person who's a potential suicide risk. Is there any part of what I've just said that you do not understand?"

"I understand everything."

Yes, I understand that he deliberately avoids the word routine because he knows that I know this is anything but routine, and he needs my trust. I understand that this is mandatory and therefore not an interview but an interrogation. If I forget that, I'll never leave here.

"Now," the Evaluator continues, "I'm not here to trick you into revealing some hidden secrets or get you to commit yourself. If I find something worth looking into further, we can arrange a visit at your convenience to discuss that issue. Is all of that clear?"

"It's clear."

"So," the Evaluator smiles, eyes crinkling behind his glasses, "Do you know why you're here?"

This is a variant of *What can I do for you today? What brings you here? or How can I help you today?* Read: Do you remember what you did to get here? Do you acknowledge and assume responsibility for your actions? A straight answer is best, then he's going to want to *come back to that later*.

"The doctor thinks I tried to kill myself." True. Eye contact, *now*.

"Did you?"

"No." True. Keep the eye contact, but don't stare. Even the most honest person doesn't maintain eye contact for more than half of a conversation. Exceed that fifty-percent threshold and you trash your believability.

"Do you mind if I ask your opinion, then, of someone who actually does try to kill himself?"

"He needs help quickly," I say it without a pause. "Something's very wrong."

"Why do you say that?"

"I don't know. I mean, people go through bad shit and they just get through it. That's the way it is. Suicide … I mean, something's wrong with his brain. I mean there's gotta be physical brain damage." I'm emphatic, and I refer to *him*. No vague pronouns, because I'm talking about someone else, not myself, and that's what he's listening for.

"It says here that you took quite a few painkillers."

"I know. My head hurt. I couldn't get it to stop." True. No pause, mild emphasis and I look him in the eye.

"Do you know how much you took?"

"I don't have any idea."

"Okay. Let's come back to that later." The Evaluator leans back, crosses his legs.

Convince this guy I'm not a head case. Whether or not I'm locked up is decided by a person who couldn't pass the same evaluation under the same circumstances in a hundred lifetimes. He's tagged me with at least one unfounded headache claim and at least one overdose, so I've got to think quickly.

The Evaluator is mixing his cue cards with instinct, like knowing when to kiss someone for the first time or push a bluffer into folding. People that survive shark attacks were never attacked. Sharks can tell with a single bite – a short fin mako's jaws can exert four tons of pressure per square inch – whether they'll burn more calories digesting the kill than they'll gain from it. Millions of years of evolution tell them whether to eat you or not. This Evaluator is going to swim in wide, concentric circles of safe subjects until he thinks I'm relaxed enough to spill my guts. Older evaluators like this one spend less time interpreting. They read you quickly, so signs are easier to convey. That works in my favor.

First, he'll assess my current mental state. This is called a Mental Status Evaluation. He's laying the groundwork for the detailed questions, the personal details that could get me sent away indefinitely, or at least until a hearing. Anything goes wrong here and the rest of his questions are null and void. He'll profile my most basic condition, such as how I'm dressed, how I'm acting and if what I say coincides with my behavior. If I say I'm fine but I'm bawling my eyes out, or *I think I'm going to die* while I'm smiling cheerfully, there's a problem.

He'll try to establish that I know who I am, where I am and what day it is. That I've got my memory – immediate, short- and long-term. Hygiene is important. Someone in the depths of depression (for which I'm a candidate) throws grooming to the dogs. No shave, white scalp flakes salting their shoulders, untucked shirts and swollen guts pushing belly hair through missing buttons, an Evaluator will mark it down. I'd splashed water on my hands in the bathroom, finger-combed my hair and chewed a handful of mints from the urology desk on the way here.

"How are you feeling now?" he asks.

"I'm all right. A little groggy. My throat hurts."

"It's swollen. Give it a day, maybe take a couple of aspirin. It should be fine," he says, and writes *Patient complaining of throat pain* on the canary legal pad.

"Mr. Fletcher – may I call you Daniel?" Turn the dial to Informal, lighten the mood and tighten the circles. The distorted fish do their back-and-forth soothing trick.

"Yeah, sure."

"You can call me Richard," he says, then continues, "Daniel, I need to go through some exercises with you in order to identify a baseline in your thought process. I need to do this to be certain you're able to accurately answer the background questions I mentioned earlier. That sound okay with you?"

"Okay." Asking my permission is a lie. I'm low on coffee.

"Do you know where you are, Daniel?"

"I'm in a hospital." I'm at Queen of Angels Hollywood Presbyterian.

Saw it on the scrubs (antifreeze blue-green, professional, calming) but don't want to look too observant. They think your intelligence is out of bounds, they get a bigger notebook and order lunch.

"Do you know which hospital?"

I shake my head, push my hair out of my eyes.

"L.A., somewhere."

He nods, writes shorthand annotations, *HG* and three *x*'s, circles the third *x* beside my abbreviated answer.

"Do you have any idea where in this hospital you are?"

"I'm on the third floor, I think. No windows in here, so it's hard to tell anything else." False. I know exactly where I am. Wallace walked me three hundred and thirty feet from the emergency room and took an elevator up three flights. Two right turns and three left, so I'm facing south. If there were a window in here, I'd be looking down onto Fountain Avenue.

I lean back, cross my legs and fold my hands. Mirror. *Trust me.*

"How do you know you're on the third floor?" *PM*, three *x*'s and circles the third, again.

"The elevator."

"Very good."

The Evaluator shifts in his seat, maintaining an open posture. He's sitting at the corner of the table adjacent to me, instead of opposite. Legs uncrossed, left elbow resting on the arm of the chair (my chair has no arms – Wallace put me here), left hand rubbing his chin or mustache. His torso is exposed to say *I'm not hiding anything.* The most important thing to remember is that all of the pop-psychology magazine articles about body language are wrong. Crossing one's arms or legs can indicate comfort or honesty just as much as it can defensiveness or barriers or deception. What's important is knowing *when* to change body language, and how frequently.

My file is out of reach, and he writes on his yellow pad, right-handed. Top left margin starting out at one point five inches and swelling inward as he moves down the page, a pattern that prematurely forces him to start a new sheet. He writes in cursive but keeps his letters far apart from each other.

"Do you know what day it is?" he asks.

"Tuesday, the eighteenth."

"You're certain."

"Yeah." I don't give up more than I have to, but I can't appear obstinate or paranoid, either.

"How is it you're certain of the date?"

"My headache started Friday. They usually last four days and I was fine yesterday when I woke up here." I mime with my hands, pointing to *here* when I say *here*. Hidden hands say *liar*.

At the mention of the previous headaches, he flips back two pages, makes a note where *we'll get back to that later* and returns. He checks my file, resumes his inward creep down the legal pad. Pen poised, thumb and forefinger rubbing his moustache, he continues.

"Okay, can you tell me the month and year?"

I shift in my seat, glance to my left because I'm remembering a fact. "It's August, 1987." Sigh, clench my left hand, then open. I'm doing *exasperated*. Without words I'm saying *Why are you asking me this?*

His first priority is to find out if I'm oriented, achieved via basic questions about where I am and how I got here, what day of the week or what year it is or who's president. Same as when a field medic is checking to see if you're coherent.

His next task is to establish that I know why I'm here, which tells him I'm aware of what I've done. That is, what did I do? And do I know that I did it? Hopefully, he'll link my *why* back to my assessment of reality.

It's a simple equation at heart, a clean chain of logic that forms a circle and bites its own tail. Question one: Do you know where you are? If you say *a hospital*, they can assume, for the time being, that you are sane. If they ask you if you know how you got there, and you say *I cut myself*, you've proven that you know right from wrong and are responsible for your actions. If they ask you why you cut yourself and you say *to stop the voices in my head*, that blows their first conclusion and you're gone. But close the circle equation and you're halfway home.

"Daniel, I'd like you to count backwards from one hundred, in increments of seven, please. Do you understand?"

I nod.

"As far as you can, whenever you're ready."

I have to act like it's not easy, but that I can still do it. "Ninety-three... eighty-six..." I close my eyes for effect, mime with my hands. " ...seventy-nine... seventy-two... sixty-five..."

"Thank you. That's far enough." They almost always stop you between five and eight numbers into a count.

Serial Sevens is a memory test, seven being the average number that can occupy one's short-term memory. Poor short-term memory is a big indicator for depression, and I need him to rule it out.

It's easy for me, like any other number. I can shuffle them in my head, easy as breathing. I can quantify objects and their units of measure with my eyes. Distance. Dimension. Angle. Volume. I know from looking. Measuring or counting doesn't describe it. I just know, in a blink. Been doing it since I was a kid.

The remaining tests: Registration. Attention. Recall. Language. Copying. The Evaluator names three objects that I'll be asked to recall later. *Ball. Tree. House*. Then, *Follow this instruction* and holds up a card: CLOSE YOUR EYES written in fat marker. I close my eyes. *Good. Now open. Take this piece of paper in your right hand. Good. Fold it in half. Now place it on the floor. Good*. Holds up his pencil. *Can you tell me what this is?* I tell him. Points to his watch, same question. It's your watch. *What were the three words I gave you earlier?* Ball. Tree. House. Usually one syllable, never more than two.

The white male doctors from middle-class backgrounds always pick Dick-and-Jane nouns: cup, shoe, chair, grass, dog, cat, bird. Those with no children always pick children's nouns: Ball, tree, house. The others, those from poor backgrounds who have struggled to get where they are, tell an abbreviated life story in single syllables: truck, street, fire, door, stairs, man, car. Female doctors wearing paisley scarves and Southwestern jewelry are more abstract: spring, fall, mom, dad, pet, sun, moon, rain. And they're the toughest ones to fool.

The Evaluator hands me a clean sheet of paper, a felt marker – can't hurt someone or cover any mistakes – and a card showing two intersecting pentagons.

"Now Daniel, I'd like you to copy this image exactly as you see it. Make certain you duplicate every point, and that the two objects intersect."

There's a lot happening here. He's testing perception, coordination, following directions, among other things. He never uses the word *pentagon*, and wants to make certain I can count the angles and faces.

Most people look at an object and see the object, force their hand to copy what their eye sees. But that object is getting filtered through a brain with years of associations to and memories of that object, so they fail. Ask someone to draw a tree and the lifetime of trees in their head says *That's not good enough*. That's why children use symbols. A stick topped with a blast of swirls. Brown crayon, green crayon. Burnt Sienna and Forest Green. Maybe a dozen Fire Engine Red dots, though they've never seen a real apple tree, much less had one growing in their front yard.

The trick is to forget those associations. If you can see the tree upside down, you're looking at a tangle of unfamiliar shapes. Draw the space between the branches instead of the branches themselves. Most people can draw better than they know, but they can't turn their amnesia on at will.

I make the pentagons look harder than they are. I pause for show, double-checking that I've drawn five points and five faces, though I don't need to.

"Thank you, Daniel." The Evaluator starts a clean sheet on his yellow pad, shifts in his seat to cross his legs, says, "Now, can we talk about this headache?"

FOUR

"Okay." Eye contact, then shift to mirror him. This part's easy because it's all true.

"You said it started Friday?"

"Yeah. Near the end of work."

"Can you describe it for me?"

"At first, nothing. It's a feeling I have. I know it's coming."

"And then after this 'feeling,' what happens?"

"Blue. Anything blue stands out, gets brighter." I use my hands again. "Then sound like the hum from a dental drill or a wood chipper. Tight and fast so it makes my head hurt. It's not in any one place. I can't handle light or noise."

"So, it comes on gradually. Does it fade gradually, as well?"

"No. Once I know it's coming, it's about an hour before it hits. Then it stays. When it stops, it's immediate." True, true and true.

"Are there any waves in between, with the pain coming and going?"

"No." Pause. "I mean yes, but from the pills. Not on its own."

The Evaluator scribbles. I'm watching his notes when he's not watching me. My answers in shorthand, then columns of abbreviations: *PS, PM, xxx* – with one circled – *HG, HE*. Maybe he's just doodling and will write whatever he wants at the end of all this, in which case I'm finished. Can't think about that.

"And you said this lasted four days?"

45

"Four days, yeah."

"And the painkillers helped?"

"Sort of. I'd take one, and the pain would fade, then creep back. So I'd take another one. Same thing. I tried to hold off until the pain was at its worst before I took any more, but I couldn't. So, I'd take two, but the same thing happened. Then three. You can take it from there." True, true, true and true.

"Interesting. What you overdosed on was a painkiller targeting the muscles and shouldn't have had any effect on a migraine. You've had headaches like this before, then?"

"Twice before, yeah," I tell him. False.

"How recently?"

"Over the last couple of years."

"When was the last one?"

"About a year ago."

If I've had just one, then it's an anomaly so he'll look for any Recent Stress or Trauma. And I haven't told him that my parents – the Fletchers, anyway – are dead, so I've got a chance to derail that conclusion before he makes it. My stories have to be solid. I wrote them out six times, every detail of every scenario, careful not to create too much consistency among their circumstances. I want him to conclude that the headaches are infrequent, random, and that I'm aware of my actions and that the overdose was an accident. He's looking for signs of depression but also for a somatoform disorder – imaginary pain.

"Tell me about it."

"It started at work. At the time, I drove a forklift at a loading dock. I hadn't been there for long, so I wasn't used to it. The noise in the warehouse was nonstop and my head hurt like a son of a bitch when I got home. I noticed the blue, but didn't. That make sense?"

He nods. I continue:

"I took some aspirin, had a drink and figured it would go away. The next day it was so bad I couldn't see."

"Where were you working?"

"At a freight forwarders in San Pedro," without delay. They never existed. I'd forged three pay stubs with different dates, then run them through the wash, and left two in the pocket of my jacket, the other in my glove box.

"What did you do when it wouldn't stop?"

"I went to a clinic to get some painkillers. I'd just started working at the freight dock, so I didn't have insurance." False. I had not gone to a clinic complaining of symptoms I did not have just to receive the latter-day version of *take two aspirin*. Clinics had to be careful about issuing pharmaceuticals to people working scams.

"Do you remember which clinic?"

"No. It was some free clinic down in Long Beach."

"And what did they say?"

"They said nothing was wrong, which pissed me off because I never get headaches. Ever. Not even with a hangover. They gave me some Tylenol and told me to come back if it didn't get any better."

"Did you go back?"

"Yeah." False. "I said it hadn't stopped." False. Sometimes I'll wrap an ice cube in foil, crush it with my teeth, spit it out. I can score a prescription for Demerol or Vicodin or something, anything, that I can duplicate for a Chinatown pharmacy that doesn't bother to verify them. "This time, he gave me a prescription for codeine. But I couldn't use it because I'd been in there until after the pharmacy closed." False, false, false. "The next day I felt okay, but a little shaky. I hadn't eaten much for those three days. I never even used the prescription." It was in my wallet. I'd made a replica, right down to the doctor's signature, but had to change the name it was issued to, since I wasn't Daniel Fletcher a year ago. And suicide/ headcase/ junkies didn't keep narcotic prescriptions unredeemed, so that would work in my favor.

Target conclusion: I had seen a doctor and did not have a

somatoform pain disorder. I had done everything possible, within reason, given my circumstances.

"Was that last headache a year ago as severe as this one?"

"Not even close."

"And how long ago was the headache prior to that?"

"About eight months before." I base my story on the truth, mimicking the current frequency.

"Was it worse? How did it compare with these other two?"

"It was as bad as this one, but it quit a little bit sooner. Really bad."

"So, you had one less than two years ago, then one a year ago, though not as bad. And a severe one that started Friday, correct?"

"Yeah." Meaning: They're not progressive. They're not getting any worse and there's nothing to be alarmed at. If I've done this right, he'll want to change subjects at this point. He makes notes, I sigh and rub my eyes.

"Mind if I step out for a smoke?" I ask. I've got a one-in-a-thousand chance he's got enough confidence to let me out alone, in which case I'm not coming back.

"Not at all," he says, "I'll have Wallace escort you."

Outside, Wallace raps with a hospital rent-a-cop, both of them standing between me and the door. We're on a smoking balcony and there's a three-story drop between me and the ground. I finish a paper cup of water, light my first smoke in nearly five days, and the flaccid synapses in my head crackle awake, I feel the static between my ears stop, the three-hundred-and-sixty-degree grain-silo information dump that I can't filter, decipher or contain when I'm like this – it all stops. Sometimes I can be so smart, and sometimes the simplest task is like playing a hundred simultaneous chess games from memory, in the space of minutes.

What I know: If the Evaluator is married, it's to his work. He looks tired behind his glasses, is on his second or third cup of coffee. Middle-aged, idealistic hippie, hence his job within the System instead of a lucrative private practice at his age.

A workaholic chained to the here-and-now, which makes me his momentary mission in life, which is bad, bad, bad. Perversely, stubbornly idealistic and like every other Evaluator I've ever met, evidently incapable of turning his expert scope onto himself.

"You about ready, sir?" Wallace calls from the doorway. Always says sir. I'm starting to like him.

"One more, if it's all right with you. I think I'll be in there for a while."

Wallace laughs, says, "Take your time, sir."

I chain a fresh smoke, inhale long, close my eyes and piece together his notebook inside my head. I'm fortunate the Evaluator writes in shorthand so he's not guarded with his notes. That's a sign of experience, which tends to be good. He's methodical, writes in chunks across the page, keeps his abbreviations in segregated columns. The electric spark of *knowing* cracks in my head and I exhale a stream of smoke.

Far left, easy: My verbal responses with his abbreviated notes beside a column of numbers. I know the questions – they're always the same subject and approximate order, so those are his numbers.

Middle column: Abbreviation codes for patient behavior, *my* behavior. Eyes, hands, posture, paralinguistics – sighs, volume shifts, etc. *HN* the moment I said that sleight of hand was a nervous habit. Perhaps *Habit, Nervous* or *Hand, Nervous*. Other *H* notes: *HG* when I push my hair out of my eyes. *Hair/Hand/ Habit, Grooming*, I think. If *H* is for hand, then I can nail *E* for eyes and *P* for posture or body language.

The right side: Three *x*'s, one circled. Never seen that before, but if he knows what he's doing, he's clocking my responses and placing them within the context of my answers. I'm guessing *xxx* with one circled is a *before/during/after*, nonverbal response key. If I'm right, and it's some mnemonic-chronology tool, then I'm way ahead of him. I'll test it out.

If the Evaluator lives for his work, and I'm his work right now, I could be in trouble. He could go digging deeper than is good for me. He could be doing that right now.

I grind my cigarette out on the balcony rail, toss it into the roses below, say to Wallace, "He's probably wondering where I am. Ready when you are."

August 18, 1987

Richard Carlisle, M.D., Ph. D.
Los Angeles County Department of Mental Health

Referral assessment of patient Daniel John Fletcher at
request of Dr. Brian Lomax, Trauma Center Director at
Hollywood Presbyterian Hospital. Per Dr. Lomax, patient
is to be interviewed to evaluate claims of unintentional
painkiller over-dose and assess potential suicide risk.

Preliminary Mental Status Evaluation

I interviewed the patient on site at Hollywood
Presbyterian. Patient was groomed and presentable under
the circumstances, though looked at least two years older
than his stated age of twenty-five. While this could be a
result of his emergency room ordeal, I will still attempt
to ascertain long-term drug and alcohol abuse.

Patient said he was "all right," and his mood and
affect is appropriately euthymic. Patient is right-handed
(see attached ER report notes on polydactyly). Patient
exhibited no outward signs of stress or discomfort.
The only fidgeting exhibited was a series of distracted,
sleight of hand routines with his cigarettes while I
made notes; patient was observed flipping a quarter
end over end across the back of his knuckles, back
and forth. Otherwise calm and cooperative with the
interview.

Patient is quite lucid and has exhibited initial signs of
high intelligence and memory, and performed well on all
tests of memory, recognition, direction, orientation, etc.
He is fully oriented as to time and place. In all, his Access

Level of Consciousness is "Alert," with an overall Mental Status test score of 30/30.

Will interview for signs of depression or bipolarism, drug use, and evidence of a somatoform pain disorder.

   – R.C.

CHRISTOPHER THORNE

FIVE

Maybe you stiffed somebody for a lot of cash. Maybe that somebody wears three-hundred-dollar sweatsuits and runs his business in a coded ledger out of a pawnshop back room or pool hall or bar. Maybe you slept with some other guy's wife while he was doing time. The worst life has to offer doesn't scare him anymore and he wants to find you when he's out. Or maybe he's a career pencil pusher, hairline making a retreat to the back of his skull halfway through his third decade and he's had one too many anonymous parking lot dings on his precious convertible and been yelled at by his boss once too often and ignored by the waitresses in the short skirts and *you* are his breaking point.

You need to disappear. Maybe find somebody your age, with your stats, with no family, friends or police record who's at death's door and will sell you his name for a few hundred bucks. But the odds are against you finding someone like that. So you need to work from the beginning.

Find a name. Check tombstones, obituaries, estate sale Bibles. Find something familiar but not obvious, distinct but forgettable: Norton, Dillon, Harris.

Occupations: Cooper, Porter, Taylor, Donner, Thatcher, Barber, Farmer.

Materials: Wood, Silver, Steel.

Flora: Branch, Fields, Weed.

Fauna: Wolf, Bird, Crow, Hawk.

Titles: Sheriff, Sage, King, Pope, Priest.

Colors: Brown, Black, White, Green.

A name people have heard before, won't think twice about, won't remember. You're not looking for a baby, you're looking for parents.

Get a birth certificate. Write the county registrar. Insist there's a mistake if they say your birth record isn't on file. I keep a list of forty-five hospitals and county registrars with pending lawsuits for mismanagement and neglect. Illicit requests slide through because they're scared of the heat another delay can bring. Sometimes I'm lucky, I'll be setting up for a change when a hospital registry or county hall of records catches fire. Birth certificate requests take longer, but they never check their authenticity because they couldn't if they wanted to.

I can make a birth certificate if I have to. Twenty-five minutes, not counting aging if I don't have a vintage paper specimen. Strong coffee, tea or chicory, room temperature, soak for one hour. Or leave it taped to a sunlit window for two weeks. Seal it inside a plastic bag with rust scraped from a nail, let the moisture make spots. Heat a bent paperclip, make wormholes. Sodium silicate on a linoleum block stamp for a watermark, because the pencil pushers will always hold it to the light. And be subtle, subtle, subtle. I saw a guy hand his fake to an SSA clerk. His overzealous paper-aging made his job look like an amusement park treasure map. They cuffed him right there, and I doubt he's out yet.

Work up a new signature, spend the time to get it right and real. Look through old yearbooks, junk-store postcards, used textbooks, Bibles, antique-store photographs stacked in cigar boxes, fifty cents each. Find the names, the letters, piece together one after the next. High, confident crossbars, forward slants. No underlines, flourishes – too arrogant. Don't cross over the name or dot an *i* too low – too subdued. Build it, write it left-handed, upside down, give it its own style, then do it right-handed, practice, practice, practice, repetition, repetition, repetition.

Then burn every sample and practice signature and every sheet of paper less than ten sheets beneath those practice sheets. Do not throw them away, tear them up or ditch them in a dumpster in another zip code or trust a paper shredder.

I started doing favors for people. Big mistake. Jimmy or somebody would introduce me with words like *forger* or *counterfeiter*, sometimes with *expert* or *master* thrown in. Like I should be proud. I hated being introduced to people, and I told them not to use words like that.

Met a guy in a DMV parking lot, said he could get me anything I needed. Probably made his money selling his work to illegal immigrants, but I caught his eye for some reason. I hate when I catch someone's eye, so I wanted to make sure he never came back. In the passenger seat of his '77 Cadillac, bigger than God and twice as conspicuous, I choked back the bile from the smell of sweat and fast food wrappers while "Eddie" fiddled with a combination lock briefcase, asked if I was a cop.

"No," I said.

"Anything you need, man, anything. Get you a driver's license, or clean record if you got a DUI. Check it out."

Half pimp, half sideshow barker, he showed me twenty driver's licenses with Sanchez, Lopez or something, photos of Mexican men all middle height and weight, blank Social Security cards, green cards, immunization documents and baptismal certificates. I rifled through, found a birth certificate that looked solid at first glance.

"Any name you want, brother," he started up again, drive-through grease fumes drifting from his glossy pimp shirt.

"Make you a couple of years older, I can give you a deal," he said.

The birth certificate, for a Carlos Mejia born in 1946 in East

Los Angeles, was artfully browned with time, all the data intact. I held it up to his windshield for the sun to shine through.

"Best you can find. I got this partner who's a real pro at this," he said.

The sun hit the paper, dull watermark letters glowed through the page, they said *100% acid free.* I tossed it back into his briefcase and got out, shut the door behind me, heavy as a bank vault.

"Hey bro, c'mon back, getcha whatever you want."

I leaned into his window and said, "Tell your partner to check his watermarks."

Barker-Pimp looks at me, like he doesn't know what a watermark is.

"And tell him when he signs a document dated 1946 that he shouldn't use a ballpoint pen."

"Where did you grow up, Daniel?"

My name is Daniel Fletcher. I was born November 6, 1961, in Corvallis, Oregon. I graduated high school in June of 1978. I am twenty-five years old. My father, Karl Fletcher, died of a brain aneurysm when I was seventeen. My mother, Elaine Fletcher, lived for another seven years and died of natural causes. I am the youngest of three siblings, Ryan, Emily and myself. They are both married, and I have one niece through Emily.

"Corvallis, Oregon."

My name is Daniel Fletcher. I was a decent student with an all-around B average and no noteworthy aptitudes or weaknesses. No extracurricular school activities (traceable), but I played in a church basketball league (untraceable). I wasn't interested in college. I wanted to travel, get out of Oregon and see bigger cities. Seattle. San Francisco. New York. Los Angeles. My parents pushed me to apply to different engineering schools.

I can tell you most anything you want to know about Oregon. 97,073 square miles averaging 3,300 feet above sea level. Population 2,617,778 spread across thirty-six counties. Admitted to the Union on February 14, 1859, a Sunday. I have a good memory.

The residence I listed on my birth certificate might or might not have ever existed. I used a housing number sequence on a stretch of rural road that had surged to postwar-boom housing tracts, degenerated to lower middle-class, to a ghetto with the state's violent crime record high, then to regentrification via bulldozers and ribbon-cutting into miles of twenty-four-hour grocery giants and shopping malls over the course of four and a half decades.

"Is that where your parents are?"

"They're buried there, yeah." I drop my gaze, my eyes say that I'm rifling through my emotional memory banks.

"And how long ago did they pass away?"

"I was seventeen when my father died, and my mother died some years later." Eyes to my shoes again, I feed him my nervous grooming gesture and push my hair from my face.

"What happened to your father?"

"Brain aneurysm," my voice soft.

"Can you remember anything specific about his death?" The Evaluator shifts position, now he's mirroring me – feet flat, elbows on knees when he's not writing, leaning forward. He's doing *empathy*, so I'll open up.

"I was at my after-school job when my mother called." I've gone through this before, checked the dates, hospital admissions records, and maps. Four nights running, I sat in the dark with the air conditioner blasting, played the movie over and over on the backs of my eyes.

"By the time I got home, they were loading him into an ambulance. His eyes were half-open and wet like he'd been crying and his skin was bright red. I followed them to the hospital but he was dead when they arrived."

"And what about your mother?" He's dropped his voice. *You can talk to me. I understand.*

"She sort of lost steam after my father died and quit pressuring me about college. She had a stroke, a while back."

"And is that how she passed away?"

"Yeah. I flew home for her funeral. I spent a week helping my sister Emily clean out Mom's house to put it on the market. She and Jeff – her husband – moved everything into a storage unit."

"Did your father ever complain of headaches?"

"Yeah. Mostly when I was younger. He took medicine, but I don't know what." False. I'm hoping that he's not completely driven, that he'll finish my evaluation without checking for Karl Fletcher's medical history.

"What did your father do for a living?"

John Vincent Senior drank, moved furniture, drove a truck, drank, bought and sold a string of motorcycles, drank, was gone for months and years at a stretch, and drank. Mom said he was helping dig a gold mine. A polished lie to keep his kids from being ashamed of him. Dad called us and sent postcards.

"He was an eye doctor. He did very well, was always getting some award or another from different groups for being a philanthropist and humanitarian."

Dad looked like the pictures of Chet Baker midway through his aging continuum, dead between the stop-and-stare handsome that made waitresses blush and the later years, after shooting four times his body weight in Mexican brown tar into his veins. Dad never shot anything, but did most everything else. I know Dad was a lady-killer at one time, but he also ate a few pool cues, steering wheels, dashboards and nightsticks in his day. Decades of vodka give you a high pain threshold.

My smile twitches, my story locked and loaded.

"What's funny?" the Evaluator asks.

"I wanted one of those games where you put the plastic on the television screen and colored along with the cartoon. He wouldn't get me one. He said they were bad for your eyes. They took 'em off the market, but I was always mad at him for that." Stop fidgeting, resume eye contact because this is more comfortable territory for me.

"I'll bet he wouldn't let you have an air rifle either, would he?" The Evaluator is smiling. His fatigue is showing but, just for a moment, he wants me to see his guard drop.

"Or lawn darts," I say.

I've given him his *rapport*: a mix of nostalgia and sugar-coated resentment over some bygone childhood toys. He's content to move on, which is good. I don't want him pressing for more detail because I don't improvise as well as I plan. I relax my posture, return my voice to normal volume. I do *unconcerned, at ease*.

"Okay, what about your mother? Did she work?"

Mom was a coffee-shop waitress. Mom drove a school bus. Mom didn't drink, or at least didn't let me or Shelly see it. Mom dated some of the coffee-shop customers while Dad was away. I could tell she was pretty compared to other women her age. She went out on her nights off. Whether she was bored, needed companionship, wanted a decent meal, rent or pocket money, I don't know. Thinking about it makes my throat hurt, so I don't think about it.

Sometimes I'd go to the coffee shop after school, when Dad wasn't home. Mom would give me a meatloaf sandwich and a soda and I was supposed to sit at the end of the counter and do my schoolwork or color. The manager, I never knew his name, was a bloated man with a sopping cigar stump permanently wedged between his teeth, always wore a short-sleeve, pearl-button shirt and bolo tie, had sideburns like two hairy Floridas crawling down his fat jowls. He was tactful to me, and very nice to Mom. I put that together later, too. Mom kept that job, thick and thin, getting progressively more bold with what she filched to bring home for Shelly and me.

I didn't do any schoolwork, even as little as there was to do in kindergarten. I drew elaborate line doodles on the backs of the children's placemats, ignoring the coloring or connect-the-dots on the front, and created huge labyrinths or perfect line replicas of the wood-veneer countertop. Or I'd play a game, watching the waitresses pause at the register to add up their checks. I'd read them upside down, add them in my head to see if I could beat their speed at the register, see if my numbers were right. Then Mom would scold me for daydreaming, put my workbooks back in front of me.

"My father made decent money, so my mother could stay home and take care of us," I tell him, moving in my seat.

"So you were close to her?" And the Evaluator moves with me. A few beats behind, thinks I don't notice, thinks I trust him. He's writing more and more quickly, shorthand abbreviations stacked atop one another – PS, HE, HN, arrows pointing up, down or to one side, x's and circles – confirming some of my conclusions, obliterating others. We do a slow dance of posture changes, eye movement, eyebrow scratching and throat clearing, and I piece together his truncated record of our conversation, one line at a time. I want to go home. I miss Keara. I really wish I could get a line.

"Not really. I wanted out of the house as a kid. I was gone right after my father died. I kept up with her after that, but we never got close."

"Can you recall the last time you saw either of your parents?

"Not sure. It's been a long time. My father, it was that morning I went to school. My mother, it was on a visit home after I'd moved away, but I don't remember exactly when."

"What about any siblings? You mentioned an 'Emily.'"

"I've got an older brother and sister. Ryan works in banking on the East Coast. Emily's still in Oregon with her husband. They just had a baby girl."

"So, you're the youngest of three. Is that correct?"

"Yeah, I'm the youngest."

Sometimes a plane will go down and FAA investigators

can't identify any remains. A fuselage explosion at 35,000 feet or 800,000 pounds of flesh and metal hitting the water at four hundred miles an hour makes it hard to check prints or dental work. And sometimes the passenger manifests don't check out. Names dead-end when they look for next of kin. Illicit lovers on secret vacations, drug couriers, battered wives, and federal witnesses die midair wondering why their oxygen mask doesn't inflate, and nobody knows it because each one is a walking, breathing John Doe. That's my family.

"Are you close with your brother and sister?"

"More or less. We live in three different states and don't have holidays at home anymore. We talk every month or so. I have drinks with Ryan when he's in town on business, and I went to Emily's for Christmas, last year."

I don't know what it's like to have a brother, so I've got to be careful. I could paint myself into a serious corner if I give him fuel for the *abandonment issue.*

"How were you as a child?"

Bull's-eye. He's not dwelling on the parental death, though it's going to show up in his report. He's moved on, looking for a psychiatric history, another indicator of trouble.

"In terms of what?"

"Bed wetter? Sleeping problems? Anything out of the ordinary?"

"Nope." False. I wasn't walking until a full year later than normal and didn't begin speaking until age five. My parents thought I might have been retarded, but they couldn't afford to have a doctor look at me.

Once I learned to match the ten Roman digits to their amounts, learning math ceased to have any curve for me, but I didn't know that. I could shuffle four digits in my head as soon as I learned how to do one. Add or subtract, not saying anything out loud or writing anything down. Feeling the new numbers bloom and swell within my chest. If I had to write it down or show my work, the numbers were silent. Math problems looked like broken numbers, their pieces misaligned for no reason. You don't need water in a dry river to know where it's going to flow. The bends, falls, banks and slopes tell you everything, water or no water. That's what numbers were like for me from the beginning, and listening to a teacher explain how to line up columns – ones, tens, hundreds – and carry digits, I felt like a bird enduring a laborious, pop-up-book description of flight.

I faded out in class one day, zeroed in on a linoleum square on the floor, the dull color of old milk, peppered with flecks and spots to camouflage its age and damage. I copied it on the back of my paper, ignoring the class exercises, matching it point for discolored point with my blunt pencil.

Mrs. McMahon stood over me. She'd called me to the front of the class to solve one of the problems on the blackboard but I hadn't heard her.

"I've already solved them," I said.

Five other kids stood at the board *showing their work*, some drawing little stick-bundle fives to help their math.

"He can't count on his hands," somebody said. Mrs. McMahon sent me to the principal's office. I went three more times before they tested me and took me out.

When you're being tested for a special program, you're lumped into a deaf-mute/brain-damaged category, longhand for *stupid*. I've seen kids in wheelchairs and on crutches, nerves that never touched in the womb so their joints are permanently kinked, the wrists, fingers and feet not fully formed, or their lips and faces struggle to give shape to the words in their brain. Someone will say *How old is she?* or *What's wrong with him?* Because clearly, *she* or *him* can't hear you or understand you or speak for themselves. When people think you're stupid, they'll talk right in front of you, like you're nothing more than furniture. People thought I was stupid, so my notion of mental hospitals comes from a frankenstitched patchwork of the details deemed worth repeating in front of me – prurient, psych-student, water cooler gossip they thought I couldn't comprehend.

I learned that:

Some patients sat in their own shit for hours before they were tended to.

Medications were forgotten or transposed, sending one patient into an epileptic seizure and rendering another comatose.

Patients were left for hours upon hours in a locked room with no toilet, then punished for urinating on the floor – a display of antisocial-social behavior.

Restraints were used less to protect one patient from another or himself, and more to protect staff lunch hours or coffee breaks.

Not finishing dessert or not wanting to watch television with the others was considered antisocial behavior.

Electroconvulsion had long since gone from a last resort to routine procedure.

Diagnoses were exaggerated to perpetuate the flow of revenue from insurance companies.

You were watched when you wanted to be alone, ignored when you needed help. An understaffed, under-qualified team of interns and trainees reported to an over-aged, overworked Board of Directors. They read *insane* into your every word and action, decided when you leave if they came to any decisions at all. And if you were a patient and a good-looking woman, then you were as good as in Hell.

In jail, visiting day draws mothers, wives, fathers, siblings and children who skip work, school, drive for hours and tolerate spot-searches, metal detectors and X-rays to see their loved ones. When and if a mental patient receives a visitor, that patient is old and wealthy. Look at their visitors, check the watches and shoes – that's how you spot money. Heirs come out of the woodwork, start spending before the judge can raise his gavel.

"Did you go to college, Daniel?"

"I did a couple of years at a junior college. Not my thing."

"And what about high school?"

"Yeah, I went to high school. Graduated in '78."

I finished barely over two years of high school. I spent most of it in jail, arrested twice between ninth and tenth grades. I logged eight fights in those two years, three of them broken up by a teacher or gym coach who had me suspended. Mom and Dad never knew. I signed their names on the forms, wrote an angry letter of apology in Mom's cursive to accompany one that I mailed back, as well as signing Dad's signature to an expulsion warning which was obviated by a stint in juvenile hall.

"What were your grades like?" he asks.

"Mostly B's, except for a D in Art." Plant the seed while I have the chance. "We had to do at least one semester of Visual Art during the four years."

"Didn't like Art, I guess?"

If you aspire to be the next Picasso or Gauguin, bury it for two hours with a guy like this. Even if you know for a fact that he owns a house full of stupid earth-hugger whale paintings or hippie pottery, keep your mouth shut. You mention art, anything creative, and your Evaluator has a mental stack of color-coded tab cards with a new question for every response that will cattle-prod you to a predetermined diagnosis. Drop your guard and some mommy-hating intern will take you by a leash to the manic-depressive-suicidal-multiple-personality-schizophrenic-sociopath diagnosis they're dying to assign to someone so they can feel like their tuition wasn't wasted.

Creativity is either positive or negative, it has zero middle ground in an evaluation. And if your evaluation is mandated by a hospital, your artistic yearnings are going to be a three-alarm warning. Listen: you hate art. You are not creative. You get outdoors, socialize, go to the beach, hike, feed the homeless, visit your family, and surf. If an Evaluator sees creativity accompanying depression, anger or any sign of self-destruction, then that creativity is going to be relegated to finger painting and puzzles with grown men and women wearing cotton gowns, diapers and head injury scars.

"I just wasn't very good at it," I say. "They had a beginning drafting class that filled the requirement and I thought I could handle that. But it was full, so I spent a semester sketching fruit bowls. My drawings stank, but the instructor passed me out of sympathy. He knew I made an honest effort." True and false. I can draw if I have to. I've got a steady hand and a good eye, but I don't understand the urge to create interpretive pictures of sunsets or fruit bowls.

"So, what were you good at?"

Math guys are loners, so:

"History. Science." False. False.

"Do you remember your GPA?"

"Three something." Zero point eight.

"Besides Art, did you have any other weak subjects?"

"English, reading, those things were tough. The grammar. Too many exceptions to the rules."

"Were you involved in any extracurricular activities?"

I signed permission slips and academic performance warning notices for five bucks a signature, sold records and pipes I'd shoplifted, and forged learner's permits for the students who failed Driver's Ed. I forged signatures on work permits and signed overtime on burger joint time cards. I did math homework for some students, charged big time to do it in their handwriting, and even more if I had to show their work. By high school I could do it, *show my work*, but it was a chore.

"I played basketball in a church league. Mostly I worked, though. Dad wanted me to save for college."

"But no outside activities related to school?"

"No."

"Was there a conflict with your working?"

"No. I wanted to be on the track and field team but I was barred from the tryouts."

"Why is that?"

"I'd been suspended. I got caught doing pot with some friends in the parking lot during free period."

Lots of parents overreact, but guys like the Evaluator know what's normal for a teenager. The one positive side of smoking pot with your buddies is that it indicates you're sociable. Loner equals sociopath. Mention sports. *Plays well with others*. A guy like me, not the right size for football or basketball, can say I ran track and it's believable. If I got barred from trying out, it means that I have the skills to participate on a team although he can't verify that participation. Team sports. Track and field. Barred from the tryouts. An infallible combination.

I read <u>marijuana</u>, the underline is Evaluator Code to revisit a subject when I'm not braced for it.

"Were you actually smoking marijuana, or were you just with the others?"

"No, I lost the musical chairs. I was taking a long drag right when the vice principal ripped open the van door."

"Okay, so the school suspended you and wouldn't let you join the track team. How did your parents react?"

"They sent me to a counselor. He was an asshole." I'm doing *post-adolescent contempt* as best I can. An authority figure mandated by my parents – if I say I liked him or that we got along, the Evaluator will be certain I'm lying.

"Why was he an asshole?"

I shrug. "Just was."

"A school counselor, then?"

"No. Somebody else. Seigelman, or something." A school counselor would keep a record and I never attended that school. Confidential or not, the Evaluator could still verify the visit. Keep the name vague – of course I couldn't remember – and the trail is too long and too cold to follow.

"When during high school did this occur?"

"My sophomore year."

He's probing, building a timeline to see if my fictitious adolescent problems coincide with the deaths of my non-parents. And I'm walking a tightrope between normal teenage trouble and coming across too straight. It's a tightrope I've built from a mental table of medians and averages culled from stats on drugs, delinquency, academic and social behavior for white middle-class teenage males. I have to hover invisibly between future ivy league and future burnout. Magritte would have been proud.

"Besides the marijuana episode, did you have any other difficulties with school officials?"

"A couple of detentions for cutting classes. Nothing else, really."

SIX

My first word was "light." *Ite*. I was five. I didn't walk until I was almost two. Before I was talking I was drawing, on grocery bags and butcher paper, on anything, grinding crayons to their stumps one after the next.

I started mimicking at seven, the year I repeated kindergarten. Mom gave me a half-used puzzle book from a yard sale that year. I finished all of the mazes so I started making my own. Bored, I copied elaborate, nonsensical tangles of lines the way other kids watched television or played Cowboys and Indians. I copied the faded, grease-fogged fleur-de-lys and surrounding embellishments from our kitchen wallpaper. I copied the border etching from my birth certificate, from Shelly's birth certificate, from Mom and Dad's marriage license. They were all kept in a Bible that nobody in the family ever read.

I wasn't doing well in school. A final, confiscated spelling worksheet, corner-to-corner covered in a labyrinth of repeating, symmetrical doodles with almost 200 intersections per square inch, and a school counselor sent for me during morning recess. She had a stack of my worksheets on her desk when I arrived, and a long list of questions and tests. She asked me to draw figure-eights with different hands, one eye closed, then the other. Right or left, with one eye open and the corresponding hand trying to draw, I couldn't move. At best, I could drag my arm with a pull from the shoulder for a drool of irregular ink. But with both eyes open, I could copy the etching on a dollar bill with a ballpoint pen and a blank notepad, and had done so several times. But the counselor never asked me to do that. They transferred me to Special Ed after that, where my first headache hit.

As I got older, I called them *godsplitters* after Dad said *Boy's been howlin'. Got a headache that could split God's own skull in two.* I was by myself during free activity time – the other kids scared me – copying the swirls in the carpet onto a piece of paper when my head started to burn. Like when you jump into a swimming pool feet first and cram fire up your nose, makes your eyes feel like they're bleeding and a thousand fingernails scraping at the inside top of your skull.

They thought I was having a seizure. They forced something into my mouth, a stick wrapped in gauze like a dog's chew toy, sat on my legs and arms and the nail scraping kept on while they waited for me to stop struggling. Through the burn, I felt out of nowhere the carpet chafing my bare ass with an aide sitting on my legs, they'd pulled my pants to my knees and shot a hornet sting into my hip. My arms, legs and throat turned to cement. Seven years old, wide awake and numb from the neck down, my tongue like a bloated wad of bread dough, my head burned like a shrieking chalkboard for three days. They thought they'd stopped it, but they had only stopped themselves from seeing what was wrong. It took time, but I figured out that these people could do whatever they wanted. Even jail has better rules.

I can copy anything now. Straight lines – name the length to the centimeter – and perfect circles. Give me an angle degree and I can do it. Any signature, even the worst doctor's scrawl. I've signed my own tickets, had the DMV OK a cracked windshield or broken tail-light citation. I kept the sample of a signature and badge number from a speeding ticket years ago. I can't afford to fix something, Officer Blaine signs off and I'm good to go. I can do fingerprints.

* * *

1968, I'm nine. I'd been admitted to the fourth grade that September, following an inexplicable leap in my test scores after two years in Special Ed. *On Speech and Vocabulary examinations, John has successfully achieved scores commensurate with his age group, and has displayed an improved ability to listen and follow directions. While there is still room for improvement in his socialization skills, we feel this can only be addressed within an environment on par with his improved intellectual performance.* And so on. Followed by two months of *Hey, kid, you're on the wrong bus* and chanting *spider fingers, spider fingers* on the playground. In truth, they didn't bother me much. I'd learned to tune things out over the previous two years, corral events into a place in my head where they happened to someone else, like watching them on television.

Dad was home for Christmas that year after having been gone for thirteen months. Shelly and I asked if he'd found any gold. *Nope, still lookin'*, he said.

Christmas morning, Mom woke up early to make us breakfast before she went to work. I was on the porch with Dad, looking at my solitary present, *Sleight of Hand Fundamentals for Beginners*. Three hundred pages, the cover was creased with wear, separated from the spine a third of the way down, the back appendix pages falling out, yellowed with age and effluviating the rotting musk of mildewed paper. The text was written in arcane grammar that took multiple readings to decipher. Dad sat beside me, feeling my emanating waves of befuddled disappointment. I'd never expressed any interest in doing magic tricks.

"Look here," he said. "That's a *cup*. And that," pointing from one line drawing to another – hands wearing tailored cuffs holding cards, coins and kerchiefs – "is a *palm*. See here," another drawing, "how he's holding the card between two knuckles? That way, he holds his palm out," Dad held his palm to me, "looks like the card's disappeared."

"How does he get it there without them seeing it?" I asked him. I'd wanted a bicycle. A pair of shoes. My own room or a real bed.

"Because," another line drawing of a hand holding a kerchief, "he uses a *misdirect*, then a *flourish*. He makes them look away by distracting them. I'll do a couple with you, then you can practice."

Nine years old, and I'm humoring my father and his best attempt to give me *something* for Christmas. I hated the book, could hardly understand the language but kept at it to please Dad. I kicked furniture when a quarter slipped through a clumsy finger-palm or a three of diamonds fell loose from a clip. But those first two months after Christmas were the longest time I ever spent with Dad, the most words he ever spoke to me in a similar period of time, and the primitive coin tricks I did for him when he took me and Shelly to the doughnut shop on Sundays were the only times he ever smiled in front of me. So I learned how to pass, top change, bottom change, switch, steal, fumble, sleeve, screen, cuff, cup, palm, clip, flourish, misdirect, and force.

By the time I figured out that Dad taught me coin and card tricks so I could conceal my hand and quit getting stared at or beat up, I'd already moved to shoplifting. Six-finger discount. A force, misdirect or flourish worked as well to help palm or pocket whatever I didn't or couldn't have. My first bust, Dad was gone again. He'd sent us a postcard saying he was off digging another gold mine, and he'd be back in a year.

Polydactyly. An extra, half-formed digit, nubs of flesh and cartilage. A toe, sometimes a finger. They're removed at birth with less formality than pulling a tooth or a circumcision. A perfectly formed digit with the skeleton reconfigured to match is almost unheard of, except in some house cats. With cats, it's cute. With people, It's Not Polite to Stare.

My left hand fourth metacarpus – ring finger – is a duplicate of the third, a virtually non-existent variety of polydactyly.

It's not a deformity in the broader sense, said one osteopath. *For what it is, it's perfectly formed*. As it is: fully formed, ossified bone tissue – base, first, second, and third shafts – with its own set of arches, loops and whorls on the print. Mom had told me the doctor attending my birth suggested amputation, in my case a simple procedure that takes only a few minutes on such a small extremity. Newborn, my fingers were like grains of rice. Mom asked how much the additional procedure would cost, and whether it was really necessary. The doctor said the procedure was elective, but they couldn't predict how the finger might grow otherwise, and there were risks of complications both with the surgery and without. It was one more procedure Mom and Dad couldn't afford. Dad said *How do you know which finger's the extra one?* Mom told me the doctor laughed, then stopped when he saw Dad's face. I can picture him looking for the joke in the hollow of Dad's black shark-stare and coming up empty.

Dad used the same logic with me when I was little, refusing to let me cave in to ridicule. *How do you know the rest of us don't have enough?* His koans dumped me into my interior labyrinth of logic in search of a rebuttal and I'd get lost every time, ditching my anger or self-pity at some dead end while I looked for a way out.

I remember how Dad would sit at the kitchen table, bite the filter off a cigarette and smoke it down to his knuckles, waiting for the phone to ring with his next job. His money gone, he drank enough vodka to muster the nerve to tell Mom that she couldn't quit working just yet. But Dad never apologized. For anything. Neither did Mom. They almost never fought but when they did, neither one of them ever backed down and the screaming would last until sunrise. I guess that's where I learned it from. God help me otherwise. If I came home from school scraped up from another fight, one flick of Dad's fingers unhooked his belt and he'd start swinging if I apologized, showed any kind of regret about fighting. If I cried, it only got worse. Since then, the only person I've ever apologized to is Keara.

Nobody sees my fingers anymore unless I'm careless, when I've had too much to drink and I'm hailing a bartender or lighting a smoke. Once, I reached into a bowl of matchbooks at the Dresden Room with my left hand and the girl next to me shrieked, the kind of razor-pitch squeal that makes every bottled-courage silverback stand up and look at you, and make certain that everyone sees him doing it. Shrieker flushed, her face redder than blood in the light of the bar candles, then laughed, covered her mouth. I put my left hand back into my coat pocket, used my right to open the matchbook and light a smoke. I'd practiced that one over and over.

My left hand is a Rorschach blotch all its own, a six-fingered, skin-blood-and-bone ink splatter. People see it and fly their worst fears and secret fetishes at full mast when they think they're being discreet. They see it as strange, fascinating, ugly, beautiful, disgusting or erotic depending on what's behind their eyes.

Grown-ups used to look right at me, point, tap each other and grab my wrist to get a closer look at my fingers. Kids can be cruel, they can ostracize you, but with adults, you're a *specimen*. As I grew older, the comments changed to whispers and the stares went from my face to my peripheral vision to my back.

Sometimes a person won't hide anything, get a good look and act like it's as common as a cloudy day. They'll make conversation as if they see this sort of thing all the time. Tantamount to calling me *stupid* right to my face.

Freaks get off on it. Like the bottle-blonde in the black mini with shotgun acne scars spackled over with foundation and blush. In her apartment, she dropped her keys, purse and clothes with all the ceremony of scraping mud from her heels. Eighty-seven minutes after *Is anyone sitting here?* at the bar. Later, she stared at my fingers in the half-dark while I smoked, said *My friend has a thing for amputees. Her boyfriend lost his hand in an accident. She liked sticking his wrist stump inside her.* I can't lie. I take advantage of this.

Models, I meet them in bars, they find out I'm not trying to take them home and *are you a model?* isn't a pickup line. I ask them for hints – head shots, I need more weight, less weight, heavier eyes, lighter eyes. I want to shift my appearance a little for each new picture I have taken. I learned to fast for four days then wear clothes a size too large. Get bold and take a razor to my hairline, knock it back a half inch so I look good and skeletal for the camera. Or gorge on milk and pasta for two weeks, chew a serrano chili to flush my skin and make my eyes puffy.

Models like talking about themselves because they have nothing else to talk about. I spend an hour asking them for cosmetic secrets, not paying for their drinks.

They see my fingers, they run. Dominique. Alicia. Penny.

They see my fingers, they want their hair pulled. Alex. Renee. Kristin.

February 1972, I'm twelve. I was a regular at Boulevard Music, lifting about a hundred and fifty dollars in merchandise weekly, spending eight or twelve bucks during a visit to look honest. I rarely took vinyl and when I did, the plain sight approach was best, and *only* if I'd walked in with a few under my arm to begin with. Cassettes were easier, they weren't kept in plastic security brackets, the eight-tracks were invisible from the front registers – the convex security mirror mounted all wrong, useless for monitoring the *N-Z* aisles.

I paid for *Stooges, The*, had sleeved both *Reed, Lou* and *T-Rex*. At the door, someone shouted *Hey!* and I bolted. One of the cashiers, post-football fat but fast on his feet, grabbed me at the edge of the parking lot, dragged me back inside, clamped in a half-nelson.

My delusion was that because I was only twelve, because it was only a couple of cassettes, that they'd call my parents and be done with it. Dad was gone, Mom would come for me but be too tired from working two jobs to care. After listening to seventy-four minutes of crap from the manager in his locked office, I spat on one of the cops when they showed up.

"You've got to be kidding." The booking officer at the police station was rolling my prints, right hand, left hand, stopped to make certain what he was seeing. "Look at this," he called another cop over. The record store was pressing full charges, and a spit wad in the arresting officer's face had made things worse.

The second cop said, "You some kinda Martian, kid?" Ah, a *joke*. "That real?" He gripped my fingertips, squeezed them together – it hurt, but I didn't say anything – tapped my palm and the back of my hand as though it were a drug-smuggling prosthesis.

"It's real," I said.

"Nobody is talking to you," he snapped. They joked about cutting it off, bagging it for evidence. He got a separate print card, stapled it to the others, and referenced it on the Distinguishing Marks section of the booking form as an Extra Little Finger.

"The little finger isn't extra," I said.

"You givin' me a hard time?" Pressed uniform, biceps almost splitting through his sleeves, black leather gloves.

"Nope."

"I said, are you giving me a hard time, *boy*?"

"No, *sir*."

"I didn't think so. Now, take off your clothes, including that sissy-ass rock-and-roll shirt." He's raising his voice at me but I'm three feet away and there's no noise and nobody else in the room. I didn't understand.

"Quit staring, *boy*, and get to it."

My clothes piled on a metal table, two uniformed cops with surgical gloves turned them inside out – pockets, seams and linings – then me. Penlight in my ears, nostrils and mouth. *Stick your tongue out. Now up. Move it to one side. Hold it there. Now move it to the other. Place your left hand under your testicles and lift.* So I grip my nuts and lift them, they search with a light, then *Bend over and spread your cheeks. Let me see the bottom of your left foot. You know your right from left, boy. We just might get along. Now your right.* They rifled through my hair like grooming chimps, kept my belt, shoes and jacket, gave me back my shirt and jeans and a pair of canvas slippers like hospital shoes.

The way Dad reacted if I buckled to a group of kids or a bully forced me to fight. Outnumbered or outsized, which was always, I fought because no other kid ever would or ever did hit me harder or longer than Dad. This was different. My defiance wasn't going to call their bluff because they weren't bluffing. I didn't learn that as quickly as I learned other things, so it took a while. After a time, I learned to be invisible, learned not to fight because that makes you visible and you do not want to be visible in jail. I learned to do *obsequious, passive.*

"John Vincent," says the cop standing in front of me. "Yeah."

"Don't *yeah* me. Yes, *sir.* No, *sir.* Now, *John Vincent.*"

"Yes, *sir.*"

He smiled, leaned right into my face, all mustache, nose hair and chili breath, said *I know your daddy.*

SEVEN

Mom showed up twelve hours later with bail. My court date came three weeks after, Leap Day of 1972. The judge handed me twelve weeks of probation for a first offense, said *Don't show your face in my courtroom again.*

I'd spent only half a day in jail that first time, had all but walked away from spitting on a cop. I still hadn't learned to be invisible. On my way home from school the following Monday, some high-school kids stopped me on a side street beside a vacant lot. They outnumbered me five to one. Three were on foot, two on bicycles, so none of them were any older than fifteen. They took their cues from a heavy kid a head taller than me, and they knew who I was.

"Hey Johnny," he said, "show us your hand."

I did, gave him the finger.

"You just flip me off?" He stepped up to me, in my face and ready to fight, and all I could think was how much smaller he was than those cops.

I shook my head.

"I *saw* you give me the finger," and he pushed me backwards but didn't knock me over. Years of this, knowing what Dad would do, my heart didn't even speed up.

"How do you know it was the right finger?" I asked.

When your nose breaks, you can hear a half-second cartilage creak like a dry branch breaking loose from its own

81

weight, then a thousand fibrous snapping sounds in auto-fire succession. It echoes inside your ears like your whole skull coming loose. Then you're on the ground, sidewalk impact making you momentarily blind and putting a lump on the back of your head. I've had my nose broken twice. No accidents, I just couldn't keep my mouth shut. After a time, you get a feel for how people fight and why. He hadn't expected to connect like he did, and he hadn't expected my tolerance, either, hadn't expected me to stand right back up with an empty glass bottle, hot in my fist from baking in the sun. They ran, and I went home bleeding down the front of my clothes.

Doctors were always a last resort with Dad. Nothing pissed him off like spending money on a doctor to find out nothing. *It's going around. Lots of rest and fluids is best for this sort of thing. If it gets any worse, come on back.* Shelly fell from a stepladder onto the kitchen floor, fell four and a half feet. She lay in bed for five weeks with ice packs and bootleg pills from Dad to kill her pain. She could finally walk with a limp and went back to school. The limp stayed for good. One month later she started bleeding nonstop, two weeks before her period. The doctor told her she couldn't have any children. I think Dad's drinking worsened when he realized that maybe he could have found help for Shelly sooner than he did, or Mom for that matter, two years later.

But Dad was gone, so Mom took me to the hospital where they set my nose, and she never said anything to the school or the cops because I was still on probation and I would have gone straight back to jail.

1974, I was fourteen and hanging out with Louis. Louis was at the tail end of a chain of kids who paid me for signatures or papers, a friend of a friend of a customer. Louis had dropped out of high school five years previous, cleaned swimming pools for a living, sold pills, and hung out with the high-school kids to whom he sold. Louis had a studio apartment full of beanbag chairs, monster stereo, and centerfold models pinned to the corkboard walls. Louis liked having me around, thought my hand was cool. He'd take a gurgling suck on a water pipe and pass it to a customer, some football jock or rich kid with his girlfriend. Louis would give them steep discounts and lots of samples, trying to get them both to pass out, but for different reasons.

The guy would do a hit and Louis would say *Johnny, lift up your hand*, then to the guy, *How many fingers you see?* and spit smoke through his nose trying not to laugh. *That's some good shit, yeah?* Every time. But Louis was the most painless way to unload whatever I was lifting from the record stores and everywhere else. He paid cash and didn't ask questions. And hanging with him, the others left me alone.

Louis was seeing some girl who was too young to drink, and he wanted me to fix her ID, so I did. I'd never done it before, but changing the birth date on her driver's license was easy, so I started working on others, from scratch in the print shop after school. I matched a random string of first and last names out of the phone book, decided on *Christopher Thorne* and made him seventeen years old, with my face, my stats and a signature I'd composed out of thin air. There was no logic to the license number and the address was pure fiction, but the craftsmanship was flawless.

"Shit," Louis said later, "you're good."

We'd gone out for burgers one night, drove for an hour before the first stop so the places and faces were new to me. Louis was hitting arcades and drive-ins, making rounds with his customers. *This is Chris*, he'd say.

And the first time he introduced me that way, I slid into a booth by some pinball machines with a group of his friends and customers all two or three years older than me, sat right down like I belonged because they didn't know John Vincent, the eleven-fingered kid who used to be in Special Ed, they only knew Chris Thorne. Being somebody else, only in name, was like wearing a mask at a party – I could do anything and nobody would know it was me.

Saturday, everyone's on the nod at Louis's place. Again, I'm eyeing the cheap lockbox on his shelf (32R-17L-26R) wondering how much is in there. But I couldn't do it. He'd always done right by me. Among his loose cash and anonymous phone numbers was a prescription slip, carbon triplicates with a red-white zigzag pattern on the back, made out to a woman with Louis's last name – his mother – for Dilaudid.

"Can you do it?" Louis asked me. He'd stolen it from his mother's house, said something vague about her chronic illness, and that he wanted to get it back that afternoon and would pay me well if I could do it quickly. I said I'd try. I kept stencils, razors, glue and correction tape at his place because I wouldn't be able to stash them at home. Dad had propped a sheet of drywall between loose cinderblocks to cut the bedroom in half so that Shelly and I could share it. I got the side with the door, she got an extra twelve feet square. My half of the room was scarcely bigger than my mattress on the floor, with enough extra space for a milk crate of books and two trash bags of laundry, clean and dirty.

The turntable dropped the next record – I'd put on Iggy and the Stooges, *Raw Power* – while everyone slept, smoked, stared at the ceiling or off-key strummed one of the Telecasters Louis owned that I never saw him play. I started on the stolen prescription, line by line, layer by layer, my head contracting into that zone where I'm not hiding my fingers or wondering if someone's staring at me or standing confounded by an obvious question in front of class. I finished four altogether, between knocks at the door, Louis shaking hands and holding muffled conversations with visitors who never came in.

Lettering took the longest. Years later, I'd assemble my

own supply of vintage typewriters, ribbons, paper samples, laminating machines, custom inks, rubber stamps, and bootleg watermarking and embossing tools. But back then, I had to settle on transfer letters that I retouched with a mechanical pencil.

"Perfect." Louis held up the replica to his face.

"No, it's not," I said.

"What are you talking about?"

I took the specimen, started pointing out minutiae with the corner of a razorblade.

"I need to better match these typefaces," I said, "and this serial number, I just made it up. I've got no idea how the sequence works. I don't have the tools to create the perforation or the watermark, and these registration marks are way off." I could tell that I'd already lost him.

"I'll put the original back," he said, "and we can still use these."

"No, *we* cannot still use these," I said.

Louis pleaded, argued, bartered, then capitulated, helping me clean up every paper scrap and specimen, burned them all on a sheet of foil.

September 1974, I was fifteen, starting the tenth grade. I'd boosted a bottle of bourbon for Louis and me, and he let me drive his car as part of the deal. Deep-sea blue GTO, liquid-shiny with an idle that felt like a cold boil moving through your bones. I was black-out drunk and sidewinder weaving across four lanes, Louis laughing in the passenger seat.

My memory jump-cuts to the breakdown lane with the bone-boiling engine off, window down, hands on the wheel, light in my face. *License and registration*. Too drunk to know better, I handed over my Christopher Thorne ID. It looked legit, but didn't hold up when the number was called in. Two years had passed, but the judge had a good memory. My second juvenile offense got me thirty days in the Hall and twelve months of probation.

Those thirty days were a crash course that sank halfway in. I learned that you came from a gang or joined one, and fast, or faded into the background if you valued your skin. If you didn't fade out or join up, you'd be singled out for a sport beating or to do courier work for the gangs' contraband traffic and shanked if you came up short or didn't cooperate at all. I learned that guards did not like to repeat themselves and had the patience of mad dogs, that protesting made your life worse than cooperating, which made your life hell, and that any expression other than bravado would get you stomped, especially any expression of fear or sadness.

I learned to keep to myself, stay in my cell and practice my moves with a deck of cards I'd bought from the commissary, do crunches and push-ups to burn off the cabin fever.

I learned that predators don't intentionally choose the weak or old or sick. They kill what they can, which means the slow members of the pack. Thus, they strengthen the very gene pool they're feeding from. The threshold for what is weak, old or sick gets raised, and the strength, speed and instincts of new generations of hunters grow. A beautiful, self-perpetuating system where evolution is the antithesis of entropy.

My first day, I remember being hit by the noise, the concrete cacophony rebounding off metal, tile and rock inside the main gallery – radios, televisions, shouting matches over card games, domino games or shower passes all trying to be heard over each other. It was the same background noise I'd heard whenever Dad called home when I was younger, that I thought was the noise of gold miners.

County Youth Authority sequestered nonviolent offenders in a separate block. Most were plenty more street-smart than I but didn't have the brains God gave a tree stump. Jeremy had the lower bunk in my assigned cell, where I'd been sentenced for the next thirty days before entering my probation. Shorter than I was but much heavier, Jeremy wore his hair in a sandy mop cut that hung over his eyes. I couldn't tell their color, narrow slits surrounded by puffy lids like he'd spent his life squinting through security peepholes in his own face. If the Hall was a microsystem of predators and prey, then Jeremy was a mollusk, fixed in place and squinting suspicious, mute, at any initiated conversation. He ignored me if I spoke, face buried in a comic book, so much so that he startled me whenever he said anything. I never found out what he was in for.

"Can I borrow that when you're finished?" I asked.

No response, he kept turning pages, returned his comics to whatever envelope they'd been mailed in (by whom, I never knew), kept those under his mattress.

"You done yet?" was the first thing he ever said to me, while I was brushing my teeth at the sink. I held up a finger, *just a minute*, finished up, said, "I've got plenty of toothpaste, if you need any."

He said nothing else, no response to my offer. He removed his own toothbrush and toothpaste from a rolled-up brown paper sack sealed with tape that had been tucked inside his pillow. He brushed his teeth, returned his toiletries to the paper sack, carefully reaffixed the tape and placed them back inside his pillow. He left for the mess hall without a word. That was Jeremy.

I passed the time dealing Twenty One to a blank wall, practiced memorizing up cards, running high-low count in my head. With four weeks of time on my hands and an antisocial cell mate, I got good, and I was getting better at reading people. Not intuitively, I don't have that. But if I watched them long enough, I could number their actions and words, work out equations for them.

A person's life story is equal to what they have plus what they want most in the world, minus what they're actually willing to sacrifice for it. You find out those things about someone and you'll know almost everything. The fractional numbers are their headshakes, facial tics or finger movements they don't realize they're doing, and they all add up if you can spot them.

I made just enough off the other kids in my block for an extra soda or candy bar or magazine. No point in winning too much, the gang kids would take it. They hung out near the commissary during yard time to see how much you were spending. You had to pay to get through them if you wanted anything. I did, they left me alone. I practiced one-handed cuts and shuffles, bottom deals and the rest in my cell, so I wouldn't end up practicing in the infirmary, and rat-holed extra scrip in my sock for when I got out. And aside from the card games, I worked hard not to be noticed. Maybe that's all Jeremy was trying to do, not be noticed, be invisible.

Gen. Pop. mixed in the gallery, the ground level of the Hall's atrium of cells and catwalks: gymnasium chairs, card tables, ping-pong tables and television. We lined up there for morning roll call, cell inspections and chore assignments. I was short-time, so I got assigned library duty. I spent mornings shelving returns and cleaning – it got inspected daily before noon. Morning chores followed breakfast. Then lunch, mail call and free time.

I had a game running one afternoon. Jeremy sat by himself in a chair at the far edge of the television viewing area, reading a white sheet from a white envelope, both typed, so far as I could see. No seal or letterhead, and by his reaction I could tell it was personal, bad news from home. He set the letter onto an empty chair beside him, dug the heels of his palms into his eyes, just once.

Say what? someone shouted. *Check it!* Whoops and jeers took flight like a flock of startled crows, then spit wads and clapping from a circle of inmates surrounding Jeremy in an instant. Two COs broke up the taunting, sent Jeremy back to his cell. My cell. His eyes were wet, I saw them for the first time when he looked my way before hiding behind his moppy hair. They were brown. I ducked back to the shit hand – pair of sevens – I'd been dealt.

Hey, a CO stopped him. *Here*, and handed Jeremy the letter he'd left behind. The catcalls and jeers chased him all the way up to our deck.

The following afternoon, I left the library early with a shower pass, on my way to check out a towel and shaving kit. The library had one of the biggest blinds between it and the gallery. Because so few kids ever wanted to read, it was a low security priority. I rounded a corner into the blind, saw a tight ring of kids from the other blocks. Some had their orange coveralls open, hanging off their shoulders or undone to the waist. It took me a second to read it, then I caught a flicker of Jeremy's face, nosebleed mixing with hot tears, then the gap in the ring closed. *Keep walking*, one of them said to me, and I did.

Showered, back in my cell, I stared at an astronomy book for seventy minutes and never read a word. Jeremy stayed gone. The same pictures of nebulae bounced off my eyes while an ice block sat in my stomach. Jeremy was moved to the infirmary that afternoon, and I didn't see him after that. A CO tapped the bars, said *Warden wants to see you*.

"Sit down, Johnny," said the Warden. I'd never met the Warden. Only Mom and Dad called me Johnny.

"I spoke with your father earlier." He relaxed in a high-backed leather chair, held a thin gold pen between both thumbs and forefingers like some delicate appetizer.

"He tells me your mother has cancer. The doctors have removed it, but still need to find out if it's spread. That's all I know." A nod to his office door summoned a CO to escort me back.

"Your father said he'd come visit on Thursday and tell you everything."

I shaved that Thursday morning, put on my clean coveralls

that I'd pressed under my mattress overnight. I practiced my cuts, cuffs, palms and clips – some of the moves that got me jailed to begin with – waiting for Dad. He never showed up, and I didn't see him until I got out.

Twenty days later, in cuffs, my toes on the yellow tape three feet in front of an acrylic security window, I signed a property slip through the one-by-six cutout. House key, wallet (minus Chris Thorne's license), watch – *Stole this, didn't you?* – sunglasses, and pack of gum. My scrip, redeemed at fifty cents on the dollar, came to thirty-eight bucks. The Property Officer slid a brown envelope through a bank teller window, buzzed me through another door. *Follow the yellow line.* A stone box of a room, two COs gargoyle-perched in the corners while I changed back into my street clothes that were folded on a locker room bench – stovepipe jeans, canvas running shoes, New York Dolls T-shirt, and my windbreaker. Cuffed once again – holding out my wrists was reflex at this point – they lead me through two more buzz-locked security doors, calling my name into an intercom both times.

"Vincent, John Dolan."

"Vincent, John Dolan," repeated the intercom.

At the second door, they uncuffed me, and I stepped through it with free hands into the waiting room – cops, plastic chairs, soda and cigarette machines, waiting families. Dad wasn't there.

"See ya real soon," they said, closed the door behind me.

EIGHT

I walked outside, heard a car horn. The October morning shone bright but cold, the sky a luminous blue, and the wind froze my ears and fingertips and the sun bounced off puddles in the pocked asphalt outside. The car honked again, it was Dad. He didn't like being there.

He drove a brown Ranchero that I hadn't seen before, the passenger-side door buckled from a collision – whether Dad's or the previous owner's was even money – idling with the uneven rumble of a machine about to die. I'd gone longer, much longer, than thirty-day stretches without seeing Dad, but this was the first time he looked truly unfamiliar to me. I remembered pieces – greasy black hair, green-blue spider webs, eagles, flags, *HD*, and skulls staining his forearms, and the inscription *13½* on the back of his left hand. I never wanted tattoos, never wanted any more distinguishing marks than what I'd been born with.

In the passenger seat, I saw his hands on the wheel, his fingers chipped, cracked, blood-blistered on the palms and black beneath the nails, battle calluses on the inside edge of his thumbs and knuckles. He'd been working, staying straight. He wore wraparound mirrored sunglasses like a cop, didn't say *hello* or *you doin' okay?* or anything when I got in. Dad put the Ranchero into gear, jutting his chin at my Personal Effects envelope.

"Take your stuff out of there and toss that. Those things are bad luck."

I dumped out the keys, wallet and gum, pointed through the windshield at a refurbished oil drum near the visitor's entrance.

DISPOSE OF ALL CONTRABAND BEFORE ENTERING.
ALL VISITORS ARE SUBJECT TO SEARCH UPON ENTRY.

"Swing over. There's a garbage can," I said.

"Roll down your window and throw it the fuck out." He turned sharply toward the lot exit, never took his eyes from the windshield. That was my reunion with Dad, like an after-school, football-practice pickup that intruded on dinner, something we did every day. An hour and a half of silence into the ride and I realized that Dad had never covered his eyes before.

With each passing minute of that silence, *Is Mom okay?* grew heavier in my head, but those space insect/trooper shades killed my nerve to ask. We arrived home and I saw for myself.

Our old place, the two-bedroom house Mom and Dad rented, was gone. Dad pulled into an apartment complex and parked the car in a covered space (#49), walked me to an apartment, a red door (also #49) in a row of other red doors in a low, white stucco barrack. With three other barrack structures, they surrounded a dirt courtyard where a tricycle sat, fused halfway underground, having sunk into the soft mud during the rain, surrounded by deflated soccer balls, headless Barbies, empty 10W-40 cans and patches of grass the color of old fingernails. Later, I found the pool, the gate padlocked and the pool drained except for a foot of black water at the bottom, in which lay three tumbleweeds the size of bulldozer tires.

Bedroom, bathroom, kitchen, living room, too cramped to subdivide for Shelly and me. Mom and Shelly took the bedroom, Dad and I slept in the living room. Everything but Mom was different. I'd expected her to wear a kerchief knotted over her bald head, her face the plastic sheen that cancer patients get when their eyebrows fall out, but she looked the same. Just tired, and she seemed to forget things more and more. She kissed my cheek and left for work.

Shelly was out of school, working full-time. I didn't know where, but she limped out every morning in a simple skirt and blouse, came back at night. Mom waited tables, went to the clinic every two weeks. Dad welded in a machine shop, made decent money for the first time in a while, but his insurance wouldn't pay for Mom. They said she had a *pre-existing condition*.

I think it was easier for Dad while I was in jail. He had enough to worry about, and as long as I was locked up he wasn't getting wakeup calls from the school or the cops, and he had one less mouth to feed.

Maybe he would rather I'd dropped out and started working too, except I had a PO who all but held a gun to my head. Officer Durrel came to the apartment every Saturday, had me piss into a cup, and rummaged through my book bag. I spent extra time to *show my work* on my math papers. Dad was always working on the car or gone when he came by. Durrel needed a signature each week from Mom or Dad, so he went for lunch where Mom worked, got a signature from her.

"I can read your mind, John Vincent." My first interview with him, he folded his hands in his lap, looked me straight in the eyes. "You think 'Equivalency Test' and I will know it, and I will violate you back. You stay in school as long as you're under my watch with nothing less than a two-point-eight. You stay outta trouble, you and I won't have any trouble."

He never said *Got it?* or *Understand?* or *Do I make myself clear?* And I didn't want to go back, so I stayed in school, kept my head low, even kept away from Louis.

You're alone, the house is quiet. The refrigerator stops

humming and the ambient static you mistook for silence is gone and you can almost hear your own heartbeat. That's what it's like right before a godsplitter hits. Like when you know something in a dream because that's the dream script and for no other reason.

I was heading home from school and by the time I'd arrived at our front door, I had one eye closed because the patchy sunlight hurt, barely held my balance, teetered on the edge of vomiting, and went straight for the couch to cover my eyes with a pillow.

I took aspirin all afternoon, chewing the bitter tablets until the bottle was empty except for the dust and cotton, started coughing them back up but tried not to, as each pulse of my lungs pushed on my eardrums like a knitting needle. Gobs of snot and spit and blood pouring out with a bile chaser to sandpaper my throat and burn my eyes. Half-dissolved chalky-paste chunks of aspirin following behind.

Mom and Dad came home after Shelly called Mom at work to tell her there was blood all over my pillow. That fixed my stomach for a couple of years. I couldn't have spicy food and my own shit burned me for a while. Twenty-four months of grits, waffles, meatloaf, and mashed potatoes in the Hall put a stop to that.

On the living room sofa for days, I wanted the curtains shut and the lights off. Mom kept trying to feed me soup and crackers. She didn't want to give me aspirin, but had other pills from Dad. Plastic bags or unmarked bottles that he turned up with after going out for cigarettes. *Give him these. They'll shut it down quick.*

Mom had come home early to check on me. She tried to put a damp cloth on my head but I didn't want it. The cold made it worse. "Sweetie, keep it there. It'll help the pain."

"No. It hurts."

"Honey–"

"*Stop it.*" The air vibrating with sound hurt. I wanted her to

CRAIG CLEVENGER 95

leave me alone, stop talking, just die altogether, but I couldn't speak. She went away.

We were already being tapped hard for medical expenses with Mom, but I knew what Dad was thinking. Some cancer is hereditary. Mom had breast cancer, it turned out, and they'd caught it too late. I wondered if there was something growing in my head, and I know that's what Dad thought. He took me to the hospital. The pain had subsided after three days, and he was able to get off work for an afternoon. I had to squeeze my eyes shut to and from the car, holding his arm.

Dark never bothered me. Dad taught me how to change fuses when I was six. I could crawl under the house with a flashlight blasting Id-fear shadows across the dirt without a second thought, swap out a twenty- or thirty-amp fuse from the cigar box, then go back inside and watch TV. But light scared me after a while. Hospitals and doctors' offices and police stations were bright, and I got to hate bright light after years of it, beginning with those first tests, when they put me through a CAT scan. I was in the hospital wearing a papery gown tied at the back and being shoved into this tunnel of light. The nurses kept telling me to sit still.

The doctor's office smelled like new leather and lemon oil. The dark wood on the desk and chairs was smooth and bright as glass, one wall covered floor-to-ceiling with books in austere leather bindings, gold stamps on their spines. *Gray's Anatomy. New England Journal of Medicine Index. Pediatric Consultation Reference.* The godsplitter had fully subsided and all I could think about was food.

Dad and I waited. An unfiltered Lucky stump wedged between his fingers, the first three knuckles of his right hand the size of walnuts, the last quarter-inch of tip missing from his thumb, sheared off with a chop saw. *Dawg ate it,* he'd told me.

"We see no signs of a fracture or tumor." The doctor spoke

with a measured cadence, no emphasis or accent, like the voice-over for a safety film. "And no ruptured blood vessels, fluid buildup or sinus infection. Here's the number for an eye doctor you might want to try."

Dad mumbled, "It's all in your head."

"Yes, there's that," said the doctor.

"Pardon?"

"Attention," he continued. "With his mother being ill, the shoplifting and drunk driving not getting him any, the headaches are a mechanism for attention."

I was in trouble and had headaches before Mom was sick and tried to say so. He held his hand to quiet me, talking about me in the third person like I was a plant that needed watering.

"But that's not really my field. I do know some people that might help," he handed a card to Dad. "They charge on a sliding scale."

In the car, Dad gripped his last cigarette in his mouth, crushed the empty package with a squeeze of his fist and tossed it out the window.

"Doctor thinks you're a fucking nut." He pushed the dashboard lighter and waited, pulled up to a doughnut stand. "More shit I do not need."

I looked out the window. Clouds the color of sheet metal hung low, scraping the tops of billboards and telephone poles. My view through the window grew hot and blurry and I kept my face turned and my mouth shut.

By now I'd had counseling from two probation officers, another in juvenile hall, one in high school when my grades were on the downside of their roller coaster and the other two that had me shoehorned into Special Ed when I was seven. Mouth off at a cop, maybe you get snapped with a baton. Maybe you get arrested for something that's got a time lock on it no matter how bad. Misdemeanor. Thirty days in County. Six months of community service. But a Psych Evaluator has a different set of rules and they can make them up as they go.

Training for therapy, learning how to diagnose or identify dysfunctions, syndromes or depression doesn't teach someone how to be patient, how to listen. Colleges don't teach empathy. Psych students don't learn how to manage budgets and paper trails or linen shortages and staff turnover at an institution.

Instead, overcrowding means you're assigned to a solitary, cushioned room whether you're a threat or not, and last resorts for therapy become first resorts for discipline.

I once read something about an orderly at a hospital. He'd been a convicted sex offender but they hadn't checked him out thoroughly. For months on end, he was masturbating over the faces of tranquilized patients in restraints. Dish towel in their mouths, the last thing a patient saw if still half-awake was the nano-second of overhead light before the orderly blew his load, wiped the sperm from their eyes and out of their nostrils and hair.

A patient complained but, as there was no evidence and as he was heavily medicated, a *severe auto-erotic delusionary psychosis* was added to that patient's file. He gave up complaining and the hospital figured the delusion had passed. In fact, he had just learned how to time the orderly's visits, learned how to numb himself to them. People can numb themselves, get used to anything.

The orderly did this with seven patients over fourteen months until someone walked in on him.

My first day at the clinic where the doctor sent me, I saw a kid who lived down the street from me. His name was Brett. He was a couple of years older than me. I'd seen him in the school lunch area by himself, eating alone and reading a copy of Circus. He lived down the block from our apartment complex in a big house. It must have been every weekend I saw him in his front yard, pushing a rotary lawnmower in precision rows across the massive lawn in front of his house. Covered with sweat, batting bugs out of his eyes and dumping the wet green clippings from the canvas grass catcher into a garbage can. Every week, without fail.

Sometimes a woman was there, his mother – baseball glove tan, shorts, rubber thongs, a blouse knotted at her waist, a tall drink in her hand. Her voice carried, dog-pitch high, and I could hear intermittent *weeds, dammit, lazy* from a distance.

I recognized Brett's mother in the lobby of the hospital where Dr. Gaines worked my first time there. She paid Dad and me no mind, her nose buried in a gardening magazine. Dad smoked, rested his face on his fists, elbows on his knees, hand bandaged from his latest cut, *piece of sheet metal went right through my goddamned gloves*, his eyes burning a hole at some invisible midpoint in the air in front of him.

The door to the lobby opened, a nurse was showing Brett out to his mother. He wore dark wraparound glasses and carried a paper cup of water.

"He'll be very thirsty for a while," the nurse said to his mother. "Give him as much water as he needs and keep him in the shade for the rest of the day. The grogginess will wear off in a few hours."

I saw him on two other visits after that. He always wore sunglasses coming out of the office, though never when he mowed the lawn. He moved a little more slowly each time. I don't know why he was there, never spoke to him at school, and he never indicated that he recognized me.

Dr. Gaines asked me about my headaches, about school, my family and friends. How did I feel about Mom being sick? Were Mom and I close? Were Dad and I close? Did I want to be like Dad? Is that why I got sent to jail?

I remembered the questions my first probation officer asked me, after my shoplifting arrest. After all of these people, the pattern shone plain as staring into the sun:

Parents.

Siblings.

Friends.
Girlfriends.
School.
Strong subjects.
Weak subjects.
Medical history.
Drugs.
Discipline.

The list was the same, rubber-stamped for every county intern, probation officer and school guidance counselor. The light came on so bright that when Dr. Gaines showed me the Rorschach blots, it didn't occur to me to ask what *he* saw in them, I was so preoccupied with putting numbers to the questions, piecing together the equation I thought he was looking for.

"John," he held up a card with a black forensic splatter. "Can you tell me what this might be?"

I shook my head.

"Try and imagine what else this might look like. Take your time."

"It's a black splatter."

They call this *marginalizing*, I came to learn, when you're faking a response in order to skew an evaluation. I could write a book on it now. With Dr. Gaines, though, I was telling the truth. And I said the same thing for the next four cards because I couldn't see anything other than black splatters.

"John." He slapped down the stack of inkblots and yanked off his glasses, closed his eyes and pinched the bridge of his nose. "I can't help you if you don't cooperate." He spoke in the short, clipped tones of adult condescension and threats that I'd tuned out long before. But the words *Special Program* tuned me back in fast, like a sledgehammer through my daydream.

"...you're failing school, you've been in Special Ed before, and now you're butting heads with the law. You're claiming these terrible headaches that your doctor says don't exist. You see where that leaves me?"

Questions had eluded me before, at school or with Mom and Dad. But I was truly stumped with this one, and I felt stupid for not seeing anything besides a white card with a black ink stain. I was back in grade school again.

"Can I draw it for you?" I asked. I didn't know what else to do.

"You want to draw me a picture of what you see? That would be fine." He spread his hands, waiting for more.

The cards lay in a face-down stack on his desk, the last one as clear in my head as my hand in front of my face. A symmetrical black splotch that fanned out like an angry butterfly after a collision with a light-speed windshield. I look back, that's what I think. At the time, saying *It looks like a butterfly* never crossed my mind.

I reached for a sheet of paper and a black marker. Dr. Gaines dealt with lots of kids, kept buckets of crayons and markers and paper right on his desk. Starting with the outside contours, I traced a single, continuous line, closed it, started filling in the shape from the edges to the center of the butterfly's exploded thorax. It took me sixty-five seconds, then I turned the last ink splatter over for comparison.

"May I have a look?" he asked.

I showed him my flawless, photomemory replica.

"That's what I see."

Sometimes I can be so smart, and sometimes I can be so stupid. The extremes of both are indecipherable to most people, and I've learned that the smartest thing that a smart person can do is keep those smarts hidden in plain sight. Otherwise, someone will slot you where you pose the least threat to their private scope on the world. Mess with their custom-fitted, rose-colored welder's goggles and you will pay for it.

Dr. Gaines brought me back for weekly follow-ups, a different battery of tests each time. More Rorschach splatters with different student interns and doctors for second opinions. The male doctors and students always called me *John* the first time, then *Sport, Champ, Slugger* or something after that. The females always called me Johnny.

Johnny, I want you to really use your imagination. Look at the picture, close your eyes and imagine what else it might look like? What else do you see?

I see:

A tumor.

A bloody nose and broken teeth from a kid who got beat up for saying fuck you to a group of other kids who called him a retard.

A six-fingered handprint.

A middle-aged woman with one tit.

A drunk man, old before his time.

A human heart full of staples, stitches and sutures.

Minnesota Multiphasic Personality Inventory. Weschler Adult Intelligence Scale. Millon Clinical Multiaxial Inventory. Beck Depression Inventory. Weschler Intelligence Scale for Children. Weschler Individual Achievement Test. Woodcock-Johnson Psycho-Educational Battery-Revised. Million Adolescent Clinical Inventory. Thematic Apperception Test. Axis I. Axis II. Axis III. Verbal. Non-verbal. True or false. Matching. Memory. Figure-eights with one eye closed, then the other. Question: *You dig a hole two feet deep by two feet wide by two feet across, what is the volume of dirt in the hole? You're being a real sport, Ace. You want a soda?* Serial Sevens: *Please count backwards from 100 in increments of seven.* Ninety-three. Eighty-six. Seventy-nine. Seventy-two. Sixty-five. Fifty-eight. Fifty-one. Forty-four. *Pretty good, Kiddo. Can you do it from, say, 322?* Three hundred fifteen. Three hundred eight. Three hundred one. Two hundred ninety-four. *You're a regular Einstein, Champ. Show me your hand. People tease you about it? What do they say?* Colored puzzles and matching shapes to holes under a stopwatch. Complete the sentence: *Dog is to cat as cockroach is to blank.*

They charged on a sliding scale and they'd quit charging Dad altogether. That was two hours every week he knew for certain where I was. A dozen graduate students padded their case-study portfolios and fleshed out their research papers while I bought time. I'd be sixteen soon and off probation. If I did what they wanted, kept my nose clean, I could keep myself from being sent to some padded boarding school or locked up. After that, I was gone. I could pack a bag and with the right window of opportunity – Mom at work or the doctor, Shelly at work, Dad at work or halfway through another bottle of vodka with bugs walking across his face on the living room sofa – I'd disappear on a bus to a city somewhere. I think everyone would have been happiest with that.

Every follow-up session, at some point, left me alone in Dr. Gaines's office for a period of time. After four weeks, I'd read the two diagnostic manuals cover to cover, had a working knowledge of organic versus cognitive disorders, knew the difference between *psychotic* versus *psychopathic*, the definitions from a cross-section of common favorites: mood disorders, developmental disorders, substance abuse disorders, depression, mania, and bipolarity. I was reading *Academic Variables in Adolescent Emotional Test Scoring* when I heard Dr. Gaines's voice in the hallway. I put the book back onto the shelf.

"We're going to try something new today." Those were Dr. Gaines's words, and it took me years to corral the itch in the back of my brain into coming out, taking shape: *We're going to* experiment *today.*

It looked almost exactly like a dentist's chair, a prop for my feet and head and they leaned me back. Dr. Gaines and a nurse ran a small battery of tests – stethoscope, *say ahh*, penlight to my pupils – after they'd told me to use the bathroom, to go even if I didn't feel like I had to.

Relax, Johnny, put your head back, rest your arms here, the nurse put my hands on the arm rests of the chair. She wrapped a nylon cuff around one wrist, like she was checking my blood pressure, then the other.

The reflex question, *Is this going to hurt?* came out and she said *No, but sometimes this causes a sudden movement and you could hurt yourself.* Then she wrapped another set of cuffs onto my feet.

I turned to watch Dr. Gaines hitting a switch on a bank of dials and lights, the nurse turned my head up, said *Open*, put a gauze chew-stick into my mouth like the one they gave me when I was a kid.

A knock at the door. I heard a guy's voice outside, the one who always called me *Champ*. He said *Excuse me, Doctor*, then the door opened without invitation. Commotion that I couldn't see because I couldn't move my head, then Officer Durrel's face was over mine.

To the doctor, "Take this shit off him."

The straps off, I stood up and rubbed my jaw.

"John Dolan Vincent. Face the wall and place both hands on top of your head."

NINE

Sometimes I can be so smart, and sometimes I can be so stupid. Louis had saved one of my prescription forgery trial runs. I'd never stopped to think about why he'd shifted gears so suddenly, from arguing with me to helping me destroy them. He wrote it out for himself, calling for non-existent 20 mg "Delauded" tablets, 500 count, and signed it "Dr. Fred Smith." He was going to sell them. This same genius froze cough syrup to scrape off the codeine. When the cops showed up after the pharmacist's call, he gave them my name before they asked for his. Mom or Dad didn't bail me out this time.

The State gave me a lawyer who gave me a black suit from the Salvation Army, a starched white shirt with pearl snaps still in drycleaner's tissue. He sent me to a barber, said *Lookin' like a leprechaun won't sway a jury. And try to keep your hand outta their line of sight.*

Tuesday, August 5, 1975, I looked like a snake handler at a Sunday funeral. My lawyer built my defense, introduced the jury to my high-school counselor, to Dr. Gaines and several members of his staff, all of whom testified as to my abnormal test scores and intelligence.

The State introduced the jury to my juvenile arrest record that was twenty months from being sealed. The State assailed my alleged intelligence with my leprous academic record and my stint in Special Ed.

"So, in this enormous battery of tests, you haven't actually given the defendant an IQ test, have you, Doctor? And how many of these tests do you personally administer? And the rest were done by students, is that correct? Students, not doctors. Yes or no."

"Doctor, how old is the average male child during the onset of speech development? And crawling and walking? And how old was the defendant? That old? Almost a full three years behind the average, ladies and gentlemen. And with less than even a single, full point GPA we're supposed to believe that he's some kind of genius. Yes, the story goes that Einstein flunked freshman math, but he wasn't counterfeiting driver's licenses or narcotic prescriptions."

My lawyer objected, had it sustained, but the judge couldn't take it out of the jury's ears and the Prosecutor knew that. He withdrew but then introduced my record of campus fights. Eight in all. I got hurt pretty bad in most of them. I'd usually been outnumbered, but I did what I could. The jury got to see the photographs of stitches and dental imprints from some of the other kids. The school didn't keep records of who starts fights, just who was involved. Jail was the same way.

My Christopher Thorne driver's license was exhumed from an evidence locker, along with the surviving Schedule II prescription forgery. The State dug as far back as when I was eight years old, salvaging from God knows where my childhood doodles of dollar bill borders. *Looks good, doesn't it?* Never mind that showing an eight year-old's perfect mimicry – by hand – of such detailed etching negated their assault on my intelligence.

My lawyer was aiming for a Not Guilty. The State had plenty of evidence against me, but my lawyer was forcing them to prove my intent, that I had larger, malicious motives behind copying narcotic prescriptions and dollar bills. Louis was his trump card, even though he was the Prosecution's witness. He knew that Louis had pocketed the slip without my knowledge.

Louis had agreed to cooperate with the Prosecution in lieu of being charged with a felony offense. Louis, I learned, didn't handle pressure too well. Louis should have left crime to the criminals. They swore him onto the witness stand, and the Prosecutor grabbed his leash. Louis crumpled on the stand as quickly as he had with the cops.

"Louis, did the defendant tell you *why* he wanted to destroy the prescription forms?"

"No, sir."

But I had.

"You have no idea why he wanted to destroy them after so much work?"

"No, sir."

"Louis, have you seen the defendant destroy his handiwork on other occasions?"

"Yes, sir."

"Can you provide an example?"

"Like… when he wanted to do something over. He'd get rid of his first tries."

"So you *do* have an idea as to why he destroyed those forms."

Louis looked wide-eyed at the jury box, as though someone there might coach him.

"Louis, when the defendant was forging a document," *objection, sustained, withdrawn,* "he would destroy previous, flawed versions and save the final, finished product. Is that correct?"

"Yeah."

"So then, Louis, is it possible that the defendant wasn't happy with the results of the narcotic prescription form in question?" He held up the evidence-tagged form for the jury once more.

"I guess so."

"Louis, yes or no. Is it possible that he wanted to destroy this in order to make additional, more accurate counterfeits?"

"Yes."

"Could you speak up, please?"

"Yes. It's possible."

I suppose I should have been angry at Louis. In truth, I wasn't. I felt sorry for him. He was going to get busted for something else – just a matter of time – and get sent down. He'd be cellblock bitch-meat inside of two weeks, washing his cellmate's underwear and doing himself up with eyeliner made from melted crayons and lipstick from blood and bacon fat. He'd be tattooed with a needle using burned newspaper mixed with toothpaste, tagged as somebody else's punk. And strange, but I felt a mixed admiration for the Prosecutor, who took a string of irrefutable facts and shuffled the deck for an altogether different truth.

The Defense countered with an assault on Louis's credibility. My lawyer attacked Louis's status as State's witness, his poor academic record, his reputation as a dealer and previous possession arrests, and the fact that he appeared to live beyond his means as a pool cleaner. And my lawyer made it very clear that it was Louis who had tried to redeem the Dilaudid prescription. He continued, hammered Louis hard to clarify that I'd never taken drugs with him, and the DUI arrest was the only time he'd seen me drink. Throughout the trial, my lawyer insisted that I not take the stand.

Thursday, August 7. Dad was the last witness. I hadn't seen him since before my arrest, and we couldn't speak since the Prosecution had subpoenaed him first.

"John Dolan Vincent. Please raise your right hand. Do you solemnly swear that the testimony you are about to give is the truth, the whole truth and nothing but the truth?"

"I do."

The Prosecution wasted no time.

"Do you recognize any of these papers, Mr. Vincent?" The Prosecutor held up a stack of forms and half-page slips from a cardboard box at his table. I recognized them all.

"No."

My lawyer raised an objection to the new evidence and the proceedings stalled for a conference at the bench.

"Make your point, Counselor," the Judge said.

"Mr. Vincent, could you please describe the forms you're holding for the jury," the Prosecution continued.

"They look like…" Dad was sober, not enjoying any of this one bit, "says here this one's a Notice of Temporary Suspension. Here's one's a quarterly Academic Performance Report."

"And what kind of performance does it indicate?"

"Says…" Dad squinted, "unsatisfactory. Says he's in danger of failing all of his classes."

"Who?"

Dad lifted his glasses to pinch the bridge of his nose. "My son. John Junior."

"Mr. Vincent, do you see your signature on any of those forms?"

Dad leafed through the stack. "It looks like mine."

"It looks like yours?"

"Yeah. My name's on all of 'em."

"But you don't recognize any of them?"

"No."

"Mr. Vincent, did you, yourself, in fact, sign any of those forms?"

"No."

I used to have to turn signatures upside down, mimic the meaningless lines. I learned how to turn off the meaning in my head after practicing over and over, do them right side up.

"You're certain." The Prosecutor was fond of imperative questions.

"Yes."

"You're saying that someone forged your signature."

"I guess so."

"Yes or no."

"Yes."

"Do you have any guess as to who might have had the reason

and the opportunity to forge your signature on a suspension notice for your son?"

"Objection. Calls for witness to speculate."

"Withdrawn." But he'd phrased it well, specified reason and opportunity in his question, knowing the coming objection, letting the jury fill in the answers for themselves. I wondered why I'd bothered putting Dad's signature on those papers. I hated school, should have let them kick me out.

My lawyer cross-examined Dad, trying hard to bring out the strain of Mom's cancer, the financial burden of both his wife and son's medical expenses, his honest attempt to go straight and keep a steady job. He both tried to play Dad as sympathetic and erode his credibility. *Do you drink, Mr. Vincent?* Then onto Dad's own jail record, skeet shooting the Prosecutor's litany of objections. *Overruled. Overruled. Overruled.* I stopped listening, couldn't look at Dad.

I'd seen the one tattoo that, unlike the others, was visible in spite of the suit he wore: the *13½* on his left hand. Over the next two years I'd come to learn its meaning – *twelve jurors, one judge, half a chance.* I figured that it was work Dad received while doing time. Digging gold mines.

The jury deliberated for two days on a muddle of forgery charges and intent to distribute controlled substances. I spent those two days in the county jail, plus the weekend. In all, a week of oatmeal, bologna sandwiches, meatloaf, apple juice, milk, seven-card stud, basketball, and one altercation with a porter whose mopped floor I walked across on the way to the toilets.

August 11. The jury came back with a Guilty verdict on the counterfeiting charge but tossed the rest. The judge gave me two years, minus time served. I ran the numbers in my head. Less eighty-five days, that would be May 16, 1977. A Monday.

TEN

Longer than twelve months and it isn't jail, it's *prison*, and if you're under eighteen it's *Youth Camp*, a euphemism that maintains local property values. And Camp regs say that when you're being spot-searched, you keep your mouth shut and your hands flat against the wall or it's considered an assault. Experienced COs know when an inmate is a real threat but the new ones, *cowboys*, they call them, or *newjacks*, are rabbit-scared. They're unarmed, patrolling the worst neighborhood on earth. Corrections Officers have the same legal authority as street cops when they're on the outside. Just like older cops are jaded and even-tempered, while the new ones want to prove themselves, COs are the same way.

When this newjack, a punk maybe twenty-five, fresh-faced and gym-sculpted to twice my size, stopped me on my way to the mess hall, *You, hands flat and feet apart, eyes ahead*, my reflexes were still intact. But my reflexes were shaped from a teenage lifetime of schoolyard fights. I was getting held up for the breakfast line and needed some coffee bad and this flunky's groping my waist, ankles, armpits, legs so he can strut for a female guard.

I said, "Don't start enjoying that."

He finished his search, said nothing, and stood back. I waited for his all clear, knowing I'd upped him.

"What did you write on your palm?" he asked me and I

knew then he was an idiot. And when I held out my empty palm so I could laugh at him, I got it.

The standard-issue baton comes in at twenty ounces of galvanized aluminum, harder than diamond but feather-light for a fast swing. Enamel coating that might chip against a brick wall or a car hood, but not your wrists, ribs, elbows, ankles or knees. In the half-heartbeat it took for me to recoil from the pain in my arm, I'd shifted all my weight to my left leg and the same whip-flash snap of aluminum blasted the strength from my knee and after that, I remember bits and blurs of trying to cover my face, throat, stomach or ribs and being one step behind where he was hitting me.

My reflexes stayed. I resumed my push-ups and crunches, worked with a deck and read whatever I could to pass the time. Found my shot five days later, pissed into an empty cup and waited, waited, waited, first balcony above the gallery, dumped it onto the guard when he passed below. Gassed, cuffed and stripped, they threw me into the Hole.

Solitary, a.k.a. *the Hole*: ten-by-ten polished concrete cube with a molded slab jutting from the wall. Toilet, stainless steel, one; tissue, individual sheets, fifty; tear-resistant mat, one; blanket, wool, one. I splashed the burning gas from my face with water from the toilet tank, kept my face down because they never turned off the lights in the Hole. Threats, screaming, gas, sticks, fists – none of them changed my reflexes. None of them stopped my spontaneous pushback when a CO crossed me or another inmate wanted to test me, say something to my face or give me a reason to step up. It was the light. Ten days of light, thirty days of light, light that pushes through your eyes when you try to sleep, burns the shadows into nothing and bleeds any remaining contrast or color out of the grey box you're in with no books, cards, paper and nothing to hook your brain to.

I'm slow, sometimes. Kids, fifteen, sixteen learn to drive, learn the value of a paycheck, long-term goals and self-discipline. I learned, after months and months of light, to make the faster-than-thought choice between drawing a line, standing my ground and keeping my pride versus being invisible.

I didn't hear from Mom or Dad for my first nine months inside, and they didn't hear from me. April of 1976, I turned seventeen. I got a birthday card from Shelly in a small package with four chocolate bars, another deck of cards and a gift notice from a science magazine that said she'd bought me a subscription. I ticked off the months with cover headlines about cell mutations and black holes.

One month later, I was reading on my bunk when a CO told me I had five minutes to clean up, that I had a visitor. I asked who and he walked away without answering. I brushed my teeth, combed my hair back with a splash of water and signaled a guard.

Overhead fluorescents washed everything in the Visiting Room in a sterile, green-white light: the checkered linoleum floor, the fifteen wooden tables, the metal folding chairs. Ask me what I remember most about those two years, and that's it.

Three vending machines stood against one wall. Your visitors had to buy snacks for you. Inmates couldn't carry coins. Anyone wanting to go to the restroom had to get permission from one of the guards flanking the room perimeter. They didn't want anyone switching clothes or pulling contraband out of some orifice.

Dad waited at a table. His beard had grown out, not long but covering the lower half of his face. White, grey, black and brown all at once, the color of snow and mud. His eyes were the callous black shark eyes that I'd always remembered, unlike the day of my trial. A cigarette burned just above his knuckles. No filter, he smoked them down to a nub of tobacco wedged between his teeth, crushed them out when he started spitting out tobacco flakes more than he was inhaling. Two cans from the machine sat on the table in front of him.

I sat down. Up close, his eyes were red at the edges, softening his dead, black stare.

"Gotcha soda." He slid one across to me.

We never had sodas at home. I only had them visiting Mom at work or when I was in jail. You had to drink them in the gallery, sitting down, and you couldn't get up until a CO took your empty can. The visiting room soda machine had a sign:

BEVERAGES ARE TO BE CONSUMED ON THE PREMISES
LEAVE ALL EMPTY CONTAINERS IN PLAIN SIGHT
FOR COLLECTION BY A CORRECTIONS OFFICER.

To this day, I hate the taste of sodas.

For nine months, I'd thought about what I wanted to say to his face when I saw him again. But the trial was distant in my head, like someone else's home movies. The only knife I had to twist was not to let him know how happy I was to see him. In truth, I was flooded with warmth at the sight of him and worried that he was starting to look so old.

I opened the can, the gaseous snap like a rifle crack in a room full of sniffling mothers and fathers holding their sons for their one chance that week. Dad flicked his ashes, took one final pull, and crushed the smoke into the embedded metal ashtray.

"Smokin' yet?"

I shook my head. He fished another pack from his jacket and lit a fresh one. "I brought a carton for ya. CO will bring it later. They're better than cash, inside. Got some toothpaste in there, too. Missed your birthday."

"I can't have cash." My voice was a whisper, pushing to crack as hard as it could.

Quiet, then, "Anyone hasslin' you?" No other fathers had the balls to ask this to their kids. Veiled as it was, it took a lot.

I shook my head. "Nope. I stay in my cell, mostly. Read a lot. Shelly sends me magazines." I stopped myself from saying any more.

"Yeah. I got some from her. They'll bring 'em to you. You like news magazines? History?"

"Sure." I didn't. But Shelly didn't know that. Parent sniffles and murmurs crept over us. Dad looked at the clock, took a pull from his smoke.

"I quit drinkin'." He looked me in the eyes, then at the ashtray. "I've gone ninety days. Feels like longer. They give you one of these." He showed me a metal ID bracelet, looked back at me.

"Drinkin' coffee and soda all the time now. I don't sleep much anymore. Can't hardly see straight." He said can't like *caint*. He took another drag, dropped his gaze, and stared straight into the ashtray.

"Your momma died yesterday. Said *John* was all, 'fore she closed her eyes."

I scratched at a piece of graffiti with my fingernail – *West Sixties* in sharp, tagger lettering cut into the table.

"You hear me?"

"Yeah."

"Not *yeah*. Yes or no." The mumbling hesitancy gone from his voice.

"Yes, I heard you."

"What else?"

If I didn't say something, I'd start crying. If I said anything consoling, I'd start crying. I shrugged.

"Look at me, boy." He put force into his voice but kept it low in the visiting room. "Your mother's dead. Yesterday. 4:57 p.m."

My memory's good, but I was drawing a blank. When had I last seen her?

"Say something to me, you little cocksucker." The voice he used right before thrashing me when I was younger.

I was about to buckle to the hot knot in my neck when *cocksucker* froze it away. I thought of Jeremy. I thought of walking into the blind that last time I saw him, how crying and/ or showing weakness make you less invisible than anything. I thought of how Dad and I weren't alone, how many people could see me.

I looked Dad straight in the face, locked into his stare, his eyes burned and unfocused at the edges.

"Fuck. You." My voice sounded like his.

He met my eyes, held his stare while I held mine. Then he looked back to the ashtray, crushed his cigarette, signaled a guard to let him leave.

I sat in the visitor's room for a few minutes, staring at my fingers, tuning out and getting lost until a CO told me to move along. In my cell, I tucked a roll of toilet paper under my head for a pillow, closed my eyes and tried to think of reasons to hate Mom and Dad. On my hands and knees, I scraped up every piece of hate I could find on the floorboards of my memory, stuffing them into my mouth and chewing, sucking on their juices to poison and drown any hint of *hurt* or *sad* or *weak*. Two days later, I had my third godsplitter.

Monday, May 16, 1977. One year to the day since I'd last seen Dad. One year and one day since Mom had died. I was eighteen, my juvenile record ordered sealed by the court. I signed for my belongings one last time, dressed in front of a uniformed guard one last time. For the last time, I heard the gates buzz open one after the next, my name called out with each one. For the last time, I heard the same joke at the final gate: *See you again real soon, boy.* Outside, I lit a smoke.

Dad wasn't waiting this time. I spent most of the day on the bus, but I got home. I stayed there for one week during which time Dad said the following:

Shelly's moved out, you can take the couch.

You need to help out with the rent.
Grab some sodas while you're out.
Empty the trash.
I'll be home late.
Hand me the paper.
After seven days, I packed a single bag and left.

I'd decided on the West Coast, someplace dense where nobody knew me or my Special Ed time or my jail record. The cops wouldn't know me so wouldn't mess with me on their slow days. I was getting good with my hands – you could know me for months and never notice my fingers. I could make coins, marbles, watches and rings vanish, pull a card out of a deck that you'd held in your head for only a few seconds, and in general pass myself off as a central casting, corn-fed, red-headed boy with ten fingers.

I knew that I couldn't make a driver's license, that the state had to give me one. And I had to show who I was to the state with a birth certificate, so I made one along with a new school ID. When I arrived in California, I'd be Brian Delvine, age nineteen.

I walked out Dad's front door and into the dark, headed for the bus station. The Ranchero was parked in its spot, #49, the driver's door open, dome light off. Dad sat sideways in the driver's seat, feet on the ground, his head down, running his fingers through his hair – still greasy-black, in spite of how the rest of him had aged. Lucky butts piled on the ground between his work shoes, another glowed between his knuckles. He held a bottle on his right knee, three inches of clear liquid remained. He didn't look up, I didn't say anything.

I can still see his face. I remember every black strand of hair, his ash-brown, snow-mud beard, the deep lines in his skin and his two missing teeth. I can't picture his eyes though, hard as I try.

The bus grazed the edge of a dilapidated residential neighborhood before reaching the highway. It was dark, but beneath the streetlights and the full moon, I saw Brett. A different house, the yard nothing but packed and petrified dirt. His hair was longer and something about his clothes said he hadn't washed in a long time. He was walking the yard, edge to edge in straight lines, one to the next. No lawn, no mower, just Brett walking the paces over his imaginary grass under the watch of the streetlights and junebugs.

"This is Erica at the L.A. County Department of Mental Health. I'm unavailable at this time, so please leave a message."

"Erica, it's Dr. Carlisle. I'm with a patient right now, taking a quick break and I need some background data. Can you locate a city or county medical clinic in Long Beach? I need to get a record of a visit from a Fletcher, Daniel J., DOB 11/6/61. He would have been there approximately twelve months ago. I'd like to know who he spoke to so I can get some details on his visit.

"Also, Daniel Fletcher's parents are deceased. They're up in Corvallis, Oregon. I'd like to track down any information on his father's history. I'll ask Mr. Fletcher about any records, but he's not likely to have anything.

"If you have any time to get started, leave me a note in my box and let me know what you find out, so I can do some follow-up this week. I'll send the specifics right over. I appreciate it."

ERIC BISHOP

ELEVEN

Maybe you're a woman and God was too good to you, and people – men – pay serious cash to look at you. Sometimes when you're naked, sometimes not. Sometimes you know it, sometimes you don't. Maybe you smiled at one of them while serving cocktails or waiting for an elevator and now he knows where you live, where you work, your phone number, and your cat went missing a week ago, and the police tell you that the note saying *I want to take you with me to the afterlife* doesn't explicitly threaten you and, anyway, you don't have any proof that he wrote it.

So you have to make what you need, whatever papers or documents to say who you want to be. Just don't expect them to stand up to scrutiny unless you're good.

I'm good. Baptismal certificate, thirty minutes. I get them in bulk at church supply shops in East L.A., artfully age them and find a recently deceased priest to sign them. Affidavit of Citizenship, five minutes. Work ID, municipal employee ID, student ID, two and a half hours, average. International driver's license – paper, *Mojave Sand*, 50# cotton bond, passport photo, custom-made rubber stamps. Two hours, eighteen minutes.

I have three shoeboxes full of samples. I used to tend bar, built a collection of confiscated licenses. Someone gives me an ID with red-eye flash in the picture or an address that doesn't match their ZIP code, I keep it. German driver's license

(Hollywood tour bus Lost and Found), three hours. British work permit (expired, in the trash at the Westwood Federal Building), ninety minutes. Drink at bars around the airport, lots of work ID badges come loose from their pocket clips.

Excuse me… anyone find a Pacific-West Expediters badge?

You Rick?

Yeah, thanks.

Every tourist theme park and gimmick-driven chain restaurant has a Lost and Found. Forty percent of European tourists are from the UK and twenty percent are from Germany. I'll take a stab in the dark and say *I called earlier about my wallet?* and let the accent do the work. If I'm lucky then someone from a different shift told someone who told someone on this shift and they don't even check me against the picture, or they can't tell when I'm doing British that I'm not from Australia or New Zealand or South Africa. Sometimes with an open-ended question or well-timed pause, they'll fill in the gaps for me. *Yes, you were with the group in the corner last night, weren't you?* or *You're Mr. Pierce?* And they'll hand me someone else's wallet without a second thought. I do *trustworthy*.

Or I'll suit up, walk into a four-star hotel. *I checked out this morning and put my bags in storage. I need to get some traveler's checks*. They never ask for my luggage ticket, never stay and watch me.

I have passports from fourteen countries, driver's licenses from eight, work permits from nine, affidavits of citizenship, green cards, employee ID badges, mug shots, booking forms, birth certificates, security passes, immunization papers, student ID cards, adoption records, and one Proof of Indian Blood Degree.

The Evaluator removes his glasses, rubs his eyes. They look smaller and more fatigued. He puts his pen down and still holding his glasses, says "Are you sexually active?"

* * *

Blood straight from a cut is red-black, shiny and thick. Mine's thinner if I've been drinking.

Early March, Keara left for San Diego to spend a long weekend with her sister. Andrea had just moved from the East Coast to go to graduate school in the fall, and wanted to see Keara before she started working in April. I spent those three days piecing our new place together, putting everything in my name because landlords and utility companies don't like actors or actresses – they want a steady check. Keara was an actress, though she did more cocktailing jobs than acting. I kept hoping she'd call but she never did except to check on me. The phone rousted me in the middle of the night – silence, then hang-up, when I answered *Hello? Keara?*

I'd had zero luck combing junk stores and cheap hardware shops for a fireplace screen, but I had salvaged an armload of sap-ridden lumber scraps from a remodeling site three blocks over. Dense knots, dry rot and resin wads swelling out of hollow pockets like old infections and hardening on the surface, rusted nails with sheared heads and the peeling residue of paint and varnish. It would still burn, and that was all the romance Keara needed in the nominal cold of a California winter.

She came back. We showered, left our half-finished Cantonese take-out on the kitchen table. I drank a beer while Keara rinsed off. She stepped out for a towel, I reached through the curtain to set the bottle on the sink and it slipped, blasted into a thousand shiny brown shards and amber foam inside the tub and I cut my foot stepping out. The red was luminous, diluted from the shower against the white porcelain and swirling into the drain like a horror film close-up. Beautiful.

On my back, still wet and soaking the rug in front of the fledgling fire, Keara crouched over my foot, mopping the cut with towels, dressing it with alcohol (that smell again) and gauze. She sat naked, her feet tucked beneath her, her belly creased as she bent down, her brown ringlets of hair hanging down and covering her face, the blast of freckles on her shoulders and the mole on her collarbone fading in and out with the popping and hissing of the flames. Rasputin sat on the couch, dead eyes aimed in our direction, following the sound of us, shrinking from the unfamiliar heat and smoke, lost in his new home.

Keara finished bandaging my foot. I took a swallow from a fresh beer, started to sit up but she put a hand to my chest, eased me back down. Kissed both of my eyes to close them (I kissed her eyes a lot, she liked that) and kissed the rest of me. Mouth around me, I reached for her face, but she pushed my wrists back to the ground and continued to move her own hands across my stomach, hips, legs.

If I tried to sit up, she pushed me back, running a hand over my face to keep my eyes closed while she climbed on top of me, slid me inside of her, and moved. Slowly. If I moved, she stopped.

"Ssshhh. Still." Whispered. She stayed quiet. I listened to the sputter of the flames and felt her on me, felt the heat of the fire on one side of my face, arm, chest. Touched her to feel the warmth on the one side of her body and she put my hand back. Kept moving. Churning. *Slooow*.

My right side burned. I sat up, wrapped my arms around her and she pushed back but knew I wouldn't stay this time and we rolled over, me inside and on top of her, she kept her hands on my face, my eyes closed. I never thought about anyone else the whole time. No one. Eyes shut, Keara not saying, whispering, a word.

Moving slowly, her arms around me, my face buried in her neck and taking in her smell and her breathing a soft *mmmmmm* in my ear. My thoughts, my heartbeat and my blood all stopped and pooled into the middle of me ready to erupt. I tried to stop it because I wanted her to go first because I thought I would pass out but I didn't want to think of something else to slow me down and finally couldn't contain it anymore and everything in me coiled back to burst when the fire popped loud from some ancient pocket of sap and one. Single. Pinpoint. Spark. Arched up and drifted down. Onto the back of my left thigh like a white-hot needle at the worst possible quantum second and I tried to push the pain out and focus on the burst and tried to stop the burst to tune out the needle and failed both at the same time and the needle and the burst both kissed in the middle of my brain and the middle of my chest and I couldn't see anything but Keara's face and felt the whisper of God deep within my bones.

On my back again, I opened my eyes to see hers, dark brown, almost black, and the edges of my vision turned purple, creeping in until everything was bright purple-blue and I might have smiled. Far from the flames, again Keara naked and kneeling, salve and gauze for the same leg, she rolled me over to look at the burn.

Every vein in my body carried the feeling like that first blast of coke years before, like all of the molecules in my body had bonded together for the first time ever. Wet heat ran down both sides of my face and I'm sure Keara thought I was in pain, but I wasn't. I was floating in the calmest hurricane eye of the deepest love I had ever felt for anyone in my life.

"I love you," I said. But not out loud.

"Yes, I'm sexually active."

In most cases, the truth is your best option, but that depends on what that truth is. And in this case, I don't know what his tripwires are. He's getting old, maybe his dick's not working. Maybe his wife/girlfriend walked out on him. Maybe he's sleeping with one of his clients or another staffer. And maybe in his eyes I'm competition. In any case, I need to be definitive:

Straight. Potent. Active. Ambiguity about sex puts capital-D depression back onto his radar.

"Are you currently in a relationship?"

"Yeah."

"And what is this person's name?"

"Molly." Don't like this. Maybe she thought she was helping me. Give them her new name as well as mine, make it twice as hard for them or twice as easy for me. But I've got enough to keep straight and I don't need any more details. Too late, Keara has to stay *Molly* until I'm out of here.

"How long have you and Molly been seeing each other?"

"About seven months, now. Maybe eight."

"What's the nature of your relationship?"

"Not sure what you mean. We're living together, if that's what you're asking."

"Do the two of you share the household with anyone else?"

"No, it's just us. We've got an apartment in Silverlake."

"How long have you been living together?"

"Since March."

"So, you've been living together for most of the time you've been seeing each other. Correct?"

"It was kind of sudden, yeah. Abrupt, I mean. We'd been going out since early January, and then she had to leave her apartment on short notice. Things were going well with us, so we decided to try living together."

"Had you known her prior to dating her?"

"Nope."

"So you met, began dating immediately and moved in together soon after that. And that was maybe seven or eight months ago, you said. Correct?"

"That's right."

"And you're as sexually active with Molly now as you were then?"

"Absolutely."

"Do you and Molly ever fight?"

"Rarely."

He's still circling tighter and tighter, every now and again a quick snap of his jaws when he sees a soft spot. Sexual activity questions either immediately precede or follow drug questions, but I think he smells my electric nerve static and will back off, widen his circle and stay within the safe zones until he can find another soft spot.

The Evaluator flips through his notes, glances at his watch.

Another moment with Keara comes back to me: eating soup on a rainy night, sharing a blanket. I can smell her, hear her voice.

"But you do fight, sometimes?"

"Sometimes, yes. But like I said, rarely."

"How would you define rarely?"

"We've had maybe three arguments, total."

"About what kinds of things?"

"Schedules, mostly. Sometimes I get stuck in traffic with a long-distance delivery and get home late. She works at a bar, so she's gone most weekend nights. We point fingers over whose fault it is that we haven't seen each other. We get over it. Makes for good make-up sex, but we don't make it a habit."

Keara threw her bag and address book onto the couch, home from another casting call. The book split open, straining against a hundred rubber bands, adhesive notes, bits of scratch paper and cocktail napkins. Among the debris was a photo of Keara. A five-by-seven studio head shot, smaller than what she normally took to auditions. I looked more closely, and it wasn't Keara.

"Who's this?" I held the photo, looking into Keara's eyes that weren't Keara's.

"That's my sister," she said, filling up the tea kettle. "That shouldn't even be in there."

"She an actress, too?"

"She gave it up."

Her sister looked almost Keara's age (twenty-three, though "Molly" is twenty-four), shared her eyes, eyebrows and forehead. The shape of their faces was nearly identical. But her sister was blonde, her lips and jaw thinner, more refined. She smiled evenly instead of with Keara's asymmetrical grin. But Keara had nicer teeth. Her sister had a gap in the center and they weren't even. But they were definitely related. And beautiful.

"So that's Andrea?" I asked.

"Yes, that's Andrea."

"Younger than you–"

"Older." She cut me off, her back to me.

"I see the resemblance," I said. "What's her story?"

"She doesn't have a story."

"You said she lived in San Diego. That's her, isn't it?"

"Yes, that's her, Eric. She lives in San Diego. What about it?" She stepped out of the kitchen and snatched the picture from me as I was staring into it.

Andrea called Keara at work, sometimes at home, but I had never spoken to her. My calls were usually work-related. Keara's were work or casting calls, and we had the periodic late-night hang-up. Welcome to Los Angeles.

"So, ask her up sometime," I said.

"Christ. Not you, too."

"What do you mean, not me too?"

"Go visit her yourself, if you want to so badly."

"Jesus, Keara."

Her cup weighed ten ounces of kiln-fired ceramic – *Beautiful Lake Tahoe* – from the Salvation Army, and it missed my face only because I ducked, tripping over a stack of magazines. It exploded against the far wall, leaving a divot that I had to spackle and repaint. Keara slammed the balcony door behind her in a burst of expletives.

I swept up, took a joint and two beers outside.

"I don't want your sister," I whispered into the forest of her curls. "Nobody but you." I stroked her knuckles, gentle, gentle. She curled up on a lawn chair, put her face between her knees and squeezed my hand.

"Thank you for your honesty, Danny." This is standard patient stroking to keep the trust intact, then he says, "You're being very helpful," and he smiles.

"No problem."

"Do you drink, Danny?"

He replaces his glasses, thinks I don't notice the shift from *Daniel* to *Danny*.

"Occasionally."

"How frequent are these occasions?"

Alcohol is linked with depression, which is exactly where the Evaluator wants to go. He's already diagnosed me, he just needs to back it up.

The trick here is understanding 'frequent.' The white, twenty-five- to thirty-year-old American male drinks twelve to fourteen beers a week, or five to seven glasses of wine a week. The average legal limit in most states is .08 BAC, which is about two beers, so two beers means you're legally drunk. The implicit question is not *How much do you drink? but How often do you get legally drunk? or How often do you have more than two beers within a given hour during the course of a week?* I'm legally drunk seven nights a week, but he doesn't need to know that.

"I go through about a six-pack every couple of weeks." False.

"Does that include weekends?"

"No. Fridays I take it easy. I don't like to go out after a week of work. I might have three or four beers between getting home and going to sleep around midnight or one." False.

"What about Saturdays?"

"I go out."

"And you drink?"

"Yeah. I drink." True. I have to wipe my forehead, bad as that might look. Can't have sweat running into my eyes.

"How much?"

"I don't pay attention. I don't get blind, vomiting drunk. Usually I go visit Molly at work, hang out until last call and drive her home if she doesn't have her car."

"Have you ever tried to stop drinking for a period of time?"

A misdirect is when you clear your throat, make a joke, or ask a viewer if they have some article in their pocket, anything to take their eyes away from where you don't want them looking. In other cases, a force makes them choose a card they believe they've picked at random. This question is a mixture of both.

Ask anyone if they think they drink too much, and they'll say *No*. Either they don't drink too much or they're going to deny it if they do. You'll never hear *Yes, now that you mention it I can't get through a single, waking moment without a drink. Why do you ask?* Someone wrestling with a drinking problem will sometimes flirt with abstinence for a week, two weeks or a month. Successful with their short-term sobriety and ensconced in their denial, they'll resume their status as a Binge Drinker, Social Drinker or Functioning Alcoholic.

"No. Should I consider it?" *Why no, doctor, it never crossed my mind. Do you think I have a drinking problem?*

"Not necessarily," he says.

He makes a final line of notes, turns to yet another sheet in his yellow pad.

"Do you use any non-prescription or street drugs, Danny?" He checks at his watch, returns to his notebook.

I've just had my stomach pumped and I know what they found in my blood. THC is fat-soluble and takes thirty days to completely flush from your system. Coke doesn't take that long, but there's no point in playing innocent. But addiction is another depression indicator, so I've got a juggling act in front of me. Give him the drugs, tell him part of the truth dressed as a lie.

"Yeah. The usual. Pot and stuff."

"Stuff?" Palm up. *Please continue.*

"Coke. I did acid once. Didn't like it."

"You mentioned marijuana in high school, as well. Have you been doing it regularly since then?"

"Yeah. I partied in high school, then slowed down after that. Didn't do it for a long time. Now it's too frequent for my own good. Part of the reason I keep a limit on my drinking." I'm halfway across the pit, ten thousand feet up without a net and the gentle breeze is getting pushy. I'm doing *Guilty, Relieved.* I lean forward, give him my Nervous Gesture and a deep sigh, look at the ground. Scale back, way back, my drug intake, but let him know how out of control I think it is. Give him an explanation for the signs the doctors found, make it good. Blend with the scenery, hold very still, and he'll keep moving.

"So how long ago did you go from abstinence to regular use?"

"About four years ago." Before my "mother" died.

"And what is 'too frequent for your own good?'"

"Four, sometimes five times a month." False.

"And how long have you been smoking cigarettes?"

"Since high school. About a pack a day the past few years."

"I noticed you've got a very upscale brand there."

"I like the wide pack. Helps me hide my fingers. Sleight of hand thing."

"What about the cocaine, then?"

"Same thing, a lot more than I should. First time, I was at a party a couple of years ago. I thought my heart was going to explode and my hands wouldn't stop shaking. I had to walk. I couldn't sit still, must have walked fifteen blocks before I felt better. Someone told me I'd just been given some bad shit, maybe cut with some low-grade speed. I tried it again a few weeks later. Same thing. I thought I was going to die from a heart attack. Tore my nose up pretty bad, like snorting a crushed light bulb. Never been the same."

False. False. False. I can't tell him the truth because it's so backwards he'd never believe me and I'd never leave here.

My after-work ritual: Switch on the lights, step over the mail, shut the blinds, and open a beer. I sit down at my kitchen table with the following: paper, white, unlined, 20# cotton bond, one sheet; pen, ball-point; cocaine, powder, four lines at three point five inches each.

The first rail is my favorite, like that first sip of coffee in the morning or bourbon in the evening. First line of the day and the whirlwind in my head.

Stops.

One thought at a time. Everything is slow and quiet. Snort hard, get it all the way back and count – one thousand, two thousand, three thousand – watch the trembling leave my fingers like fading pond ripples. With the pen and paper, stare at the white space and measure six inches with my eyes. Hold the distance in my head until I can see two dots on the empty page and connect them with a line – a single clear, straight stroke. I'm accurate to the sixteenth of an inch. Do another rail and feel the pond ripples leave my chest and head, hands steady like glasswater. The next line, also six inches, intersecting the first at their mutual three-inch midpoints at a precise ninety degrees. Hit number three, then draw line number three, exactly six inches, at a one-inch parallel to the first. For the fourth and last hit, I turn the paper to the clean side and wait for the dot to appear. I used to mark it by hand, but I don't need to anymore. When I see it, it stays, and three inches from the dot I start, drawing a perfect circle with a three-inch radius.

Close my eyes. Deep breath. Lower right bicuspid coke-smeared and numb. Could be a cavity. I should get that looked at. Sweet, syntheto chemical drip down the back of my throat and the world feels so *right*.

The cobwebs and noise in my head are gone, the world is quiet. But with every ounce I cop, I'm forced to tolerate the other clients in Ray's apartment sucking rails off his mirrored table, chewing their lips, chain-smoking and shoehorning their political conspiracy ramblings into my line of focus. Some people, coke makes a stage for them in their head, makes them think they're more interesting than they really are.

Me, a few lines and every stray thought, split-moment flashback and frustrated impulse is magnetized in a quantum instant into a single here and now, and my internal swarm is gone. I'm not watching the world behind glass anymore. Calm enough to sleep, but happy to stay awake.

The other drugs – the quality stuff that I find in Mexico or scam from a pharmacy – all share the same pseudo-tease of relief before their effects fade out and I need more. They start to work, convince me that I'm going to be okay. Like the girl with the baroque stage handle – *Champagne, Christy, Ariel* – wearing the sequined T-back and sitting on your lap who might leave with you if you pay for one more dance, buy her one more drink.

Maybe one more.

For certain this time.

Like that, the candle flicker of relief fades out, and I'm still conscious so I take more. Then a gloved hand is slapping me awake, asking me to count fingers or say my name or the day of the week or name the President and I'm here, explaining to an Evaluator that I don't want to die, but that I want my head to stop hurting. And it does. Like a jig saw through my cortex, it burns for days and then stops, quick as a light switch. I'm in a trauma center, parched, tubes coming out of me and needles going into me, answering the same set of questions. I'm bruised in places from sleeping or cringing in some ungodly position that felt so much more comfortable than the blue sparks behind my eyes. I'm rug-burned from random twitching, spasms where I couldn't control the nerve signals running for their lives and I'm soaked in my own piss.

"How often have you done cocaine since then?"

"Too often. A couple of times a month, Molly and I will get

some to party with. I'm careful about where I get it, though. I don't want anything like those first two times, and I don't want the legal hassles, either."

"Danny, when using cocaine, have you ever seen or heard something that was apparent only to you?"

I do *puzzled*, but I know where he's going. Hallucinations are a clear sign of organic dementia or severe depression. Most people who claim to see ghosts are grieving or in extreme pain. Not to mention what's known as amphetamine psychosis, which is a result of long-term abuse.

"Do I hallucinate?"

"Have you ever?"

"No."

"Do you mean 'no' whether you were intoxicated or not?"

"Right. It's never happened, whether I've been stoned or otherwise."

TWELVE

When you're in love, your brain secretes endorphins into your blood. Organic morphine leaks out of a gland in your skull, feels like a low-grade opium rush. Some people confuse the two, the head rush and the love. You think you're in love with a person, but you're in love with a syringe. Skin like liquid silk, hair, eyes, laugh, smile, impulses, trust, confidence, curves, perfume, sweat, affection, but still a syringe. You're high and hooked, and soon comes the *more, more, more*: marriage, career, mortgage, children, school, it's harder and harder to feel that rush.

Happens all the time, men and women. Body clocks twenty years out of sync between genders, the rush dries up. You look for new hooks, new fixes, anything for that *more, more, more*. Some people burn their lives to the ground doing so, fodder for talk radio and daytime television. These same people assail the evils of drugs and urine-test their own children.

Sudden turned me on to coke. That was her real name, *Sudden*. Mine was Martin Kelly. I hadn't had any headaches since I'd left home, but Brian Delvine had worn out his welcome in Los Angeles after three traffic warrants, one eviction and one post-employment random drug screening. I kept changing names, records and histories, getting better and better at it. I finally learned I could afford to live alone, keep the eviction notices at bay with multiple lines of credit under multiple names. It was a game that kept my slate perpetually clean. It wasn't yet something I had to do to save my life. Then the godsplitters came back. Right after I met Sudden.

I had been born to Mr. and Mrs. Liam and Fiona Kelly twenty-seven years prior. I found them in the *Boston Globe* obituaries, Liam Kelly having unstatistically survived his wife for seven years after her death from a stroke. They were survived by seven children, excluding "Martin."

It took seven weeks of correspondence with the Massachusetts Bureau of Vital Statistics, insisting they'd made a mistake, that they must have my birth record on file. I used a ream of misprinted (wrong phone number) letterhead for McKinney, Watterson and Ross from a copy shop trash bin – MW&R had an imposing chain of WASP surnames that meant either an accounting firm or legal partnership, which always greases civic wheels. Ultimately, the Bureau was willing to shoulder the blame and right a wronged birth record for the good of the tax coffers.

My landlord happily accepted an extra twenty bucks a month for one of the surplus mailboxes in our apartment building. I used that for an address, then started building a history. I secured a credit card with a $1,000 cashier's check, charged things, paid it off. I made a list of defunct business references from a four-year-old phone book and built a résumé.

Some people say they can read handwriting the way others can read palms or cards. I didn't believe it, but since some cops did, then some doctors might. I learned the rules and shaped my writing to fit.

Martin Kelly wrote at a near-vertical ninety-four degrees, with just enough forward slant to indicate *positive attitude* and *looking to the future*. He wrote his crossbars two-thirds up from his baseline and perfectly balanced his ascenders and descenders. I was Martin Kelly: cautious, careful to decide, intelligent with a high self-esteem, inclined neither to carelessness nor to depression.

I'd made a mold of my left thumbprint, pressing it into a lump of firm putty, made a latex cast of its arches and loops that I fixed to a thumb tip from a Hollywood magic shop. The DMV never noticed. *Look straight at the camera, please. Smile. Thank you. Now please press your right thumb firmly onto the green light.*

Misdirect: My left hand on the counter gave the clerk something to stare at. Cup and switch: slip the prosthetic sheath over my right thumb, press firmly, back off again. Martin's right thumb print was Johnny's left. A fingerprint database search would take them through a dead-end maze. I can count on their officious boredom for each successful change.

I met Sudden when she tried to strangle me. We slept together three nights later, but the night I met her she stripped, rubber-band-shot her panties at my face, and dry-humped my work jeans to the rhythmic distortion of Motley Crüe.

The doorman's name tag said *Jimmy*. Jimmy looked like a size forty-eight, but his black suit in the dark light of the club made it hard to tell. He handed me my change, stamped my wrist and said *Have a good time* in his gravelbox voice.

If I need to get out but want to be invisible, I go to a strip joint. None of the customers are sizing you up, they're looking at the talent. The talent isn't sizing you up if you aren't loose with your cash, and the doormen ignore you unless you get rowdy.

Sudden wore a sheath of white gauze from her armpits to just below her hips, weaving through the tables of solitary men or silent, staring groups. She touched shoulders, whispered into ears, moving from one person to the next on her white stilettos, holding a clutch purse the size of a large fist. She caught me staring, gave me a long-distance look with her honed bedroom stare. I ignored her – I knew better than to believe that stare – ordered a coffee.

She appeared over my shoulder, the warm weight of her bare arm snaking across my chest, and I smelled alcohol-heat mixed with coconut skin lotion.

"I am *so* drunk," she said, then, "You're coming with me," pulling me by the wrist to a curtained booth, past another doorman with a tie and a clipboard, marking her down for a dance. Her eyelids sagged, she breathed whiskey fumes from her lips into mine, closer, closer. Five minutes for ten dollars and she was straddling, stretching, writhing and grinding, pulling at my hair, shirt collar, pressing her breasts into my face against every posted rule of every club in Los Angeles.

Then Sudden was choking me. Her hands around my neck once, twice, a third time, her grip firmer each time then relaxing. Her smile an inch from my face, *Just kidding*, it said. And then she wasn't. Opposite sides of my windpipe touched and I stayed – she'll stop in a second – but she didn't and the pain in my throat was half from not breathing, half from my neck being twisted out of shape. I peeled her hands away, hoping a bouncer didn't catch me touching her. She pushed me back onto the couch with her knees pinning my arms, curled her fingers around my throat once more and squeezed. When I reached to take her hands away, I was too weak to move. The room lit up, the lights seeming all at once to flood purple and green, and Sudden looked straight into my eyes. Hers were the green-brown of bayou mud – what the DMV calls hazel – and I was filled with a bursting love for this woman. I mean an absolutely undying love and rush of gratitude for her, enough happiness to split my heart open. And that's when I first asked her name, or tried to.

I coughed, heaved and choked for air, realized she was blowing breath back into me, the sharp odors of whiskey, chewing gum and spit pushing into my lungs. A slap, a blast of stings across my left cheek, right cheek, and when I opened my eyes I didn't see Sudden at all, but a skinny blonde woman who probably got a lot of attention at the club but not a second look in the clear light of day.

"I'm good," I said. "Don't hit me."

Then the shock of ice water in my face. Sudden stood next to her, naked, holding her gauze dress in a rumpled ball. The blonde kept telling her *Go backstage before Jimmy comes over.*

"I've got to go," I said.

"Are you okay? Are you sure?" The blonde asked with rehearsed concern while torquing my elbow toward the pay phones, restroom entrances and back door with No In And Out Privileges next to a fire extinguisher. Then I was standing in the gravel lot with my wallet in my hand and all of my money gone. I found Sudden three nights later and we slept together.

You call a strip joint asking for a dancer, they'll tell you the girl is working whether she is or not. They know that once you're there, you'll spend money anyway. If they think you're a stalker and they don't know if you're out to slash one of their dancers in the parking lot, they'll still take their chances because you're going to spend money. Maybe. I figure there's no way to find out for certain when she's working. I return two nights in a row and blow sixty bucks each night, four-dollar coffees and singles on the brass rail until the third night, I find Sudden. I didn't see her for an hour and ten minutes while she was soaking some Japanese millionaire for her condo payment. I knew if she took too long, he was probably dead of asphyxiation and she was sneaking out the back door by the phone booths.

But that didn't happen. I flagged her down and she came and sat beside me. *Hi, Honey*, like she didn't recognize me. I picked up the tiny lamp from the cocktail table, tilted the shade to throw the light onto my face. Two streaks like red lash marks ran along the left side of my neck, one on my right. She was right-handed. The skin had been chafed raw, and a crust of scabbed welts stippled over yellow-green bruises otherwise invisible in the dull club light. My throat still clicks when I swallow.

I met her at work again the next night, and the following night met her for a drink after her shift. Three consecutive nights in her Sherman Oaks condo followed. I liked watching her walk naked to her dresser, liked staring at her ass while she did a post-coital line.

"Try some?" She held the vial to me, brown glass the size of my pinkie tip.

"Okay..." I knew I had to snort it, but it still didn't seem right. Things going into my nose usually burned.

"Take this," she handed me a metal straw – stainless steel, .20 gauge – cut two lines an inch and half long each. "Sniff hard and follow the line. It won't burn at all."

She was right, it didn't burn at all. Picture a shattering window, each piece of glass – from the biggest shard to the tiniest sliver – is a thought, a memory, an idea or an impulse, tumbling end over end in every direction at once, every minute of your life, from your first heartbeat to your last. Imagine stopping the film in a split moment, then running it backwards. Imagine the billions of jagged fragments magnetized in an instant, pulled back into an unfractured whole, crystal clear. That's what it feels like. The perpetual whirlwind of vaporous memories and regrets goes away. Sudden changed everything.

So, I'm standing in her room, the first waves of that first hit collapsing my thoughts into *here* and *now*, eyes fixed on the mirror and razorblade thinking, *I like this.*

"This used to be part of my act," Sudden said. I looked over as she took a pull from a bottle of rum.

"What did?"

At the same instant, she spat a ball of bright heat across a candle, daylight flashing into the bedroom for a moment.

"Where did you learn *that*?"

"Didn't you ever want to join the circus when you were little?" she asked me, laughing at my amazement.

"Yeah, but not to get my face set on fire."

"What would you have done, then?"

"I wanted to be a contortionist." In one second it seemed funny and in the next second I forgot why.

"C'mere," she said. "Have another line."

Sudden's connection was Jimmy, the doorman at her club. Jimmy took me on as a customer. He had some of the dancers as customers too, as well as some regulars. The owners knew, and they took their cut. And I'm sure their bosses took a cut, guys working with ledgers in card rooms or Vegas bars. I didn't ask. After a time, Jimmy connected me with Ray, with whom I stayed through every other change, but he never knew about those. Jimmy introduced me as his friend, and Ray only knew me as Jimmy's friend thereafter. He never saw my left hand, would meet me at his place in Culver City whenever we did a deal. Ray didn't seem too bright, but I wasn't falling for that. He wore a black knit cap year-round and a patchy beard. He had hearing aids in both ears, the putty-colored, median pigment of the hard-of-hearing demographic, every race and none.

The expense added up. I did things for Jimmy when he needed them or when his employers said he needed them. The first time I did what I do for money, I'm thinking, *I shouldn't do this, but I'll make an exception. Just this once. Maybe one more time.* I procured Social Security numbers or printed birth certificates. I did passports. Mia and Lenka from the Ukraine, Pavel from Budapest. I can feel the brain-rush when I start working. Lay out the pieces, look for what's missing and seal the gap, brain cylinders firing to reshuffle the puzzle, and it makes my face and fingers warm, feeling my brain work.

Some people wonder how others go on the run, leave one place for another when they're being tracked, watched, and they slip away anyhow, wonder how guys get through the

Canadian border with opium bricks or up through Mexico with uncut coke. I don't.

I made an exception for Jimmy, and now I've got Jimmy and his people to worry about, and they've got me to worry about. But that exception for Jimmy was the catalyst for the exception I made for Keara. *Make me someone.* Taught her everything I know. Wanted to learn the ropes. And if I hadn't trusted her with my real name, then I wouldn't still have her. And I can't have that.

I spent five months with Sudden, through August of 1985. I was living in North Hollywood, some nights staying with her in Sherman Oaks. My last godsplitter had been years prior while I was in jail, before I had moved west. The infirmary had done little more than restrain me to a bed and shoot me with just enough Thorazine to shut me up. That lasted three days and I had almost forgotten about it. I'd written the headaches off as a childhood phenomenon, some anomaly of my growth.

Sudden was working a day shift, and I stayed at her place that afternoon, reading. In those first few minutes when that unearthly quiet muffled every ambient sound of the city and the blue walls of her bedroom started to glow, I remembered every single second of those first three headaches. The pain started as I was ransacking her bathroom for anything that might help. I found a bottle of Percocet, started taking them and they didn't do anything. I lost count and took them all, found other pills, took them but shouldn't have. The godsplitters have been returning ever since.

"Can you hear me? Can you say your name for me?" Loud, clear, persistent. Latino Med-Tech with close-cropped hair, cradling my head with rubber gloves. Blue windbreaker, L.A. County Paramedic patch, and shining a light into my eyes. Might as well pry my lids open and scratch his name onto my retina with a coat hanger.

Again, "Can you say your name for me?"

"Johnny." My tongue was a fist of tar clogging my mouth, unable to make the complex twist into the required *j*. Ellis Island butchered a lot of names that way, lice inspectors armed with rubber stamps and naturalization documents, unable to hear through the blurs of Gaelic or Slavic accents. *J*'s don't happen until the tail end of speech development around age four. In my case, seven. Narcotics like Percocet hit the speech and memory regions of the brain first, making my answer moot. *Shonnie.*

"His driver's license says 'Martin.'" Another voice. "John's his middle name."

I tried to say *yes* but could only grunt.

"Do you know what day of the week it is, Martin?"

Yesterday was payday, so that made it Thursday. But I'd been locked inside and hadn't been able to pick up my check and I'd have to do it tomorrow if I wasn't stuck in the hospital. I didn't have any cash and had spent my last five on two pints at the Dresden Room. Jimmy owed me big and was supposed to come through. But I cut him slack so he'll cut me slack.

"Jimmy owes me money," I tried to say.

"Martin, I need you to open your eyes. Come on, Martin, open up. Look at me."

After the Emergency Room, I passed the evaluation, the back of my head virtually touching my heels, the psychiatric equivalent of coughing up a half-swallowed hairpin and picking locks with my teeth. I had to forage through my memory for every scrap of reading I'd done in Dr. Gaines's office, and I kept preparing my answers in my head, just ahead of her line of questioning because I knew the checklist well.

The Evaluator was a frazzled, female graduate student intern wearing thick-soled running shoes, a rumpled, ankle-length skirt, mismatched sweater and a blast of frizzy hair screaming in every direction against the call of gravity. Spider-thread scratch lines and freckle-puncture scabs covered her wrists, hands and fingers. No jewelry.

She reveled in the interview process, enjoyed looking through my file, such as it was, and consulted an interview crib sheet that she did a shitty job of keeping from me. In short, she was everything I've ever come to hate: the authority of the State with the mind of a child fighting for sandbox territory. I could tell by her hands that her closest companion was her cat, which meant she had no husband, boyfriend or girlfriend. She hated any life more colorful than hers.

"How are you feeling now?" she asked.

"I'm exhausted," I said. "I want to get out of here."

"Are you happy or sad right now, Mr. Kelly?" Tense.

"I'm happy," I said. This was not going to be easy. I hadn't spoken with an Evaluator since I was a kid, and back then I hadn't been lying to them. Back then, I didn't know just what damage they could do with the stories I told them. But I did now.

She made a single line of notes, then asked Why? Twice she held up her hand to quiet me – a gross breach of APA protocol – if I embellished my answers. Her three nouns were *cat, blanket,* and *baby*. She incorrectly used the word *symptom* instead of *sign*. I doubt that she ever finished getting her license.

"Mr. Kelly, I'm issuing you a conditional discharge. I believe your overdose was accidental, but you're showing symptoms of a somatoform disorder with these unfounded migraine claims. I'm going to keep you on file, and I need to see you in three weeks. I'd like you to take some tests when you return."

Read: She couldn't tag me with anything then and there, but still wanted me to come back for further evaluation. This, in spite of the fact that her sole charge was to provide a single, written opinion for the attending ER physician. I promised her that I'd return and when I left, made another promise that I'd be prepared for this next time. I never went back, and I knew she'd never find me.

Sharon had quit working at the club with Sudden. Sharon needed to turn her life around. Sharon needed money, methadone, urine screening and weekly counseling to stay clean and, if Sharon had all of those things, then the State would let her keep little Paul, born six pounds, two ounces. Daddy had gone AWOL as soon as she said *I think I'm pregnant* and her arrest for possession followed soon after. Sharon had to work, and work meant carrying trays at Ships or Denny's, just like Mom used to do. Work meant making ends meet on a minimum-wage graveyard shift with a newborn to support and the State clocking her and her bodily fluids. A hard change after years of making six figures in undeclared cash and spending every bit of it.

Here's a thousand bucks, I said. *You're my wife, and that's our son. We're getting him a Social Security number. I'll give you another thousand when we're finished.*

He's already got one, she said.

I know.

Baptismal Certificate and hospital birth record, fifty-five minutes total. When the County Registrar's Certified Record Of Live Birth arrived in the mail, it was for Paul John Macintyre.

His middle name is Michael, she said.

It was Michael. Now it's John.

I applied for a passport and Social Security number, awaited the inevitable written denials. Baptismal certificate and hospital record, round two. Four letters of complaint sent back to the County Registrar with the accompanying rejections from the SSA and State Department. I insisted that they'd transposed *1958* with *1985*, that they'd made a serious mistake.

It took time, but that didn't bother me. They were slow, which meant they were inefficient, which meant they wouldn't see that the birth certificate's serial number showed I was lying. And I was right – the rubber stamps, corrections and form letters followed, just to make the problem, me, go away.

Martin Kelly ended when Sharon took the money, took Paul to live with her parents in Virginia so she could start over, and I had a new birth certificate with a new date. I also had a spotless driving record, perfect credit and no psychiatric history. I was Paul MacIntyre.

I didn't know what to tell Sudden, didn't know for certain how I felt about her. Knowing her precarious balance with human relations – she dealt with men at their lowest, and that came out during sex – I doubted she'd miss me. And Jimmy's needs were getting bigger. Kept saying he wanted to introduce me to some people, that they appreciated what I'd done for them so far, and that they had plans for me.

I opted to not tell her anything, to not meet Jimmy's people and see what plans they had for me, to not say goodbye to anyone. I vanished.

THIRTEEN

Natalie wrote me fifteen love letters altogether, with the rounded printing of a young girl – circles over her *i*'s and *j*'s, sometimes a smiley face or heart. She was twenty-four. She owned her car free and clear (an opulent BMW 320i, oil-slick black), paid a mortgage on a Marina Del Rey condo. And she was gorgeous, likely as attuned to sidelong, surreptitious gawks as I had been as a child. But dating Natalie meant swimming out of my depth. My best clothes, dishrags in contrast to the New York acronyms, baroque Italian and French labels of her social set. I tried, but my wardrobe was based on anonymity, economy and function, in that order.

We'd made eye contact seven times during a show at the Coconut Teazer, each look compounding the seconds from the previous. I hadn't seen her with anybody. When the bartender handed her a drink (I guessed rum and Coke), I ordered a bourbon, tipping a twenty in her direction to indicate I'd be paying for both of us. She said something, too many syllables for *Thanks*, but I couldn't hear her over the music. I leaned in, *'Scuze me?*, still deaf. Whether she said *Thanks for the drink or I've poisoned yours*, I don't know. She ignored my words, kept her face close to mine. On that thin, anonymous, Sunset Boulevard pretext, we kissed, hard, almost not breathing for three minutes. I was right, rum and Coke. She pulled away, took me by the hand to the patio.

Outside, we made out through the rest of the set. She was too hammered to notice my eleven fingers on her ass. When the band stopped, she said *What's your name?* I said *Paul*.

We kissed again, I got carried away in my drunkenness and pulled her hair and she moaned. I let loose but she moaned again, *No, pull my hair*. The courtship was all of forty-one minutes.

A week later, I rang her number from her condominium guest entrance. Her voice mixed with static and the anonymous, implied plural that women living alone use on their answering machines: *No one's in to take your call, but if you can leave a message...* The matchbook had her name (heart over the *i*), address, the date and time. Twenty-two minutes and three messages later, I left. One bourbon, phoned her once more from the bar, left a message. *No one's in to take your call...* then, *Hey, it's Paul, gimme a ring when you get this* and drove home.

She phoned two and a half hours later, blathering apologies but with no explanation.

"I completely forgot... I'm so sorry... I never do that... Let's hook up tomorrow..." She suggested we meet at a place called Magnolia on Beverly Boulevard. The sign out front had letters cut with a plasma torch from a sheet of aluminum, backlit with pale neon. The décor inside, polished concrete, halogen lights and space age furniture, had been profiled in every Los Angeles magazine and newspaper. Her condo gate and Magnolia were the first indications that I was out of my league. Status symbols and invisibility are mutually exclusive.

The next night, Natalie showed up wearing a grey business suit, the skirt too short for business, the blazer both hinting at and flaunting her cleavage. The conversation wound down (I drove a truck, she was a publicist, I wasn't listening) and she checked her Cartier – the circumference of a nickel – for the third time.

"How big did you think this place was?" she asked.

I spat an ice cube back into my glass. "Pardon?"

"Did you think we could just walk in here and pick a table? It's Friday."

"You've lost me, Natalie. What's wrong?" I'm slow sometimes. I can't hear between words like other people.

"What's wrong is that it wouldn't have killed you to make a reservation. We've waited for over half an hour. Jesus."

"Twenty-eight minutes," I said. I don't own a watch. Then, "Fuck you," and knocked back my last finger of bourbon. "You blow me off, then cop an attitude because I don't know your debutante protocol." Halfway into the drive to meet her, I realized I should have done a line or two, taken my edge off.

"What did you say to me?" She looked at me, her eyes and mouth locked open.

"I said twenty-eight minutes."

"I mean after that."

"I know what you meant. And I know you heard me."

She slapped me. Her practiced force made a sharp leathery crack against my face.

Restaurants – crowded, Friday-night restaurants – go dog-whistle quiet when that happens. Stares assuming unheard, succulent details, waiting to see if I'll hit her back (not my style). I ran it back through my head, tagging words with values trying to see what I missed, what didn't equate, what didn't add up – when she hit me again. Same cheek. My face blazed, the purple brightness on the edge of my eyes swelled and I dragged her by the wrist (an extra finger does miracles for my grip) out to Beverly Boulevard, to her car. In the parking lot of a nearby church, she wrapped around me – her clothes on the driver's side floor – said *Pull my hair*. I watched St. Francis through her windshield, laughing to myself. True. True. True. True. True.

* * *

Natalie and I let our contrast speak for itself, watched nanosecond conclusions silently congeal behind eyes at cocktail parties (office birthdays, promotions, contract acquisition celebrations). I'd shake with my left hand, hold the grip for the small talk and watch someone's fog of bewilderment envelop them, too nervous to look down and see what they were feeling. I'd prolong a post-*Nice to meet you* conversation for the pleasure of watching someone's fake smile strain and collapse, and then tally their excuses – *Doug just arrived. I should go say hello. There's one of our new clients. Can you excuse me?*

Natalie thought she was better than I was, that I drove a delivery truck because I couldn't do anything else. I didn't tell her that I liked driving because I got to wear a uniform and look like a hundred other drivers and not have more than a few minutes of interaction with any given person on any given day. I didn't tell her that I liked the paycheck and health coverage that gave me stability, anonymity.

At a birthday party for one of her co-workers, she introduced me as *Paul, a truck driver*. When someone said *I thought you were a mechanic*, I realized I wasn't her first. *We've got a job in our mailroom, if you're interested,* one guy said, and his buddies laughed. Fifteen years ago, I would have said or done any number of things in response, but I'd learned better. I looked at Natalie in her short denim skirt and tank top, her runner's calves and firm belly, and kept my mouth shut.

I clocked wedding rings and accents and scars, felt for calluses when I shook hands, checked watches and shoes, measured weights at a glance, guessed ages and silently ran the equations I'd learned as a kid and had improved over time. What did they want most, what had they settled for and what were they compensating with?

I did *polite*. I did *harmless* and *charming*. I listened, nodded and smiled, broke and resumed eye contact at specific intervals. I mirrored postures and stances, repeated half-phrases of their

own back to them while they spoke to me. They always said
Exactly. You know what I'm talking about.

Most of the time I didn't, but I just said something open-
ended and let them keep talking.

Where did I just read about that?

*Somebody mentioned that same company, earlier. I forgot his
name…*

Put on an empty look and they would fill in the blank for
me.

Right, that was Thursday's Wall Street Journal.

You mean Mike? He's one of our freelancers.

Every time.

I lit nobody's cigarette, paid no compliments. But I would
listen, match their drink brand for brand, from the bottle or
a glass, ate what they ate, chewed when they chewed. They
loved me. Natalie told me so, later.

On her balcony that night, I kept her clothes on but pulled
her panties down to her ankles, held her hair at the roots in
a tight tangle around my left fingers and did her while she
moaned.

We fast learned to skip the arguments. We took nights out
on her dime, attended her social functions, had sex. Slapping,
hair pulling, ripping and rending her DKNY office-fantasy,
power-suits *sex*. I'd cut her bra straps with a broken shot glass
and split her panty hose crotch with a stiletto heel. I could rip
her thong away with a single pull (I'm right-handed, but my
left is much stronger) – a half-twist at the seam of her left hip
(never pull forward or backward, always against the bone) and
tug with a full-body jerk like a reverse boxing punch and the
right hip seam pops like a frayed shoelace.

She tore three of my necklaces from me, slicing me each
time. Shredded my shirts and left Bruce Lee nail marks on
my chest. She replaced everything with a vengeance. Armani,
obsidian-black, single-breasted, four button. A Tag Heuer that
looked like a submarine depth monitor and worth four and a

half months of my salary, easy. On her floor, new nail marks, my boots on, work pants around my ankles, Natalie in nothing but stockings and heels, tortoiseshell comb snared midway down her waterfall of half-undone hair, bra, shredded skirt, and panties draped over her answering machine, ashtray and wine rack. *Stay there, I have a present for you.* She'd leave for her bedroom while I did a three-inch rail from her coffee table and then *Here, try this on,* followed by dinner. Four nights a week. I could set my watch by it.

Sex without that adrenaline was strictly a pre-shower, weekday-morning pressure release valve and not our first choice. Like anything else you put into your bloodstream again and again, we needed more, more, more for the same rush. She gave me a scar and I gave her one.

When I saw her next, it rained. The evening streets were shiny, wet, and grey. We met for a drink after work. Natalie was having her carpets cleaned and the condo association was spraying for bugs at the same time. She hadn't mentioned renting a hotel room, so I'd spent the afternoon scouring and scrubbing my apartment. I'm clean to begin with, at least very organized but, in truth, I was nervous. In five months, she never once stayed at my apartment. Four nights a week at hers. I never had a key.

Portico was in Brentwood, had a marble bar, marble tables, a connoisseur's scotch list, and leather booths that heaved a luxurious sigh beneath your weight. Normally not a place I'd go without Natalie, but weeknights were dead quiet and they didn't care how I dressed so it was a good hiding spot. Then somebody at Paramount held a production wrap party there, and somebody at Universal held an opening night reception there a week later. Both events hit the fashion and entertainment magazines simultaneously and my quiet spot was gone. And this was where Natalie wanted to meet, in a crowded public place where she said *We should talk.*

I squeezed into an open space at the bar near a cluster of players – six guys, a year or two either side of my age with caramel-orange tans and halogen teeth. Four women, whippet-thin, their faces the plastic sheen from multiple surgeries, spaghetti straps pulled their cocktail dresses tight, stretching them across half their weight in subdermal silicone bags. Wallets out, rounds bought, key rings on the bar – BMW, Audi, Mercedes, Jaguar.

My chest was still glowing from the last rails of blow I'd done in my car. I'd pulled into a dark residential street on the way, sucked up a line after fourteen days of nothing. Ray was in jail so I had gone elsewhere for my stuff. The guy had said *Good shit, straight from Bakersfield, not cut with nothin'. Just 'cause I like you.* And he was right, it was good shit, but I wasn't going back. Guys who *just like you* for no reason will always want something later.

Natalie showed up. She'd assembled my accumulated belongings from her place into a brown leather duffel, another gift that I would have never bought for myself, set it beneath our feet at the bar. We finished our first round, she held out her hand and shook mine with a polite, firm, post-interview grip.

"I can't see you anymore." Thanks for your time. We'll keep your application on file. We'll definitely consider you should something open up in the near future. Please take a brochure on the way out and be sure to sign our mailing list.

"I don't understand." True. My fingers were cold. I couldn't feel her grip. My left hand started cramping. It does that sometimes, from the mutant muscles configured for the extra digit.

"Paul... I love being with you. I do, honestly. But I need to grow up. I can't explain, but I can't do this anymore..."

I started to speak. She put her finger to my lips.

"Paul, you're an Aries. So am I. It can't work."

She kept talking but my ears filled with a humming sound

that muffled the music and bar noise. My hands grew colder, colder, colder, and my mouth dried out. I held my glass to the bartender, *Bourbon*, and when I turned back to her, she leaned in and kissed me.

"I do love you. I'm sorry."

I called Ray's substitute – which I'd sworn not to do – from a pay phone. Left a message, said where I was, said *Do you still have that girl's phone number?* Hung up and waited. He came by an hour later and palmed me two half-gram vials. I bought him a shot – clip, switch – set it down in front of him with a folded bill inside the napkin. He knocked back the shot, then another, feigned sympathy. *Just when you think you know someone*, he said.

Yeah, *now leave me alone.*

The coke faded, the light in my chest died and, eight ounces of bourbon later, the bottom of my brain started leaking, and my calm, focus and reason drained into the black hollow left by the waning rush. The mnemonic slide show – Mom, Dad, hospitals, Natalie, jail – started up, my own private lash. I thought of my sister who couldn't have children and I had no idea what's become of her and Dad who will never be a grandfather. Dad all alone without Mom, living on the street or dead for all I knew and his daughter by herself and a son nowhere to be found. I remembered, between the dead coke rush and the dull glow of the bourbon and claustrophobic heat of three hundred people with whom I have nothing in common, that this is why I hate crowds.

Weird. Shit, no. You ask him.

I'd been careless. My fingers were wrapped around my glass and I was two feet away but they acted like I couldn't hear. Shouting at each other over the din and they thought they were whispering. *Probably doesn't...* and I lost the rest, they started laughing, loud at first, and they tried to cover their mouths because they thought I hadn't noticed.

Dude, how many fingers your hand got? The voice was familiar.

Jocular and happy, secure in its ten digits and backup drinking crew, so it says whatever it wants.

The Players waited, muffling smirks behind martinis and spritzers.

"One for each of your mothers," I said. The predictable followed – widened eyes, lowered drinks and a spokesman stepping forward.

"What did you say? I didn't catch that."

"You caught it," I said. My old habits coming back.

He was tall with the spongy girth of an ex-high-school football player. His cologne burned my eyes. He squared off with me, gave me his best hard stare.

"You lookin' for me to kick your ass?"

Physically, I was no match for him, not by a long shot. But it's funny how guys with nice jobs and German company cars always want to *kick your ass*. Guys who can afford private gyms but have never thrown a real punch are going to *kick your ass*. Big tan white guys who lose their hair but hang onto their Alma Mater yearbooks will say they're going to *kick your ass*.

Nobody ever got their *ass kicked* while I was in jail. They had filed-down chicken bones or sharpened toothbrushes punched between their ribs, jaws broken by socks full of gravel, corneas split by wet paperbacks tied inside of towels, faces and necks cut by the plastic soles of county-issue slippers sharpened on the concrete floor.

Guys who want to *kick your ass* don't know the look in the eyes of somebody who knows how to seriously hurt you or worse, and who doesn't have anything to lose from doing so. It's a look you see in the eyes of a stray dog. Not a look of aggression because aggression is personal. It's an assessment: *Are you food? Are you a threat?* The answers take half a second and if the answers are both *no*, then the dog keeps moving.

That's what you see in the eyes of someone who can finish you off without a second thought. No face-off, no name-calling. *Are you going to hurt me? Yes? Then can I kill you?* and in the space of a heartbeat you, your life, your kids, your car, your job, and your bright promising future don't matter dick. Pampered fraternity students who grow up to be six-figure-income advertising executives or luxury car accessory dealers or this guy in my face don't have those eyes and have never seen them, but I have.

I felt my heart pounding, like I hadn't for a very long time. The adrenaline burned through the liquor and blow like so much nothing and I was wide alert in my head but frost on the outside, my brain running the numbers in a fraction of the time Mr. Player needs to figure his next move. He was six-foot-two, two-fifteen and right-handed. His eyes told me he was on his third drink and his breath backed that up. He had no peripheral vision and poor balance and I had a foot of space behind me, the bar on my left, and twenty-three inches on my right.

Think. Bars hate fights, hate cops. Liquor licenses are expensive. They've got the police, the Fire Department, the ATF, and ABC watching them, so they want a low profile with the city and a high profile with the weekly club listings.

Think. This is *not* the way to be invisible.

I was holding a full gram, couldn't afford to get searched, and if I was forced to do another change, soon, I'd need a driver's license photo and passport photo and couldn't wait for a broken nose to heal.

"Here," I said, and I fanned my fingers wide at his eye level, "check it out."

He didn't say anything, the others moved closer to gape. I kept talking, doing *backing down*.

"Look, I get sick of people talking about it," I said. I flagged the bartender and paid for a round. "It's on me. Have a pleasant evening."

I heard them talking and laughing as I left, but I chased their words out of my head. Stomach burned, old aspirin damage flaring up, and the bile backed up to my neck and every boot-licking sir from two years in Youth Camp roared through my head.

Drove into Hollywood, did four shots at Boardner's and then walked for a long time. Let the adrenaline run its course. Burned off the coke. Then did more.

At La Brea, where Hollywood arcs into Sunset. *How did I get this far?* I was past – long past – the calm centering of the first four blasts. My left hand twitched and I swatted imaginary bugs out of my eyes. Talking to myself but *loud*, floating like a hawk on the warm current of her memory, but at the same time a reservoir of hatred creaking seams and popping rivets. *Bitch!* at the thin air. Tourists, runaways and failed musicians stared, and no matter how well I was dressed I was going to get stopped and searched, cuffed and stuffed.

Legs hurt. I found my car down Cherokee, a block from Boardner's. More hits during the walk back, miming calls in phone booths or lighting a smoke, cupping the vial cap for a snort while I do so. Screen and cuff. Mouth dry as dust and I couldn't blink, my hands quivered like small angry dogs, and a thousand moments with Natalie blasted through my memory like a pillow torn open in a high wind.

I wasn't cold anymore, but my hands were still shaking. Then I was in my car holding a medallion, elliptical with a four-centimeter shear along one edge, the rest of the key buried in the ignition and I hadn't felt the snap. Dug in with my fingers but it was in there tight. Needle-nose pliers would get it. I had a pair, but not with me. My spare key was in the ashtray on the wine crate beside my front door. But which front door? Which door? Sorted through the apartments and names in my head, couldn't remember where I lived or which name I was using. *Paul* sounded right, but I couldn't remember my last name, only apartments. Paul Ridgecrest. Paul Los Feliz Gardens. Didn't know, couldn't remember. Felt for my wallet.

It was in a brown leather bag with my clothes and toothbrush. I'd left it at the bar, but couldn't remember which one. Which bar which bar which bar?

Snow White's Coffee Shop down Hollywood Boulevard. I ordered four eggs, easy, wheat toast, white toast, hash browns, tomato juice, orange juice, coffee, iced tea, a side of bacon, an English muffin, slice of ham, and a glass of water. I'm staring at a mound of food that I ordered because I could pronounce the menu but couldn't eat. Might as well have put it in my ear. My stomach was a thousand miles away.

Stared at my food. A crumpled T-shirt that smelled of gasoline and shoe polish from the floor of my car – *when did I grab this?* – and I used it to stop the blood but my nose insisted on flooding black-red all over the shirt Natalie gave me and my jeans and my eggs. Luminous red Rorschach drops on the white paper napkin – two dogs fighting, a bug trapped in a jar. I tried to stop the bleeding, but my nerves were shrapnel and I did another blast in the toilet stall of the bathroom just to even out, inhaled the sweet dust through my smoking septum, microbits of glass slicing their way through my sinuses. Rinsed my face in the sink. Tried to keep my nose covered but my left hand was cramping worse and worse and worse and it was hard to hold the cloth in place and I'm not even caring about hiding my mutant fingers and I thought I should eat. I should really try to eat.

Sir, I'm going to ask you to leave or I'm calling the police.

Hollywood Boulevard.

Lost my car again.

Pulled my coat tight and tried to sleep.

Natalie Natalie.

FOURTEEN

The sun cut through my eyes, woke me like a slow hammer from the scant rest I salvaged from the night. Fingers and feet were cold, stiff, couldn't feel them, had to force movement. Sat up, hurt from the wood slats, back resting against ARE YOU PAYING TOO MUCH FOR AUTO INSURANCE? Red block letters screamed the question against yellow. A black-and-white head shot, confidence beaming from the superhero jaw and walrus moustache, promised to save me hundreds of dollars.

A Korean woman on the bus bench near my feet. She probably didn't want to sit anywhere near me, but was too old to stand. Aluminum cane, plastic grocery bag, clutch purse and RTD pass. I needed water, needed to rinse the cotton out of my mouth. Needed to find my car, fix the ignition, and needed to get home. My brain said *Natalie* left, and I didn't care anymore.

My head felt like it was packed full of sand. My bones hurt. It hurt to stand up, hurt to stand still and it hurt to walk, but I had to. I needed juice, water, fluid. My wallet was gone, I had less than two dollars in my pockets and, without ID, that made me a vagrant. I started down the block, foraging through my memory for my car and my wallet and my bag as Hollywood Boulevard was waking up – street kids moving alone or in clusters, trash pickup, maintenance workers with high-pressure hoses blasting the previous night's biohazards from the Walk of Fame.

A shop window caught my reflection and my own face startled me. A head of shiny, rust-colored hair, skin stretched over my skull and ten years added to my face over the course of the night. The window reflected another window and I saw my other reflection, just as bad, staph pocking the forehead, picking at it with my left hand.

My left hand had five fingers and I wasn't scratching my forehead and I wasn't *that* sick and I turned around. There I was, or a kid who looked just like me, same hair, same skin, same face, same height with an army surplus jacket and jeans that he'd probably worn for a year or two straight. Whether he saw his own face or mine but didn't notice, I couldn't be sure, but he walked, face watching the ground in a second-nature scan for spare anything that might have hit the sidewalk to his good fortune. He had junkie-fidgets – sneezing, wiping his nose and trembling – and they'd get worse before they got better.

People do what I do, they call it the Zombie Method. You find someone who's a marginal *someone*, someone who's physically similar to you within reason, has good credit or at least manageable debt and a clean legal record. Someone whose days are short-numbered, someone nobody gives a damn about, and you buy that someone's name and history.

Runaway Junkie Double worked his way down the block, parked on a bus bench with a girl, maybe fifteen, sporting a mohawk, and another kid, really big kid, wearing a Black Sabbath T-shirt that was too small for him, and I could smell them all from a distance. They knew each other, knew the same soup kitchens, rescue missions, sympathetic Samaritans and drive-by tricks and they probably shared the same freeway underpass or squatters' hovel or youth shelter.

He looked so much like me it was spooky. Minus one digit. I doubted he had any credit history at all to worry about, but his jail record was going to be ten times mine or more. That alone was enough to keep me walking, but he verged on being my clone, and I couldn't waste that.

Bigman in the Sabbath shirt caught me staring, tapped the other two and they looked my way. The girl shouted *c'mere*. I turned and walked. I was in no shape to talk to them, needed to come back when I was clean, rested, and with cash. Kept walking, hoping Bigman wasn't following me.

I stopped at a corner deli, tried to buy some juice with the last of my change but I was eight cents short, so I left the bottle on the counter and walked out with another tucked under my coat. Outside, a white Taurus sat parked in a fifteen-minute zone with a ticket flapping beneath the windshield wiper. That's a good car if you want to be unnoticed, the least likely to be pulled over and non-existent on police profile lists, and I'd already passed it when I remembered, fog in my head starting to clear, go back and crawl underneath. Spare key in a magnetic box, I climbed into the driver's seat and the severed key slid out of the ignition on my first attempt with a ballpoint pen, now that my hands weren't quaking from a bloodstream full of blow.

"Stove!"

Strange word to hear called out, but I heard it again, *Stove!* Shouted like a name. I recognized Bigman from my post-coke jag. He wore a Goodwill dumpster denim jacket and a dog collar, black trousers cuffed over blood-colored Docs, sat with a dogpack gaggle of other street kids at the nether edge of a strip mall off Sycamore, a block from Hollywood Boulevard. I was dressed in a black suit with an open collar and wore shoes that would have cost me two months' rent (thanks, Natalie) and stepping up to a homeless group of runaway panhandler teenage street hustlers. Me, dressed the way I was, approaching these kids, I knew it wouldn't look right if a patrol car spotted me. But I want to see my double again.

The dog pack of runaways whistled, stared as I walked toward them.

"Look at him."

"Shit, you score or what?"

"Check out Stove."

"Hold up," Bigman said to the group, and they went quiet. He squinted at me in the parking lot light.

"You ain't Steve," he said. "You his brother? Didn't know he had a brother. Twins or what?"

Let the question slide, let them infer an answer, find *Steve*.

"Why do you call him 'Stove?'"

"The fuck you care?" said Bigman. The ringleader.

Did *acquiescent but firm*.

"Because it's important that I find him." I took out a pack of smokes, tapped one loose and pulled it out with my teeth. Kept my left hand in my pocket, held the pack out to Bigman and he pulled out three at once, tucked one into his mouth, one behind his ear and the other in his pocket.

There are predators, prey and mollusks. And there are scavengers. After jail taught me how to stop fighting, it taught me the pecking order of groups, how to spot them, play them or disrupt them and with what currency.

Bigman squinted at me with the cigarette hanging from his lips, said, *Light?* and I had control now because he *asked* for something. I tossed the pack to a kid at Bigman's knee, little guy, shaky, with a TSOL shirt.

"Take one, give one to your buddies. The rest are his," I pointed to Bigman, "whenever he asks for one. Understand?"

"Says who?"

"I do, fuckhead." Bigman thumped the kid's ribs with the toe of his boot.

My lighter made a high chrome snap like a sliding gun chamber. Tossed it to another kid, said, "He needs a light." Then I stepped closer, voice lower, "Any of your friends know where to find Steve?"

They shook their heads.

"Then let's just you and I talk."

"Fuck off," Bigman said to group, and they did.

"Do you know where he is?" I asked.

"Not now. He's off doing shit. We need money. I'll see him at the place."

"Where's that?"

"No way."

"Right." I handed him another pack of smokes. Held a folded twenty on top, more cash than he'd seen in a long time.

"Tell him to find me here tomorrow night. Nine o'clock. I've got good news for him."

I figured I had a strong chance of wasting my time. In twenty-four hours he could be on the nod, trying to score, in jail or in a dumpster. But Steve was waiting, probably had been since eight. Didn't own a watch and didn't need to tell time.

He was exactly my height, with my same hair color and eyes but much lighter, which made him *really* thin, with one digit fewer on his hands and I guessed less than a year to live. It's a strange thing to be looking at your own face from a distance, covered in staph with the teeth falling out and a snotslick upper lip. It was my face, minus a few years plus a hundred more bad ones. He'd had to get used to things I didn't even want to imagine – ways of sleeping or finding places to sleep, finding food or making money – and for a second I wondered if at the rate I was going, I wouldn't have to do the same. My cash flow spikes and plummets like a heart attack EKG, I have no next of kin and don't know if my next godsplitter is going to knock out my remaining grip on reality for good.

I was half a block down and I watched him pace, flashed my brights when he was facing me. Don't know what Bigman told him, but he'll know it's me. He stopped outside my car, junkie-hustler caution mixing with hope. I opened the passenger door so that the dome light flooded my face, let him see me and wonder.

"Get in."

He looked at me, knew this wouldn't be his usual ride, but hope won out over caution and he climbed inside.

"There's smokes." I pointed to the dashboard, fresh pack, and he jumped, ravenous. "Keep 'em."

I punched the dashboard lighter, said, "What else do you need?"

"What else you got?" He looked like me, but he had the voice of a teenager.

"Why do they call you *Stove*?"

Pause, like he was repeating the question in his head, had to say it. I could see his lips move, silent before he said anything out loud.

"It's like Steve, only slower. *Stove*. I'm slow."

"What's your last name?"

"How 'bout money!" Loud, flip-switch tense, fight or flight. He had nothing to lose and obviously shifted gears quicker than most but didn't know he was doing it, and that made him dangerous. I needed the edge here, so I had to hope he bought my approach.

"You need to lower your voice, Steve."

"I *need* to do shit. Maybe you'll just let me out."

"Maybe, Steve-only-slower, you'll stop to figure why a guy who looks *exactly* like you only wearing an expensive suit wants to talk to you. *Maybe* you'll get something out of this. Maybe you'll be cool."

I didn't know where I was going with this pitch, but it didn't matter. Blood-red cherry light hit my rear-view, bathed the inside of the car, and the static megaphone voice behind me said *Pull over to the curb and turn off your engine.*

Steve did not take this well, panic shuddering and murmuring *fuck, fuck, fuck, oh fuck.*

I drove, slowly, looking to stop without double parking or blocking a driveway, which isn't easy in the middle of Hollywood, and that bought me time. Wanted to stop Steve's panic, slap him but I couldn't, cops would see that. I gripped his leg, hard.

"Be *cool*, Steve."

"I'm going to jail. I can't do it. I'm going to jail."

"Breathe, Steve. Now shut up, just nod *yes* or *no*. Quick. You got a warrant?"

Yes.

"More than one?"

"I think."

"Just nod, Steve."

Yes.

"You high right now?"

No.

"Don't bullshit me. They'll know."

Yes.

"Tell me. Say it."

"Crank."

Pull over and turn your engine off.

I stopped, finally, hoped I had at least fifteen seconds while they were on their two-way.

"Look at me." Steve did, his pupils bloated.

"You holding?"

No.

"Anything. Set of works, razor, knife. Anything."

No.

"Got any ID on you?"

Yes.

"What?"

"Rescue Mission card. Got my name on it."

"Give it to me."

Fumbled in his pocket, I knew they could see that. We'd parked, and the cops were running my plates. They were clean. They'd probably seen me pick him up.

"Steve, can you remember 'Macintyre?'"

"Who?"

"The name. Can you remember it? 'Macintyre.' Think, *mac* and a car tire. *Mac and tire.* Say it."

"Mac and tire." He handed me his Rescue Mission ID card. *Steven Edwards.*

"They ask, your last name's *Macintyre.*"

The wrong time to be passing anything between you and a passenger is when the flashlight hits your window, which is precisely when Steve was handing me his card. Steve knew this, but all the cop saw was me handing over a pack of smokes, one tapped loose from the top. Steve looked surprised.

"Take it," I said, firm.

Cop said, "Sir, please place your hands on the steering wheel."

I took out a smoke for myself, closed the pack and tossed it back onto the dash. Cup, clip, palm, switch – Steven Edwards's Rescue Mission ID tucked behind the foil and nobody saw a thing.

Light in my face, turned to show him my eyes. Another cop on the passenger side, his own light on Steve, and the two lights crossed back and forth in my front seat, once, twice, both cops scanning me and Steve-only-slower, Prince and Pauper.

"Would you step out onto the curb, please?"

I unbuckled my seat belt, said, "Steve, it's cool. I'll have you at Grandpa Macintyre's as soon as we're done."

Outside, the drill began.

"License, please." Not a traffic stop, they didn't ask for insurance or registration. Which meant they did indeed see me pick him up. They think I'm a *john.*

"Something funny?"

"No, sir."

"Have you had anything to drink this evening, Paul?"

"No, sir." True. I wasn't taking any chances.

"You haven't had anything to drink tonight, correct?"

"That's correct."

"What about earlier?"

"I worked all day. I haven't had a drink since yesterday."

"Where do you work?"

"Messenger service."

He was my height, his voice measured, doing what he was paid to do. If Steve didn't blow it, I had no problem. He handed my license to his partner who took it to the squad car for the check. Paul Macintyre was clean. I wasn't worried.

He gave me the standard field test, *Place your feet together and look straight ahead, now follow my finger.* Held his index finger at the far edge of my field of sight, kept it there, waited for my eyes to strain, break their hold. I'm surprised when he unwraps a breathalyzer.

"Now, Paul, I want you to watch what I'm doing, see that I'm breaking the plastic in front of you, so this is a fresh test."

I'd just palmed a card and stuck it into a pack of smokes right under his flashlight, so telling me to watch what he's doing meant nothing. But he refused to believe I hadn't been drinking, until I blew a 0.0.

"So, Paul, if you're not drinking, what are you doing out here?"

"Been looking for my brother," I said. "Trying to get him cleaned up, get him some dinner, see if I can convince him to let me take him back to our mother and father."

"That's your brother?" He'd seen us side by side, but asked nonetheless.

"Yes sir, that's my brother." Obsequious, jail-house etiquette in over-drive. The word *sir* coming out of my mouth made me sick. One more time I'd had to kowtow to some asshole who could wreck my life. And this one because I thought I could score a set of new papers.

I heard the other cop's voice, then Steve's, stuttering with adrenaline-fear.

"Has your brother been drinking?"

"I think so."

"Anything else?"

"I'm sure he's stoned, sir. I don't know on what. It's taken me a while to find him."

"What's your brother's name?"

"Steve."

"You two twins?"

"No, we just look alike. People can't tell us apart, sometimes."

His partner returned, handed me my license with an all-clear nod to the cop talking to me, then said, "The other one's got no ID, but said his name was Steve *Mac-and-tire*."

Stupid dumbass junkie panic punk.

"Yeah, that's how he learned to remember his name when he was little. He's–" pause, one, two, three "– not very bright. Lots of problems as a kid. Like I said, he's probably stoned right now."

"Okay, Paul, we just had to be sure. He looked like he might have been hustling when you picked him up, so it's his lucky day. He's definitely intoxicated, and without any ID or cash, we could have hauled him in for vagrancy. The resemblance is the only reason we know you're related, otherwise you'd both be at the station."

"Understood, sir."

"It's good you found him. Maybe get him some help." He switched off his light, *we're finished*. "Have a good evening."

"Thanks. Same to you."

Back in the car, Steve was a ghost of his former ghost.

"You like whiskey, Steve-only-slower?"

"Yeah."

"I'll get us a bottle, then. But I'm keeping it in the trunk until we get where we're going."

"Where are we going?"

"Wherever it is you sleep."

FIFTEEN

Steven Edwards led me to an alley that led to a hole in a brick wall that led to another alley that led to a chain link fence peeled back at one corner. At each juncture Steven Edwards asked, *You a cop? You gotta tell me if you're a cop*. Steven Edwards was slow.

"No, I'm not a cop."

Through the fence, we entered the back door of a boarded-up single-story house. No light, no heat, no plumbing, no furniture and from the smell, no ventilation. But no landlord, no rent and, for now, no police raids. I'd expected worse, a dumpster, bus station or freeway underpass.

Steve-only-slower crouched on a foam mat. In the dark, I made out spray paint on the walls, broken glass and puddles on the floor.

"Everybody's gone," he said. "They'll come back late. Do you have my ID card?"

"You need it?"

"It's mine."

"Listen, Steve-only-slower, I'd like to buy it from you."

"No shit? Nothing less than ten bucks. Or else give it back."

"Tell me what else you have, then we'll discuss price."

"No." He shook his head and the word barked out like a half-sneeze, groove-stuck in the last turning wheel still in his brain. "No. No. No. No. No." Sputtered over and over, the same snap to his head.

"Ten bucks. Deal. What else do you have?"

"Like what? Why?"

I crouched down in front of him, showed him my empty right hand, made a fist, then fanned out five twenties. He laughed, a stunted child's crude amusement.

"How did you do that?"

"Magic. That's a hundred dollars, Steve-only-slower. It's yours, but only if you show me anything else you're holding."

He lifted the foam mat, pulled out a rumpled brown bag.

I dumped it out, tore it in half to make certain I missed nothing and sifted through the contents in a patch of streetlight with my foot, not wanting to cut myself.

Socks, three. Pants, one. T-shirt, black, one. Comics page from a Sunday paper, one. Plastic bag containing a small bottle of liquid soap and a toothbrush, one each.

Then, jackpot: twenty-three Polaroids of Steve-only-slower as a Hollywood punk posing with tourists. Steven, younger and healthier, with a liberty-spiked mohawk, leather jacket and tartan bondage pants.

A diary, the inside cover inscribed *To Steven, to help you on your journey* from a Father Riordan at a local rescue mission. Three pages of misspellings and drivel dated with each entry, eight pages of ballpoint pentagrams and band logos – *TSOL, Crass, Christian Death, Catholic Discipline, Lords of the New Church.* Pentagrams, lightning bolts, swastikas, skulls, knives, amateur ink drawings of female sex organs and a hundred and thirty-nine blank pages. I held the journal upside down, fanned the pages once, twice, nothing fell out. I tucked the pictures inside, kept looking.

Pack of condoms. Wallet-insert card with St. Jude, Patron Saint of Lost Causes. Tucked that into the book. Laminated card with his name and patient number from a methadone clinic. Business cards: One from Father Riordan, another from a cop on a homeless youth task force, one for a shelter. A high-school ID card from Detroit, Michigan – Steven Edwards as

red-headed all-American boy. All of the papers, cards, traces of
his contact with anyone, not counting the journal, weigh less
than seven ounces and will fit in my pocket.

The smell was starting to swell in my stomach. Rapid, frame-
splice thought: Godsplitter kicks in while I'm here, I scream
my teeth loose for three days, crawling over broken crack
pipes, kinked syringes and coagulated afterbirth, I'm stripped
clean and left to die. Flask in my pocket, still wrapped from
the liquor store. I took it out, snapped the seal and took a long
pull. Felt the burn below my eyes and let it grow, fire inside my
nose then fade, took another because I wouldn't want it back
once Steve-only-slower put it to his mouth.

"Here," I said. "Keep it." I held the book up, the front cover
bulging with the pictures and papers crammed inside. "We
have a deal?"

He nodded, grinning at the money.

"Anything else, Steve-only-slower? You have anything at
all on you in paper?"

"I got a number. Guy gave me his number to call if I needed
something."

"Let's have it."

He fumbled, found a matchbook, black with a white outline
of a gloved fist on the cover, phone number written on the
inside. I kept it.

"Another twenty bucks if you answer some questions."

"Twenty bucks," he grinned, whisper-shouting the words,
barely able to contain himself.

"Yes, another twenty," then, "Steve-only-slower, you got
any tattoos or scars? Cops check out any distinguishing marks
on you?"

"Yeah."

"Show me."

He pulled up his left sleeve. A sewing-needle A for anarchy,
three inches across on the underside of his forearm, black
ballpoint ink seeped deep into his skin.

"Anything else?"

He shook his head, took a drink.

"Hold off on that, I'm almost done. Do you know your birthday?"

"March 11, 1962."

"What's your middle name?"

"Benjamin."

"You ever had a job, Steve-only-slower?"

"Yeah. Paper route. And I worked at a hamburger place for a week."

"So you have a Social Security number then?"

"No. I used my older brother's."

"What's his name?"

"Jeffrey." Jeff Edwards.

"With a *j* or a *g*?"

"A *j*."

"Any other brothers or sisters?"

He shook his head, *No*.

"How much older is your brother?"

"He's four years older than me. He was my mom and dad's favorite."

"Were both you and your brother born in Detroit?"

"Yeah, both of us."

Birth certificate for Steven Edwards would be a snap. I could track down an SSN for Jeffrey Edwards, born in 1958, maybe late 1957. While Steve-only-slower had a bad post-juvenile record, the lack of an SSN would work in my favor to wipe his name clean.

I coaxed as much from him as I could, which was as much as he could recall through a fog of chemical damage. He'd never driven legally, had never been issued a license, had been sent to a psychiatric hospital at thirteen, had been shocked, drugged and strapped down. Like most any psych patient not completely delirious or catatonic, he had a photographic memory of his string of conflicting diagnoses and battery of forced medications:

Tranquilizers.

MAO inhibitors.

Neuroleptics.

SSRIs and SDRIs.

Haldol.

Prolox.

Thorazine.

Schizophrenia.

Manic-Depressive Disorder.

Disassociative Borderline Personality Disorder.

He was held, indefinitely, against his wishes – he was a minor and his parents wanted to be rid of him – and indefinitely for Steven Edwards came to three and a half years.

I was looking at Steven Edwards there in the dark, my own face staring back at me. Homeless, half-insane, dying proof, the existence of everything I was afraid of happening to me.

Steve-only-slower continued, "The hospital closed down and I didn't want to go home, so I ran away. I've been out ever since."

"Anyone looking for you?" I asked.

"You mean my parents? No."

"Then you're not a runaway," I said. I could see his confusion setting in, so I kept pressing. "How many times you been picked up, Steve-only-slower?"

"I dunno. Buncha times."

"What for?"

"Stuff."

"Stuff?"

"All kindsa things."

Figure purchase, possession, possession with intent to distribute, prostitution, evading arrest, loitering, public nuisance, vagrancy, lying to a peace officer, assault, public intoxication. No credit history, no driving record, good. Big jail record, not good.

"You sick, Steve-only-slower?"

"Need to hook up, that's all."

"You got money to do that now. What about those bruises and spots? You sick?"

"I get hives."

"How long you had those hives that you have now?"

"Dunno."

AIDS, hepatitis, staph, delirium tremens, liver failure. "Steve-only-slower, listen up." I crouched down low and looked into his eyes. "You get picked up by the cops, tell 'em whatever you want to. They've already got your prints, so it hardly matters."

I could see my words bouncing off his android glass eyes. I slowed down.

"But you talk to anyone else, if you go to a rescue mission or a hospice, you're Steve Carpenter. You're taking my money, so I'm Steve Edwards from now on. Your name's Carpenter. Say *Steve Carpenter*."

"Steve Carpenter."

"Steve Carpenter's a good guy," I lowered my voice, "Steve Carpenter was a straight-A student, trained for the Olympics before he got into an accident. He couldn't compete and he couldn't work. It's not his fault."

His glass eyes gave way to a weak smile. I needed him to erase everything and a good story would help him do that. I was being thorough. He wouldn't last a year.

"You're not from Detroit," I said. "You do not have a brother. And you cannot carry anything, ever, that says *Steven Edwards*. And when you feel really sick, you go to a hospice and tell them that you're Steve Carpenter."

They'd be too inefficient or under-resourced to check his records. He'd die as a quasi John Doe, and Steve Edwards would stay off the Social Security Death Index. I stood up to leave.

"Hey," he said, still smiling. "Could we be brothers? You related to me? I mean..." He trailed off, but the light stayed in his eyes.

"Steve Carpenter," I said. He missed it. "Steve Carpenter." Louder.

"Yeah," then animated again, rapid-fire speech kicking back in. "I think I was abducted. I know I was. They took blood from me, and I'm missing all of this time that I can't remember, and I think they used my blood to make a baby. I've got a half-alien baby. Fight that in court," and he let out a blast of laughter, then blank, then alert and calm again, all in the span of three seconds. "I was wrong. They cloned me. You…"

"Steve."

He stopped.

"Can you count backwards from one hundred–" he cut me off, started with *ninety-nine, ninety-eight.*

"Steve," I said, stopping him, "can you count backwards from one hundred by groups of *seven.* Can you do that?"

"Yeah." Pause, one, two, "One hundred," pause, "seventy…"

"Steve, we're not related."

Paying off street kids with cash, smokes and cheap whiskey, risking jail, walking into a squathole to inhale piss, bribing some kid who happens to look like me into handing over a name buried in criminal charges I wanted nowhere near me. Thinking it over, the physical similarity seemed minor next to the risks. I wrote for his birth certificate anyhow. I'm thorough.

For nine months, there was no one. I remained Paul Macintyre until a godsplitter warning tapped me on the shoulder, halfway into my second round at the Formosa. Counting the minutes in my car – twenty to get home, ten to leave a message at work, unplug the phone and tape heavy-duty garbage bags onto the windows to seal out the coming light.

Godsplitter panic cut up my memory and made me careless. I fished through my glove box for the film canister of painkillers and knocked them all back in two swallows from a cup of day-old coffee still in my car.

Empty stomach after two drinks, the dosage hit fast. Halfway through Hancock Park, my right rim scraped against a residential curb when my wheel became too heavy to steer and I felt the top of my skull trapped beneath a rain of invisible welding sparks, fifty minutes ahead of schedule. The Demerol wire-clipped my nerves, my arms and legs inert like the dreams where you can't run from the thing chasing you.

Tapping on my window. Flickering cherry light rebounding off trees and regal Hancock Park houses. Curtains slit, eyes suspicious, curious and afraid all at once. My last lucid thought: Pull my keys from the ignition so they couldn't nail me with a 502.

Paramedics peeling my eyes open and strapping a mask to my face.

My name is Paul Macintyre.

The hospital didn't detain me, but the cops were waiting when I was discharged. Along with a fine and community service, the judge sent me to counseling, a ten-week course with fourteen other drug-related offenders. We met Thursdays to share our feelings with a court-appointed Evaluator. Sharing our feelings included watching documentary films and listening to guest speakers – recovered addicts who came to share their feelings. We wrote lists – three things we'd rescue from our burning house, the three most important people to us, five things that triggered us to drink or smoke or snort or shoot, three happy and sober memories. And we took turns in the circle, sharing our feelings.

I compared the other stories, watched their eyes and hands while they spoke, tagged and numbered tics, fidgets, squirms, scratches and pauses. I clocked how the Evaluator reacted and when, snapped his notes with my eyes when I could. My turn came, I told the truth, that I'd mistaken the dosage. Then confessed that I shouldn't have had them at all, my eyes downcast and my fists clenched. I did *Contrite*. The Evaluator signed me out two weeks early.

I quit my job and moved after I burned Paul Macintyre's papers in my sink. License, birth certificate, Social Security card, diploma, rental agreement, credit card, pay stubs, bank statements and utility records. I bought baby name books and salvaged old phone directories, sources of infinite name combinations. I scoured library microfilm archives for news of defunct hospitals or civic record halls destroyed by electrical fires or ruptured water mains. I used two hundred sheets of blank paper, practicing new upstrokes and downstrokes, serifs and crossbars. I had five new names and histories in different stages of completion lined up for when it came time to use them. I owned thirty-five mail drops, twice as many ghost addresses and a tangle of double-intersecting mail forwards for all of them without a single written record for anything. I have a good memory.

The headaches kept coming. Raymond O'Donnell almost died, so did Barry Miller.

Do you know why you're here?

How are you feeling now?

Can we talk about your mother and father?

Is there a history of drug use in your family?

Dog. Rain. Trash.

Baby. Door. Lock.

With each interview I got better.

I used a San Francisco mail drop as a return address so I could put some distance between the old Steven Edwards and the new. After three months, I had a birth certificate, a Social Security number, and a California driver's license with a San Francisco address, all for a Steven Edward. I dropped the finals.

I made a replica of his birth certificate, down to the last detail, except for the spelling alteration. If anyone bothered to back-trace it, it would prove legitimate and the misspelling would look like a clerical error. The kind I depend on.

All said and done, including the Northern California address and minor spelling change, I was still left with papers for a repeat-felon-junkie-runaway-prostitute-street-hustler picking the lock to death's door.

But I'd do it all again, even if I knew the risks would be two or three times worse. Because when I came back from my last drive north, I stopped for a drink in a place I'd never been to. And that's when I met Keara.

SIXTEEN

They used a bag of cat litter to track me down. Sealed inside a 12×12×12-inch cardboard box, ten pounds four ounces, they shipped a dozen of them in a slow ricochet among their offices, knowing that eventually one of the couriers making the drop would be me.

Hazard flashers blinking in a Century City loading zone, I jogged inside to the lobby desk of the glass tower. The guard has seen me before. Not me, but a hundred other names just like me, guys with boxes and parcels and letters and fat envelopes in uniformed trucks and bicycles with nylon bags over their shoulders. All one and the same. It's why I liked the work. Always moving, never remembered.

"Need a signature from Suite 1154," I told him, and he waved me to the elevators with barely a glance up from the sports page.

Out the elevator, down the hall, and two raps on the door with no name – just 1154 – opened and went inside, and it took me a second to get a read on what was wrong.

"Help you with somethin'?" Guy on a couch in the front room, big guy, in a black sweatshirt and work pants, buzz cut, watching a game on a black-and-white pinhole television, he dug at his nails with a toothpick.

"Need a signature," I said, set the box on the desk.

He said nothing, just heaved the bulk of himself from the couch and walked through a door into the deeper office.

My scanning reflex kicked in, I measured the room with my eyes, counted the tables and chairs and wastebaskets and phones and which lights were about to die. Got a feel for the air, where it circulated and where it didn't.

Like some people keep glancing at a television when you talk to them, the way a certain flutter of movement pulls at the corner of their vision and they have to follow it or it won't stop pulling. Passing reflections in a peripheral window or the breeze rustling a newspaper on the edge of their sight. Same with me. Gotta know where I'm standing. Just have to. Count the flights up in the elevator, feel the speed of the cables and the gentle slowdown, keep my clipboard in my left hand, fingers hidden, package in my right. Eyes to my shoes so I won't see someone else's foyer when the doors open and not know the dimensions. I can't let that happen because if I see it and don't measure it then it's like someone flicking the back of my skull with their fingernails for the rest of the day. I'll have to go back and look.

That office, the numbers didn't add up. Wastebaskets overflowing, piles of half-open boxes, new office supplies and phone books worn with age. They'd been there a while, but nobody came to clean the place. The furniture was worn, but no pictures on the walls, no calendars. No name-plates, no desk plates. I knew what I was looking at and I didn't care. Laundering money, sports booking, importing God knows what, it wasn't my problem. So long as I didn't have to deliver any heroin or plutonium or severed hands or dead fish. Sign by the *X*, print your name below and I'll be gone.

Except there, I wouldn't be. Except there, Jimmy walked through the door with Fingernails, who resumed his seat at the couch, now behind me, between me and the door.

"Six of Diamonds," Jimmy said, grabbed me in that manly shoulder-backslap hug that men do, said, "The fuck you been?"

He was friendly, smiling, and *the fuck you been* could have meant either 'How' or 'Where' and it wasn't good either way.

He had his hand on the back of my neck, that way of looking like a friendly shoulder grab to a stranger but with enough force to let me know I'll be turning blue if I did anything but follow him.

The guys that worked the strip joint where I met Sudden used to call me "Red," predictably. When Sudden tipped them to my hand, they wanted to see, so I showed them, and some of them started to call me "Six," like it was a much more clever nickname. So, Red and Six quickly became Six of Diamonds, but usually just Six, for short. It never bothered me. Anytime somebody was compelled to give me a different name, I let it happen. That made a lot of things easier for me.

Through the labyrinth of gunmetal grey cubicles, more boxes and half-used furniture. A guy worked an industrial-grade shredder, pushing phonebook-fat mounds of paper through its jaws.

"One of those can take your hand right off," Jimmy said. "So fast you won't even feel it. At first."

I counted four other men, sitting in arbitrary desks and chairs throughout, reading newspapers. Back office with a large glass window and a door, Jimmy walked me through, two big men in suits stopped talking when we entered. The smaller one smiled. Tailored black suit with a bright red floral tie and a screaming white shirt. He's older, and aside from me, he was the smallest person I'd seen in the office, and the only one dressed like an executive instead of a labor foreman.

My portable two-way radio kept blaring out pickups and re-routing orders, like shattering glass in church.

"Put it down there," he said. The light bounced off his brown eyes in little white pinpoints. With the faint curve to his mouth, it looked like he was smiling, but he wasn't. I set the package down. The other man didn't move or speak. Huge and inert, he didn't stop staring at me.

"My associate," he nods in Jimmy's direction as he signed for the package, "speaks very highly of you."

I was quiet.

"He says you're a real self-starter. Highly motivated. A valuable addition to the team."

I tried to say *thanks*, but my mouth was dry.

"James, can you fetch our man here something to drink. We'll meet you outside."

The big, quiet man opens the door and the executive walks out first. Quiet Man nods for me to follow. I'm loosely sandwiched between the two of them, down the hallways to a door labeled EMERGENCY EXIT ALARM WILL SOUND but it doesn't.

Outside on a gravel rooftop, no rails, just the breeze and a brown ring of Los Angeles haze all around us, and we walked to the edge. I slowed down. The Executive kept ahead and Quiet Man was behind me, walking fast and not letting me out of his way.

My eyes couldn't measure the open space and it felt like I was spinning, so I looked at my feet, got it to stop. My radio hissed again.

"Turn it off," said the Executive. That same curve to his mouth, the same slivers of rebound light in his eyes. He turned away from me while I did so, staring out at the empty air just beyond the building's edge, two hundred feet above a steel sewer grate.

"I owe you a rather large debt of gratitude," he said, his back to me. "The State Department, INS, and who knows who else would have delayed the immigration of my colleagues for months, perhaps years, and at considerably more expense."

The fire exit door opened, I heard Jimmy's footsteps on the rooftop gravel. He handed me a soda, warm. I snapped the tab open, drank the thin, sweet-flavored tar syrup and had to choke back a ballooning memory of juvenile hall – Dad's chipped and scabbed fingers fiddling with his sobriety bracelet.

"No problem," I said.

"That's good," said the Executive. "I'm glad to hear it's no problem, because we'll be in need of your services again, very soon."

I tried to work it, figure out how I could explain to him that it was harder than I made it look, that I was going on a fraction of the information that I normally use for myself, that the risks were far greater when dealing with the State Department or the INS than with the DMV or a county hospital, and those risks increase with each attempt. I tried to keep it simple, but my thoughts ran rampant in every direction without the confines of walls and ceilings. The Executive turned to face me again, smiling, but not.

"We have a business to run here," he said. "By 'we' I mean my partners and me, and our investors overseas."

He took a few steps to the right, then to the left, back and forth while he spoke. I watched him pace, just so I could keep from fixating on the monstrous, empty gravity in front of me.

"We have operational expenses, production costs, research and development, distribution," he continued, then said "legal costs" and couldn't contain his own laugh. On cue, Quiet Man and Jimmy snickered. I took another swallow of soda and got more thirsty with it.

"But our chief asset," he continued, "is our personnel. Talent. Intellectual property."

He stopped pacing, stepped up to me, sunlight rebounding off his eyes and his nose an inch from mine. He had three thick hairs between his eyebrows, a flake of chapped skin on his lower lip, and he'd had a very strong mint, recently.

"People who know things," he said, "are our most valuable resource. We're in a highly competitive business. We can't afford to get sloppy with writing things down. We can't risk having names and papers and numbers and records lying about for our *competition*…" his eyes move in the direction of a distant siren, then back to mine, "our competition to get their hands on and use against us. Do you follow me, so far?"

I did.

"People like you, who don't have to write things down, who have a certain talent for keeping their records here," he tapped my temple once, twice, with a manicured forefinger, "are very valuable to my investors and me. Consequently, when we don't know where *this* is," he touched my temple again, firmer, "we have what is known as a security risk, or a leak. Some call it a 'brain drain.' And nothing scares our investors like a security risk. Nothing damages morale like a brain drain. That's the sort of thing we have to rectify very quickly. All sorts of people get involved. Public Relations," he nodded to Jimmy, "Personnel," he nodded to Quiet Man, "all sorts of people. It gets very complicated, doesn't it?"

"Very complicated," said Quiet Man, at last. "Very messy. It means we have to mop up."

"Exactly," said the Executive. "We have to bury a mistake like that immediately. It could be a media disaster for us otherwise."

He held my gaze, taking in my heat with the pit between his eyes. Without a glance to his watch, he said, "Goodness, I've made you late, haven't I?" He sounded genuinely distressed for me.

"It's all right," I said. "I've got a flat and my radio's broken. I just need to phone the dispatcher."

"Well, I appreciate your time," he reached into his pocket, pulling out a reptile skin wallet. "Orientation is tedious for some, but I rather enjoy it. It makes me happy to meet the new members of our team. James has an eye for talent." He handed me a sheaf of stiff bills. I didn't count them.

"I understand that you prefer your status as an outside consultant. For now, as long as you remain a valuable member of the team, I see no reason to change that." He turned his back to me.

"Don't be a stranger," he said.

SEVENTEEN

Keara. Five-foot-five in her bare feet, with almond skin that straddled some blurry border between sunshine and vestigial ethnicity, brown eyes. Her hair was a chaotic blast of auburn-copper curls with pale streaks spiraling out from her forehead and temples. Straight nose, almost pointed, and perfectly straight teeth behind a strange smile that stretched more to one side of her mouth than the other. I liked the way the leotard strap stretched taut, suspended above the pit of her collarbone. A dark pierce of a small mole beside it, cluster of freckles on her neck, like a star map, the slope of her breasts.

"My name's Keara," she said. She held out her left hand – clever woman, she'd written my order with her right hand. "I saw you at Raji's about a week ago."

I had been there – Raji's was a basement club at the eastern, nether-edge of Hollywood, and this woman had seen me and remembered me. I work hard not to be remembered, don't like it when I catch someone's eye. But I'm willing to make exceptions.

I kept my left hand on my pint, extended my inverted right hand to meet her left and introduced myself, *Eric Bishop*. Had I liked the band? Where else did I go? Where did I work? The same conversation kickstarters that men just can't do as well as women. Moments like that one come back to me, like when her voice or her face or her smell flickers in my brain, and I'll close my eyes and hang onto that flicker for as long as it lasts.

Business was slow, so we talked. She said Come back and see me tomorrow and I did. When I left at midnight, she stopped long enough for a kiss, and the next time I stayed until the lights came on and followed her home.

Keara went to change, said *Make yourself comfortable*. I opened a beer, sat down on her couch, a sidewalk throwaway leaking clots of upholstery stuffing, half-covered with a sheet. A paint-chipped window with four panes of glass lay flat, milk crates beneath each corner for a table, buried under a mound of fashion magazines, junk mail, nail polish bottles and an ashtray peppered with bong flakes.

Fine grey hair stuck to my hands and the bottle, then I noticed it on my jeans, recognized the smell of a cat. When I heard him yowl, I saw him in the corner of her living room, looking in my direction with empty eyes like chunks of glass. Looking at me but not. *That's Rasputin*, she told me later, scratching the side of his neck. *He was in an accident.*

Sounds: Running water (sink, shower, sink again), the scrape of particle wood drawers. The phone rang – 2:40 in the morning – once, twice, and on the third ring, Keara darted out to catch it, wearing a T-shirt and a triangle of red silk with shoestring straps, an inch-wide band of belly curving over the top of her underwear. *Hello...? Hello...?* She hung up, stood with her back to me.

Behind her, I slid my left hand onto her stomach, spread all six digits wide. I drummed my fingers, feather light, skin-on-skin count to six. Her hand on mine, matching me digit for digit minus one. I held it up, let her stare, back down again, brushing her belly. On the couch, she held my hand to her face, taking each finger in her mouth slowly and back out again. One, two, three, four, five, six. I couldn't tell if she was a freak or not.

Three weeks later, I was washing my hands in her bathroom sink when I fell in love with her. A shelf by her window, covered with a paisley kerchief – candles, a jar of bath salts and an eight-by-ten black-and-white print bowed inward from the repeated and prolonged assaults of bathroom humidity: Keara on a couch between two other women. She held a glass of wine and looked at the camera, a spark in her eyes and a Mona Lisa smile that was bigger in your memory than in the picture. I never asked about it, where it was taken, the occasion, who the other women were or who took it – ex-boyfriend or not, I didn't care – nor why she chose to display it on the wall of her bathroom. I didn't tell her how it cemented something within me. That being with her became as important as changing my name, stopping the godsplitters, or reading and learning whatever I could to stay out of a hospital, only I couldn't put a number to it, couldn't measure it. That wanting burst inside my head and inside my chest fast as striking a match, and it stayed. My heart has a mind of its own. I don't decide these things.

I stood holding a towel in my wet hands, staring at her frozen silver print face staring back between two candles, air-pulse flickering from my movements in the small space, when I heard my name.

"Eric, you still in there?"

In her kitchen, she was opening a bottle of merlot.

"I'm back," I said.

She was playing Dave Brubeck while she cooked. I recognized the opening percussion of "Take Five," the soft, precision drumming like grains of sand hitting glass, you had to listen for the shift from cool to manic and back, the first pulses of sax vacillating from menacing to playful.

"I like this song," I said. "I don't follow jazz, but this one is different."

She handed me a glass, said "My mom used to play this on the piano when I was a girl. I'd sit under the piano and watch her feet work the pedals."

Brain flicker slide show: I'm picturing her as a girl, then trying to picture her mother and brothers and sisters and the rest of her life before she met me, and the rest of her life now that she has met me.

I took a swallow of wine to loosen my tightening throat, then kissed her.

"Hey," she leaned into me, wrapped her free arm around me and put her face next to mine. "What was that for?" Softly.

"I need a reason?"

"No." She laughed.

"I need a permit? A waiver? There a form or something?"

"Stop." She kissed me back, and we stood there by her counter with the saxophone, drums and piano doing their cautious mating dance. She kissed me again and went back to her cooking.

Moments with her leap to mind when I'm alone. We were celebrating one night – she'd found a better-paying cocktailing job and done a week of work on a film set as an extra. Things were looking up for her, and I kissed her and put a small package into her hands.

"What's this?"

"Open it," I said.

Weeks earlier, I'd sat at the bar during her slow shift, and she'd told me about a woman that had come in earlier. Keara had been struck by the woman's perfume, so much so that she kept lingering just near the end of the bar where the woman sat with a girlfriend. Keara finally worked up the courage to ask her what she was wearing. She'd told me that story midway into my fourth bourbon, having smoked the last of a roach out back during her break.

When she opened the package and sampled the perfume on her wrists, she stared at me in amazement.

"How did you know?" She put her wrists to her face, breathing deeply.

"You told me, remember? The woman you met at work? But it was too expensive."

"You remembered that? I can't believe you remembered anything from that night."

"I remember every waking second with you," I said, and kissed her.

Memories like that made my throat catch. Each new detail I learned about her added to the bits and flashes that I remembered while I was away from her. Like when I was younger, that eager ache of knowing I would see Dad soon, when Mom said he might be coming home.

Apart from her sister, whom I never asked about again, she never spoke of her family. I wanted to know, wanted to ask her about school and when she moved and why she decided to pursue acting, but I didn't want to answer the same degree of questions in return. It's different with someone who's not writing it down, who wants to know because they do, and for no other reason.

Sometimes I couldn't sleep, because I wanted to tell her everything, but instead I'd hold her so tightly I thought I would hurt her. She never said anything, just moaned, quiet. I'd measure her breathing, count how many times she'd stroke my knuckles before she stopped, and then I knew she was asleep. I'd draw her profile in the dark, over and over, happy except for knowing that everything she knew about my life was fiction.

En route to Mexico, where I knew a place that stocked the drugs I needed, I had between sixty and eighty minutes before the buzz saw cut through the middle of my head, and I held onto the wheel trying not to roll my car and kill myself and

a hundred other people on the freeway. I gutted my bag –
notebook, change of clothes, toothbrush belched onto the
floor – for the bottle of Darvocet I'd stashed.

Over-Nite in yellow block capitals and Motor Hotel in pink
neon script atop an arrow trimmed with bulbs pointing to an
asphalt courtyard. I'd passed it before on this route, always in
the dark. That evening, I saw the blue background behind the
letters, clear and bright and loud, and the sky – almost black
moments before – shone like the still, Jamaican ocean. These
minutes of beauty, when I can see blue so easily, tell me I need
to get inside quickly, somewhere quiet and dark where there's
not enough light to see any blue at all.

In the office, beyond the pink Vacancy neon that would
soon make me squint, sat the couple running the motel. They
were old, watching a religious talk show blare from a black-
and-white television the size of a mailbox opening.

"Can I help you?" The woman approached the counter,
cigarette wedged between her first two fingers. The man, in
a cloud of cigarette smoke, remained sitting in an ancient,
leprous barcalounger, oblivious. He wore a flimsy, V-necked
undershirt and his legs weren't crossed so much as draped
over each other like wet seaweed. A cadaverous five and a half
feet of sun-weathered bone and nicotine stains. I didn't see a
wheelchair, so someone must carry him.

"A single room for the night, if you have one, please."

The ritual ensues: driver's license, credit card, license plate
number. I needed to stay for three days and I needed to be
left alone. But if I paid in advance and told them as much, I
might as well give them my real name and tell them I've got
a corpse in my trunk. Grizzled truck stop and roadside motel
owners can smell junkies, prostitutes and trouble in general
from miles away. Most of the time they don't care, unless they
think they're going to get saddled with a blue body in one of
their rooms.

"What time's checkout?"

"Ten ay-em," she said, the last syllable catching, and she heaved a brown glob into the wastebasket next to Seaweed Man.

"I need to sleep in, tomorrow. Can I make it for two, maybe three nights?" I do *casual*, hoping there's still color in my face. If she was suspicious, she didn't show it. She ran my credit card while I guzzled tepid water from the drinking fountain in the lobby. My mouth was drying out and it was getting harder to speak.

She handed me a key, a routine lecture on the amenities and rules of courtesy while I nodded, *yeah, uh-huh*, on cruise control. There was a 24- hour market across the street and I had to get there quickly. I needed tape – gaffer's tape, electrical tape, almost any kind of tape – and liquids, lots of liquids and something to eat for when I came to, three days later. If I wasn't accidentally dead.

Room 15. Light is the enemy. I pulled the curtains tight and sealed the edges with the gaffer's tape (hotel curtains can withstand a neutron bomb flash), used the tape to cover the bathroom window with a towel (I used foil at home). Do Not Disturb hung outside, secured the door chain and propped a chair under the knob. Off with the clothes because I was going to get hot. Dug the extra blanket from the closet because I was going to get cold. Pissed, shit, emptied my guts so they wouldn't empty on their own. Four Darvocet, 100 mg per, cold shower, laid on the bed and waited for the worst. Right as the purple light was beginning to wash out the edge of my vision, I saw Mom.

She sat in the chair by the bolted-down television, looking at me. Hair parted down the middle, draping past her shoulders, blurry, green tattoos on her wrists and ankles, a pair of jeans and a Lynyrd Skynyrd concert T-shirt. It swelled under the slope of one breast, hung deflated in the absence of the other. No expression. Not pain, remorse, sadness or condemnation. Just looking at me.

My whole body seized motionless, I couldn't move, couldn't see.

Shower. Water was cold, building up around my ankles. How long? I got out, dried off with a stiff towel, the smell of chlorine bleach stabbing through my haze.

Bed. Television spitting blue noise, the light cutting through my eyes. I shut it off and the light went away but the pain didn't.

Someone knocking on the door, shouting a name. Mine, I think, but I couldn't recall it at the moment. On the floor, twisted up in a bedsheet, felt cold water soaking through the carpet at my feet. Something running in the bathroom.

On my back. Voices. Someone shone a light. My head was under the nightstand, I could see splintery stipples in the particleboard underbelly. I heard, *Alive. Overdose. Check-in. ID. Shower. Damage.* I asked if they'd seen my mom.

Vomiting black. A spew of activated charcoal and water pumped into my stomach, but it was supposed to stay down. Through the receding pain of the headache, I felt the acidic nausea that Darvocet brings on, like a gut full of hot snot and sandpaper kicking at the roof of my stomach.

I spent seventy-two hours in the hospital. The vomiting and dry heaves cleared my system but my blood pressure and temperature rode a three-day roller coaster, my head screaming every minute of it. X-rays and spinal taps yielded nothing (I knew this, couldn't stop them) and on the second day I had to be treated for shock. They forced my blood through my veins to keep my organs from dying.

When I met the Evaluator after the Darvocet OD, I'd lost six pounds, six that I didn't have to spare.

"Are you Mrs. Bishop?"

Keara had driven south, waited for me at the hospital during my third-degree with the Evaluator. I made it through the interview, the cold brick in my stomach telling me how much I wanted out, how much I wanted to see her again, telling me that I had to change names again, and telling me that I couldn't walk away from her. Not this woman, not this time.

"No," she said. "I'm his girlfriend."

The cold feeling in my stomach melted. They wheeled me out – hospital insurance won't let you walk out – and I climbed into Keara's car. The rental company had taken their car from the hotel lot, sent me a bill in the mail. I never made Mexico pickups in my own vehicle.

"How you feel?" She brushed her hand against my face.

"Better. Tired."

She pulled out of the hospital lot, headed toward the freeway.

"They said you were being examined by a psychiatrist."

"It's the law," I told her. "If they're not sure whether or not you made a suicide attempt, you gotta talk to someone."

"So, what, they'll lock you up if they think you did it on purpose?"

"Yes, they will," I said.

More than seventy percent of the Evaluators who handle people like me don't have licenses to practice. They're students logging in their hours to meet certification requirements. And like ninety-five percent of everybody else, most of them believe in astrology or UFOs or the power of crystals or crop circles or reincarnation or something else. And if these people think you're a threat to yourself or others, they're obligated by law to intervene. I haven't found a solid definition of intervene yet, but I didn't want to be within a dog's light-year of knowing firsthand. Yes, yes, yes, they would lock me up, Keara.

Staring out the window, wondering how I was going to tell her the truth, I took the cigarettes from her dash, lit one. They always feel so good after three days. A deep drag, I held it in for as long as I could. I was laying the groundwork for another change in my head, preparing to grab the next name in line and make Eric Bishop disappear forever.

In a rare moment with Dad, when he was home and we had a conversation of more than eight or nine words, he once told me, *As bad as somebody wants to hear a secret, that's how bad they want to tell it to somebody else.* Keara hadn't asked why I'd tried to make a surreptitious trip to Tijuana, why I'd rented a car while she was on a two-day shoot, but I knew she was wondering, and I wanted to tell her. She pushed a tape into the deck. I finished my cigarette and I closed my eyes. Neil Young sang "Sugar Mountain" while Keara and I held hands – her right, my left – in silence for two hours. I'd never done that before.

I slept at her place for an hour when we arrived. After a shower, I made coffee while she dressed for her shift that night. "Listen," I sat Keara down. "I have to move. No big deal, I'll be staying in L.A. But I have to move."

"Eric, sweetie, what's the matter?" She was fitting a silver hoop into her earlobe.

"There's something else." My mouth had dried out, fingers got cold. The truth, that everything she knew about me was a lie, could mean I might never see her again. "My name isn't Eric. My name is going to be Daniel. Or Danny. Daniel Fletcher."

I told her about the headaches, their history and that no

doctor could explain them. I told her about the overdoses, how nothing seemed to stop the pain and how I couldn't risk any records being cross-referenced, couldn't risk having any documented link between identities. I couldn't stay at a job where people knew me, couldn't stay in an apartment where my new name would conflict with my name on the lease. I'd have to sell my car and pay off my Eric Bishop credit card because I couldn't risk a collection agent tracking me down. I didn't tell her about Jimmy and the Business. I didn't tell her about the Executive.

I pointed out her balcony window.

"See that building there?" I said. "There's a vacant lot behind it. That's where I live." I explained that I used that lot's street number for Eric Bishop's address, but had a forwarding request at the post office that routed my mail to a drop in Pasadena.

And I told her that she was the only person in the world who would know me as both Eric Bishop and Danny Fletcher, if she wanted to.

"And if you really want to know," I said, "and it matters to me that you do, my real name is Johnny." I hadn't said that name out loud, on purpose, in years.

Her eyes were wet. She forgot about getting dressed.

"Johnny? That's your real name?" she whispered.

"John Vincent. After my dad, John Dolan Vincent. I'm John Vincent Jr."

She wrapped around me, hot tears on my neck and I couldn't understand why she was crying if she wasn't hurt or angry. But the cold left me, and it hasn't been back since.

"Johnny," she whispered again, in my ear.

"But please, don't call me that. Please call me Daniel. It's very important that you never call me John."

"I'll call you Johnny very quietly, when nobody's around. Okay?" She squeezed again. I had no words.

"I have to get ready to go, sweetie," she said. "Are you going to stay?"

"I'll be here," I said.

When she left, she kissed me and said, "I've been shopping, so there's plenty of food. Please eat something, Mr. Fletcher," and smiled.

"I will."

"And rest." She leaned in and whispered, "Because when I come home, I want to talk to Johnny."

I ate, poured a glass of bourbon and played "Sugar Mountain" over and over, smiling alone in the dark.

EIGHTEEN

The dispatcher relayed a message from Keara to me while I was making a delivery to Ventura. I worked a lot of courier and driving jobs. New identities with clean DMV records and short résumés made them ideal. I called her from a lobby phone after making a drop.

"Hey," her voice sounded thrashed, 976-bedroom rasp about to crack.

"What's wrong?"

"They're kicking me out," she said. "The neighbors have been complaining."

"About you?"

Someone in a truck had been blaring the horn and shouting outside her complex one night. The neighbors thought it was her name being shouted, and when a used spark plug took out a tenant's front window after a second horn-blowing incident, the manager called the cops and gave Keara her thirty days – a pink A4 sheet, Notice To Vacate The Premises, pinned to her door while she slept.

"Sarah's helping me pack. I'm moving into her place this weekend." I'd met Sarah once, a cute redhead she knew from her previous cocktailing job. She let Keara register her car in Sarah's name. Keara's driving record left her with horrible insurance rates, she told me.

"Slow down," I said. "You've got a month to find a place and pack. I'll be there tonight and we can talk. You can contest the eviction. It won't hold and you won't pay a dime in rent while it's in dispute."

"No, Eric. I want out of here. I don't want to deal with any of it."

I'd already paid for two previous broken windows, one on her apartment and another on her car. I kept telling her to park closer to her complex, but she insisted that she could never find a spot when she came home late. Each time, nothing had been stolen but both events filled her with a paralysis, a hopelessness out of proportion to the damage. The fearless woman I was contemplating going clean for would retract, become inert for a whole day before resuming her old persona. I kept saying *This is Los Angeles, this happens to everyone*, but I was wasting my time.

A flattened cardboard box fixed in place with duct tape covered Mrs. Phelps's downstairs window. She smoked, wearing a pink bathrobe at her open front door, a talk show blaring from the television inside. "You the one with the horn?" she barked. I walked past her, eyes straight ahead.

Keara's apartment was directly above. She and Sarah had consolidated her belongings into boxes – music, books, toiletries, makeup, cleaning supplies, dishes, cutlery, pans and miscellaneous effects (*junk* written in red marker), and three plastic bags of clothes and linens. Anything non-functional, aesthetic, she had carefully placed into another box already in Sarah's Volvo: rolled-up posters (Van Gogh, Kahlo, the Ramones), paisley blankets she had tacked to her walls, candles of sandalwood, jasmine, sage, rose. She owned less than I did, because of my behemoth reference library that I'd culled from a thousand yard sales, junk stores, and used book dealers – Bibles, out-of-state phone books, expired medical references and outdated engineering texts came cheap. I read a lot. Keara's ten boxes and six bags of personal possessions looked like a life in microcosm, a core sampling of accumulated strata salvaged in haste. Rasputin yowled, confused by the presence of three distinct voices.

"Sarah's in the shower." Keara handed me a joint, said, "We're going to take my stuff to her place, get some Indian food. She brought me a housewarming present, too," and tossed me a small tin of throat lozenges. That's what it said on the outside. Inside, half a gram of coke in a brown vial, and nineteen pills, cream-yellow tablets with a butterfly puncture. Valium, 5 mg.

"Can they deliver?" Sarah asked. She opened the bathroom door, expelling its bayou steam into the bedroom. Wrapped in a towel, she ran a comb through her hair, sat down on the bed.

"I'll check," said Keara. "I'm not paying this phone bill, might as well get some use out of it," and left the room.

"My turn," Sarah said, eyeballing the joint.

"Here," I tried to hand it to her.

"My hands are wet."

I started to put it to her lips for her, but it died. It wasn't until after I'd fished out my lighter and held the joint back to her that I caught myself using my left hand. She leaned in to take a pull, her lips grazing my left thumb and forefinger and I snapped my lighter, held it for her.

And that was our position – Sarah's towel draping looser, looser, Sarah not using her wet hands to close it – when Keara returned with a door-hanger delivery menu.

"Go easy on that, you two," was all she said, reaching for the phone.

Guys write about this stuff, lie about this stuff. I should have seen it coming but I'm slow sometimes. I never asked Keara if they planned it, not wanting to press my luck. We never left that night, or the next day. I called in sick. We never slept. And when Sarah had to leave for her shift the next afternoon, Keara and I used the Valium to come down, finished the leftovers and slept.

"Maybe you and I should find a place together." She smiled, put her head on my chest. I was looking for the compliment in her words, certain it was there but addled from twenty hours of Keara and Sarah naked, eating take-out Indian and Mandarin, the three of us crammed into Keara's shower, on the bed, the living room floor.

"Definitely," I said. "We should definitely do that."

I enjoy a certain feeling of new freedom after each change, each time I crawl out of that small airless box and breathe again. I have a clean name and a clean start. Then the rabbit-reflex tension returns on day twenty-two, like I could set my watch by it. I wonder if someone's on to me, a subtle paranoia that a coke habit only encourages, and it's worse with each passing day. I squint, glance over my shoulder when someone asks the time. Look for vans, delivery services – flowers, parcels, plumbing or electrical repair – stop at a pay phone and call the 800-number painted on the side. If I get a dead connection, I'm going to run. Disappear. That's what I tell myself. Then I start seeing blue and the cycle starts all over again.

I held Rasputin in my lap, the room quiet and lightless when a knock at the door kicked the *disappear* wheels in my head into high gear. Through the peephole lens, the Executive's bloated, fish-eye cartoon face stared back.

"Yeah?" through the door, fire-code sturdy but it seemed so thin right then.

"Conference," he said, " I need some face time with you."

I sat in the passenger seat of a pristine Mercedes while he drove. "We've just closed the books for the quarter," he said. "In a manner of speaking. We've exceeded projections, and the investors are quite happy." He meandered the side streets, so far not going anyplace I didn't recognize. I knew my way around.

"Costs are down. Revenues are up. Market share is increasing and we're penetrating new territories each week. Everyone, including you, is up for a bonus. We're putting together a bonus plan. Nothing on paper, you'll just have to take our word for it. But right now, there's a few more board members I need your help getting into the country. I can count on you, can't I? It will count as overtime pay."

"Okay."

"Where you been?"

"I don't know what you mean."

He turned his head, eye contact for the first time during the drive, looking at me and not the brake lights in front of him. I must have flinched or something because he stopped, just short of plowing into a BMW with a BABY ON BOARD sign in its rear window, but he never took his eyes from me.

"I never repeat myself," he said.

"I was sick," I told him.

"Sick? Sick, how?"

"I have migraines. Jimmy told you, didn't he?"

Trying to piece it together for him, but it all seemed too obvious to put into words.

"They hit me every few months. I'm never certain, the intervals vary. I usually end up in the hospital."

"Then get something for them."

"That's the problem. The doctors won't give me anything, they don't believe me. And it's the stuff I get on my own that puts me there."

"We couldn't find you."

"I change everything. Phone, my name. You know that. That's why you hired me. I changed my address." I'd given them a mail drop for messages, instead of the apartment. I wanted to protect Keara, but one secret confessed only made more room for the other.

"I'm aware that you changed your address. I picked you up, remember?"

"I don't understand. I'm still here, you knew how to find me, I'm still doing the work. I'm keeping in touch."

The Executive pulled to a curbside parking meter and stopped, and when I looked outside I saw the broad, neon-trimmed windows of the bar where Keara had just begun working. I could see her through the window, and so could he. All at once, I felt like I was on that rooftop again. Should have known.

"So, 'Fletcher' is it? For this week? Well, Mr. Fletcher, I get headaches, too," he said. "Stress and worry, night and day. Mergers and acquisitions. Liquidations. Hostile takeovers. Will we make our numbers? Will the deal go through? Is our competition growing? Mr. Fletcher, I get headaches like you wouldn't believe."

The drone of an LAPD helicopter dopplered low overhead, and as the rotor-thumping faded, the Executive looked upward.

"Hostile takeovers," he said again.

My eyes were on Keara and I thought my chest would burst. In my head I went back to jail, squaring off with Dad. Freezing up because I was dead, or Keara was, if I did otherwise.

"I've learned that I can't do anything about them," he continued, "so believe me, I understand where you're coming from. I finally learned to attack the problem at its source – stress. If I get rid of the cause of my stress, I don't have any more headaches. Am I getting through to you?"

"I told Jimmy as soon as I was discharged," my words gush out almost ahead of my own breath. "I had everything set up and gave him all of my new information, along with that last passport you needed."

"Do it beforehand, next time."

I listened to eleven seconds of traffic drone while watching Keara.

"You understand this isn't the sort of errand I would normally do myself," he said. "Usually when there's a personnel problem of this kind to sort out, I have people that do it for me. But I'm hoping that's not necessary, in your case."

"I appreciate that."

"Can I give you a lift back?"

"No, thanks."

"Buy yourself a drink, then." He handed me a crisp hundred. "And don't be a stranger."

I stepped out of his car, closed the door behind me, and heard the electrohum of the lowering window.

"Got it?"

"Got what?"

"That's the second time I've said 'Don't be a stranger,' and I told you I hate repeating myself." Then, "There won't be a third time."

In a blink, he'd merged with the traffic and vanished.

Dr. Carlisle –

Had to leave early today. Called multiple clinics in Long Beach/South Bay. Most could track visits back to twelve months ago, but no D. Fletcher turned up. Still waiting on call backs from others. I doubt we'll find anything, regardless. These places are always overloaded and short-handed, and files go missing quite often, so I'll be very surprised if we find anything.

I've attached time sheets for the department and a schedule of upcoming performance reviews.

Rgds,
– E

P.S. One of the clinics said the Soc. Sec.# was showing up as issued in Oregon less than a year ago. I double-checked that I had the correct number, so this didn't make sense. I'll ring the Trauma Center admission desk before I leave and see if they can verify the number.

JOHN VINCENT

NINETEEN

Maybe you were born with some strange abnormality, like a six-fingered left hand. Maybe some doctors think that it's linked to some organic brain disorder but they can't be certain, and your parents could never afford to find out.

Maybe you walked late, talked late, were held back as a child and diagnosed as retarded. Maybe you've got some strange aptitude for numbers that offsets that diagnosis. Maybe, just maybe, you get hit with a screaming skullache every six months that doesn't register on any X-ray, blood test, MRI or spinal tap, and the pain is so bad you almost kill yourself trying to stop it. Maybe if they see you more than once, they'll quit believing you when you tell them it was an accident. You go by your real name, they find your medical records and decide since you've done this before you're a *danger to yourself*. And the State can shoot you full of Thorazine and children's TV and puzzles in a room full of mumbling, head-bobbing, grown men and women who can't wipe their own asses, if the State thinks it's the same you over and over again. And the State decides how long you stay and when you leave, and they can make up the rules as they go.

Trying to pass yourself off as a twenty-one-year-old dead baby to some bored civil clerk is going to get you sent down to where there's no sunlight, no God, and no clocks.

So you learn to do it all, learn the ins and outs of the System, learn how to forge some pieces and learn how to have the others certifiably issued from a civic authority so the old you can disappear.

The Social Security Administration wants a driver's license, and wants to know why I don't have a number yet.

I worked at my father's shop until a few years ago. I never had my own paycheck.

I've been in jail.

I been living overseas with relatives. I just moved back, my passport's being renewed, but I have this. Trifold international driver's license, two hours, eighteen minutes.

I bring a birth certificate and a work ID to the DMV. They want a Social Security number and want to know why I don't have a driver's license already.

I been living overseas with relatives. I just moved back, my passport's being renewed, but I have this.

I've been in jail.

It was revoked after a DUI in Arizona, four years ago. SR-22, ninety minutes.

I've lived in New York my whole life.

I own stacks of blank 1040s, W4s, baptismal certificates, time cards, thirty-five mail drops, three typewriters, résumé paper, large vintage books, correction fluid and strips, rollers, seals, laminating machine, four-in-one- exposure passport camera, surgical gloves and vintage fountain pens.

I subscribe to magazines, rent videos and check out library books to correspond to fictitious interests. I don't register to vote and I don't sign petitions. I stay out of every municipal database that I can.

Yes, I'm paranoid. But I'm a walking assemblage of federal offenses, outstanding bench warrants and psychiatric referrals. My paranoia is greater than the sum of its parts and, because of that, I am free to come and go.

I'll pause between steps, admire the work, watch the pieces fuse together in front of me or in my head. Clean the table, do a line, another, then another, then another, lay them out in front of me and admire a job well done, though not yet finished. Birth certificate. Work ID. Security badge. Baptismal certificate. Social Security number. Address. Driver's license. Bank account. Secured credit card. The economy's good right now, and credit cards have been easier to get for the past couple of years.

That last overdose? Not me. That last psychiatric referral? Not me. Failed drug test? Lost job? Not me, not me, not me, not me. You must have me mistaken for somebody else.

I'm not scared of being caught. I'm scared of being caught twice. Maybe once, a doctor won't believe me and I'll go down for seventy-two hours and the State will keep me off the streets and out of harm's way and save me from myself for three days. But I go down a second time and some clip-on-badge clerk will match one name to another and the domino-chain of whispered rumors and palmed favors ricochets from a county holding cell to Jimmy's boss and I won't live to see those seventy-two hours end.

Maybe Jimmy gets nailed, or someone he works for does. Nobody's taking the heat for anyone else, so the giant blame-boulder starts rolling, fingers pointing downhill, naming names and gunpowder-pelt bartering for shorter sentences and better meals in lockup until somebody says, *Red-haired guy with a fucked-up hand.*

House of cards and vicious circle at the same time, a crapshoot that shoots back if I slip just once. All because I made an exception for Jimmy, so I could rationalize the exception I made for Keara that I would willingly do again and again, even with God's own gun to my head telling me to do otherwise.

"Are you presently employed?"

"Yeah."

"What do you do?"

"I work for a messenger service."

"How do you like it?" The Evaluator is pulling back, lightening the tone after digging too deeply. Wants me to breathe easy, trust him. Holding very still so I'll move closer.

"It's cool. I drive my own car, have flexible hours. Gets me outside."

And I can do it with a virgin driving record, which I get with every change but which makes for ugly insurance premiums.

"Is it ever stressful?"

"Sometimes. Traffic or a rush delivery can make it tough, but it beats working in an office."

"How do you sleep?"

"On my side."

"How *well* do you sleep?"

Light sleeping, insomnia and oversleeping are big depression indicators, which leaves scarce room for the average person to deviate from the recommended seven-point-five hours of sleep without being tagged as a suicide risk. I can't remember my last full night of sleep, can't recall not needing six cups of coffee and a rail to wake up, but the Evaluator doesn't need to know that. Ice on my eyes in the morning, eye drops, iron and B-vitamin supplements keep the pallor and bags away.

"It takes me a while to pass out sometimes. But once I'm under, there's no waking me up."

"And how early do you wake up?"

"On a workday, about six."

"Before your alarm?"

"Rarely."

"So," he starts a new sheet of paper, and here it comes, "can we talk about your hand?"

"You noticed that?"

The Evaluator laughs, says, "I had to re-read the report, then I saw you doing those tricks earlier. Hard to miss."

I don't say anything – smile, nod, wait – let him fill the pause.

"That thing with the cigarette," the Evaluator continues, "that have anything to do with your hand?"

"My dad bought me a magic book when I was a kid." The first of only

two complete truths I tell him. "Said I should take advantage of what God gave me, maybe I could do something so that the kids at school wouldn't hassle me." I'm calmer, my front dropping for a moment.

"But nothing ever came of it?"

"That's right." I feel the pause, so I give him one last piece of truth. "After a few years, people telling me to learn magic or play guitar or something pissed me off worse than the ridicule. Most of the teasing stopped after grade school, but then grown men and women keep saying *I'll bet you could be a fantastic musician with that, or something*. They think they're being helpful."

"And they're not?"

"Nah. They're being charitable, which means they're looking down their nose at me. It gets old."

"Does anyone say anything about it now? Besides the unsolicited advice?"

"Like I said, mostly when I was a kid. Now and then somebody says something rude. Bound to happen."

"How does it make you feel?"

"Pisses me off." Another down gaze, clench my fists, unclench. Show him *angry but subdued*.

"What do you do?"

"Walk away. Ignore them. Not worth getting sued or arrested over." Show him that I know right from wrong, that I act from reason and not impulse.

"Danny, did you suffer any kind of injury to your head when you were younger?"

"I was in a motorcycle wreck a few years ago. I broke my hip socket and fractured my wrists. Got a concussion, but didn't fracture my skull."

"A few years ago? Before the first migraine?"

"Yeah. Before the first one."

"Other than the concussion, you've had no other physical head trauma that you know of?"

"That's right."

He's not supposed to lead my answers like that. He's been at this too long to be an amateur, so he's slipping, showing his agenda.

"Danny, I know we covered this earlier, but I still need to ask you specifically, have you ever thought about killing yourself?"

It takes years of practice for an Evaluator to ask this casually, without a hint of emotion.

"Nope. Not a chance."

"Has there been any incidence of suicide in your extended family?"

"None." Dad, maybe. He put a bottle to his head and pulled the trigger for years. That's what the Evaluator wants to know. Depression's hereditary.

"And aside from high school and our visit today, have you ever seen a psychiatrist?"

"No, I haven't."

"How about any other kind of counselor or mental health professional?"

"No. I mean there was a little therapy after the concussion. It was all tests though, she didn't ask about my childhood or drugs or anything."

The Evaluator places his pen down onto my file, folds his hands on the table in front of him.

"Okay, Danny. It looks like we're about finished here," he says.

"What do you think?" Do *nonchalant*.

"About your risk factor? I don't think you're at risk at all. Am I wrong?"

"No. I'm fine. Honest. I just want to get home."

"We'll have you on your way shortly. I should add that I'm concerned about these migraines you're experiencing. While they're not getting any worse or more frequent, there's no apparent trigger or source. They could be genetic – from your father – or long-term trauma from your accident. With many such migraines, the causes are never known, but if yours are serious enough to cause an overdose, then we need to look into them further."

"I'll do that. I'll take one of your cards."

"That's not what I mean. I think the headaches are real, Danny. Presently, you're covered through your employer, correct?"

"Yeah."

"I'm going to make a referral to a specialist, so your insurance should pay for most of it."

"Thanks. I appreciate it." Do *calm*. Do not do *impatient*.

"The blue color is strange. It could be optical trouble, but it sounds much worse."

"It's just my eyes getting sensitive. There's fewer photoreceptors for blue than for the other colors, so I see more of it, that's all."

He pauses, not timed, not calculated.

"How do you know that?"

Do *quick-thinking*. "Like I said, my dad was an eye doctor."

"Right. Which brings me to him. He suffered migraines and died of a brain aneurysm."

No, he's still alive as far as I know. Likely broke, or back in jail, perhaps once and for all. Or he's on the street. Maybe he's looking for me. Maybe I've passed him as he slumbered by a sewer intake with a one-hundred-ten-proof teddy bear.

"He was taking medication for them," the Evaluator continues, "but I don't have a history for him. His history would help you greatly."

"I'll track that down before I go see that specialist." Do *not a care in the world*. Do *cooperative*.

"Don't worry about that. I've already contacted my office. They should be able to obtain a history for him."

Do *panic*.

"It'll take a while," he continues, "but we can usually cut through the red tape faster than even a relative like yourself. It might help if we could contact your sister in Oregon, if she's the custodian of your parents' estate. She might have something that could help us."

Do *get out of here right now.*

"I'll ask her."

"Are you all right, Danny?"

"I gotta eat. I want to get out of here."

"Certainly. Can you tell me your sister's married name, though? Or give me any contact information for her?"

"Explain something to me, Richard." I'm doing *lost* it. "Where do you get off tracking down my dead father's medical records?"

"Danny—"

"I had a migraine. You said so yourself. But they stick me in here with you, a complete stranger, and I'm supposed to tell you about every drug I've ever taken, every woman I've ever screwed, and any 'episodes' I've ever had, dredge up shit about this," and spread my left hand out, inches from his face, "and relive the details of both my parents' deaths after I've had my stomach pumped, after I've been shocked in the chest, after I've overdosed, after not eating a thing after a four-day, godsplitting migraine."

"Danny, you need to lower your voice immediately."

Double-tap at the door, Wallace's simian brow ridge scowl fogging up the wireglass.

Deep inhale, through my nose, out my mouth, conjure up Keara's perfume, clench my fists, unclench. The Evaluator waves Wallace off.

"Danny, is everything all right? Is there something you haven't told me?" Soft, forward, sympathetic. "I'm here to help," he says.

The worst cards I've been dealt were from people helping me when I didn't want it.

"Don't help," I tell him. "More shit I do not need. Please write your assessment report and let me go home."

"Danny."

I wipe my face, surprised at the wet heat coming out of my eyes and trickling shiny down my fingertips.

"Danny, can you look at me?"

I look at him. "What?"

"Have you done this before?"

"I've already told you."

"Danny. You said 'assessment report.' How do you know what it's called?"

"Psych class. Junior college." *Breathe.* "All the case studies had them."

"I'm sorry, Danny. I know this must have been rough. I'll finish things here immediately. If you can wait here, I'll write this up and have your belongings brought back to you. I can get you a voucher for the cafeteria, if you'd like."

"I appreciate it. I'm really sorry."

"Don't sweat it, Champ."

He's gone, I'm alone with my thumping pulse and the phantom drone of the fluorescent tubes above me.

I almost wasted everything. I can be so smart sometimes. And sometimes I can be so stupid. Slide a chair back to the wall, scoot the metal table close and lean back, put my feet up. Watch the fish. They swim in a slow, oblong Coriolis circle, all the same direction, different speeds, different degrees of ellipse, all clockwise. Soothing. I close my eyes.

Sometimes I know things before I know them. Memories stare me in the face, one after the other, mute. The freckle-mole on her collarbone, the three on the side of her neck like three corners of a constellation. Her eyes, their color. Her smile, the way one side of her mouth stretches more than the other, almost staying still when she laughs, like it can't move at all. I remember the woman in the emergency room, metal finger splints and ring-stain bruise on her neck, staples running along the edge of her jaw, left eye socket purple-black and the white of her eye dark with blood. She mustered a smile for the nurse who brought her a paper cup of water. *Thank you*, trying to look grateful, one side of her mouth stretching into a smile while the other side couldn't move, teeth bolted together with industrial braces. She'll have to carry wire cutters in her purse for emergencies. *Thank you*.

Why did Keara put clothes on me, give me my wallet and keys after calling an ambulance?

Double Wallace-rap on the wireglass and I snap awake, the question from my half sleep hovering like a flashbulb afterburn. Door opens and Wallace says, "You got a visitor. Girl named Keara, someone named Jimmy." Said *Jimmy* like someone would say *asshole*.

Something's stuck, no room for shock or fear. The numbers aren't adding up, the waterfall flowing backward-wrong like an Escher print. She dressed me. Wrong wrong wrong. No need for that. And she told the hospital her name was Molly.

"What's she look like?"

"Cute. She your lady? Tall, skinny blonde. She got a sister?" Wallace laughs.

Hot-cold bone melting is back.

"Can I go?" I ask.

"As soon as I get the 'all clear,' you can go."

"Ask 'em if they can wait. Thanks."

Door closes and I'm awake, cattle-shock fear awake. Think. Think. Think. That's not Keara, but they want me to think she is. Coax me out of here. Jimmy shouldn't have said anything to him, but I'm glad he did. Think. She okay? Has to be. Else she'd be with them, and make sure I knew it. Can see the Executive's reptile eyes, no smile, if I close my own.

We're downsizing. We've decided to eliminate your position. Through the dead alarm exit to the rooftop. *Thanks for your dedicated service. Please follow me to discuss the terms of your severance.*

Now, I need those seventy-two hours that I've worked all morning to escape. My biggest fear coming true – what I've been trying to escape all along – is the only way I'm not leaving here in Jimmy's trunk. I should have threatened to slit my own throat as soon as the Evaluator introduced himself.

Where's Keara?

To: Brian Lomax, M.D.
Cc: Wayne Kelly, M.D., Ph.D.
From: Richard Carlisle, M.D., Ph.D.
Date: 8/18/87
Re: Suicide Risk Assessment of Daniel John Fletcher

Referral Summary:

Patient admitted to Queen of Angels Emergency Room on 8/17/87 suffering from an overdose of Carisoprodol. Chief complaint was a chronic headache for which physicians could find no basis. I have been asked to assess the patient on two fronts. a) validity of the chief complaint, above and b) the potential risk of suicide. Given the parameters, I have looked for evidence of a somatoform disorder and signs of depression (or a possible bipolar disorder) from both the patient's personal and family history.

Interview Summary:

See attached Mental Status workup. Following that, the interview was conducted according to standard measures, beginning with inquiry into specifics of the chief complaint, followed by questions including family, school and current employment status. Having developed a comfortable rapport with the patient, the interview probed more sensitive areas such as sexual activity, interpersonal relationships and drugs and alcohol. Further, specific signs of depression such as any past suicidal thoughts, family history, sleep patterns, drug dependency and recent life changes were probed.

Overall, patient shows virtually no signs of depression, chronic or otherwise, nor any potential accompanying mania. Patient is clear-headed, with a sharp memory, mild sense of humor and appears highly intelligent. He is currently employed in a blue-collar fashion and involved in a monogamous relationship. These factors most strongly negate the argument for depression. He shows no history of suicidal behavior (as indicated in the interview and an absence of any other medical records) nor has anyone in his family, and speaks fondly of his late parents (see below).

However, given the death of his father during the patient's adolescence, the death of his mother several years later and the distance (both personal and physical) from his siblings, I would place him at a high risk of substance abuse. He readily spoke of his drug experimentation, though I do suspect some malingering here, in light of the above and given his acquisition of a prescription painkiller and the inexplicable headaches.

Specific questions about drinking alcohol yielded benign answers that conflicted with the patient's repeated mention of drinking during the course of the interview. In particular, he was very quick to answer the 'abstinence question' negatively, when asked.

Regarding his polydactyly, I personally am not equipped to remark on organic mood or cognitive disorders that might accompany such a pronounced case of polydactyly as with patient. However, it undoubtedly acts as a stigma that could exacerbate his risk of substance abuse, above.

Further, his above-average intelligence, coupled with a body of answers so deliberately pointing away from suicide or substance abuse suggests a certain degree of malingering, as mentioned previously. However, given that the patient has no medical or psychiatric record, and has not requested additional medication for his headaches, I cannot make myself liable with any further statements about possible malingering on the patient's part.

Diagnosis:

Severe but aberrant migraine led to an accidental overdose of prescription painkillers. Subject is of sound mind and poses no immediate threat to self or others.

Recommendations:

Discharge immediately, though making notes in the patient's file. In the event that Daniel Fletcher is readmitted under even remotely similar circumstances, a detailed psychiatric recommendation should immediately follow.

– Richard Carlisle, M.D., Ph. D.
County of Los Angeles Department of Mental Health

TWENTY

"You're free to go, Danny," says the Evaluator. He sits back down, my file nowhere to be seen, his notebook shut. He hands me a card with his name, office number, and a separate emergency number.

"In the future, if you'd like to discuss anything else, please feel free to call me."

Face, chest, hands, pinprick tingling numb. No panic, no fear. Nothing. Try to picture my apartment, Keara, my job, the bar. It's like remembering scenes from a movie I saw a year ago. So this is what resignation feels like, a warm and weightless relief is just behind it, and I can have it if I want. Need to think, think, think, but my brain is cold.

"You ever play chicken?" I ask him.

"You mean with cars? No, never did that sort of thing when I was younger."

"No, I'm talking about pills."

He pauses, one eyebrow arched, waiting for the other shoe to drop.

"Usually one-on-one," I say. "Two guys face off, alternating Seconal or Nembutal, back and forth, swallowing them with whatever they happen to be drinking."

"Sounds dangerous. Have you ever played chicken, Danny?" He's measuring his reaction, staying in neutral.

"Alone, yeah. Plenty of times."

He wants to start writing again, but won't make a show of re-opening his notebook. He meets my eyes, clicks his ballpoint pen open and shut with his right thumb. Nervous gesture.

"The pain gets so bad that I don't care," I tell him, "So bad that I don't give the threat of death a second thought. I just start taking something, anything. One after the next in measured intervals and I figure that either the pain will stop or I will. That life-or-death equation is as simple as making change for a dollar. It's that bad."

"Daniel, do you think you might do this again?"

"Not might. Will. I've got six months before it starts. I *will* do this again."

"Danny, we can talk about this as much as you'd like. I'd be very happy to see you at any time, and I can work out an hourly rate that you can afford if your insurance doesn't cover it. But what I won't do is send you away with a prescription or green-light your discharge if I think you're a suicide risk. Is that clear?"

Need to hit him, hard. I cannot walk out of here. No room for error. Dig backwards, remember:

The undistilled fear I felt earlier when I met him, the shame of almost groveling, of actually apologizing to him later. Think of how much I hate my own fear and don't pull any punches.

"Pick a number."

"Pardon?"

"Pick a number."

"I'm not following you."

"Any number. The bigger the better."

Puts his pen down, shrugs, says, "Two hundred twenty-three."

"Two hundred twenty-three, two hundred sixteen, two hundred nine, two hundred two, one hundred ninety-five, one hundred eighty-eight," rapid-fire. "Serial Sevens. I could keep going but testing mandates that you always stop after five. Am I wrong?"

"What are you getting at, Danny?"

Pull the bowstring back, wait for him to move, show his Achilles' Ego: his work, his dedication, his long hours, to cling to whatever ideals he harbors or hide from whatever reality he can't go home to. Then I let it snap loose and fly.

"What I'm getting at is that I skated through your decade of expertise in half a morning. While I'm thinking about it, your shorthand could be more inventive, or you could at least make an effort to shield your notes. H is 'hand,' that was the first one I figured out. Therefore, *HS* means 'hands, static,' *HE* means 'hands, emphasis,' which indicates honesty, versus *HC* or 'hands, concealed,' which indicates deception. Am I right?"

He's still. He's feeling for the first time how one of his involuntary patients must feel, having someone look right through his eyes and into his brain.

"Those were easy because I spoon-fed you my Nervous Gesture," I brush my hair from my eyes, "and I watched you write *HN*. After that, your codes for eyes, posture and everything else might as well have been in longhand block capitals."

"Listen, Sport, this isn't a court of law. Double jeopardy doesn't apply here."

"There's more laws that don't apply here than do."

"Danny, if I have reason to believe you might hurt yourself, then I am bound by law to disclose that. What you're telling me now is enough to warrant seventy-two hours of observation. Do you understand what I'm telling you?"

His voice is droll, impassive, punctuated with the condescending, cryptic chuckle of the coward with the desk, the badge, the bankroll, the executive nameplate. I give him one more push. He won't be compelled to act until he thinks he's lost control.

"You're blind, Richard."

Pause, one, two, three. The Evaluator takes off his glasses in a practiced show of indignation.

"What do you mean by that?"

"I mean that you take your glasses off to look me in the eye so that I'll think you're being more sincere. But it's easier for you to hide that way because you can't see a goddamned thing."

"We're finished, Danny." He starts to put his glasses back on.

"It's the same thing you do when you have to talk about sex."

He stops cold, stands up and stares at me, or at least toward where I'm sitting, stares at my blurry outline with his blind, pinched, mole face.

"Sex, *Richard*. Sex, *Dick*. Molly and I fucking on our living room floor. And the only time you took those fish-eye lenses off during my entire interview was when you had to address the topic of sex, on which you dwelled for a proportionately longer time than on the rest of the questions."

His glasses are back on, the color gone from his face.

"I want to help you, Danny."

"Is 'help' being shot full of sedatives so I don't feel it when your unbackground-checked, pervert orderlies have a speed-jack-off contest over my face while I'm asleep so I can wake up with sperm in my nostrils?"

"Jesus, Danny."

"Spare me. Don't try to tell me those things don't happen. Observation, my ass. Next time I'll remember to rip the phone out, put a stop to some damned Samaritan's 911 call."

Up, he taps on the wireglass, gives a hand signal. Wallace enters, two hundred sixty very quiet pounds, the Evaluator steps out. Wallace stands by the closed door, smiling, his arms across his chest for three minutes of silence. When the Evaluator returns, he's flanked by two shorter but thick-shouldered men, nearly identical. Same height, hair color, mustaches, and khaki uniforms with Los Angeles County Sheriff's Deputy on their badges and shoulder patches.

One of them says, "We're the men in white coats."

I'm going to become a name on a file in a cardboard box in a moldy basement in County records, and my chest and stomach begin to warm up and relax, and I'm thinking *finally*, and it doesn't feel so bad, doesn't scare me anymore. So long as Keara's safe. This is what resignation feels like.

The Evaluator ignores the "white coats" remark and says, "These gentlemen are going to escort you to an observation facility. I'll speak with you tomorrow, Mr. Fletcher, after you've rested and eaten."

The equation's not right. Wallace can handle me. I'm thinking these guys don't belong here, and then I get it. Someone in the chain figured out Daniel Fletcher. And I think *what took them so long?*

One last middle finger to all of them:

"My name isn't Fletcher."

TWENTY-ONE

The door to the interview room is propped open. The deputies don't want secrecy here. The Evaluator and Wallace are gone, nowhere to be seen. A nurse hands them a yellow piece of paper, an administrative carbon triplicate slip designating me for a transfer to a County mental health facility.

The cop who said *white coats* steps up, gun belt at my eye level, radio at his hip stuttering garbled static.

"If your name isn't Fletcher, then what is it?" Don't know how much he knows.

"Doesn't matter anymore," I say. For once, not thinking about where my eyes are moving or what my hands are doing.

White Coats pulls out a field interrogation card, wants my basics. No more Daniel Fletcher. My real name is on my lips when a blast of hazy transmission hisses from his radio, whipcracks the side of my brain like a slap to an old television, and knocks a memory loose: talking to another cop on a Hollywood side street when my name was Paul Macintyre.

White Coats says, "Look at me. One more time, Champ, I need your name."

The memory, saying *Paul Macintyre* into a flashlight, starts the synaptic-domino reaction through my head, the heat-rush of putting the puzzle together like a flash behind my eyes and it burns all my resignation into a ghost.

"My name is Steven Edwards."

"What's your middle name?"

"Ben."

"As in Benjamin?"

"Yeah."

Their own checkbox procedure follows, the other cop steps out of earshot, talking into his radio. He returns, shows White Coats something on his notepad and White Coats looks at me, half scowl, half eye roll.

I've got a less than even chance that Steven Edwards, five-ten, red hair and blue eyes, age twenty-six, is already in custody or dead.

"Can you stand up for me, Steven?" The second cop is polite, because that's how he gets people to cooperate.

"You carrying anything we should know about?" Without waiting for my answer, he begins a standard search of my pockets, seams, waistline in case I cavity-smuggled a revolver into the hospital while I was dying. My fingers are locked behind my head and I don't remember putting them there, dormant reflexes waking up from a long slumber.

Polite Cop, he's gentle, brings my wrists down one at a time and I cooperate, feel the first nickel-plated cuff, then the second.

White Coats is back in my face. Raising his voice, getting tough now that my hands are locked behind my back.

"If you're lying to me now, I'm gonna find out. You're telling me the truth? That's your name?" His voice is the bark of a chained dog, thrashing against its own leash, wants so badly to get a few inches closer.

Not sure what he knows, but if I buckle now, I don't have a chance.

"That's my name."

"Did you bring any ID with you to prove that?"

"I came here in a coma, so it sort of slipped my mind." The hospital has my Daniel Fletcher wallet, but I'd rather he not know about that. Gotta hope White Coats runs a check on

Edwards before he finds my Fletcher ID. He's finished for now, pissed off but can't show it in front of three dozen hospital staff.

"Take this kid to the car," he says. He's keeping his cards close, doesn't say where they're taking me so I can only hope. I hate hope.

Any formal requests to have Fletcher, Daniel J., taken to County Mental Health have been superseded by three outstanding felony warrants for Edwards, Steven B.

Booking, strip search, surrender my boot laces, two and a half hours in a holding cell, low-profile reflexes up and alive. Guys mumbling to themselves or talking in groups, amplifying tales of street bravado, and I'm staying invisible, far away from anyone's radar.

Guard calls my name, "Edwards, Steven. Your lawyer's here."

Steven Edwards must be a serious wack job. They've got me a four-piece – wrists and ankles cuffed and locked to a D-ring at my waist. I penguin-waddle with four pounds of nickel-plated chains under escort to another cell with a bolted-down steel table and two benches. The deputy escort – four times my size, all of it chest and shoulders – leaves me alone in the cell, standing watch through a shatterproof window.

My lawyer, Steve-only-slower's lawyer, shows up, a court-appointed drone who knows my file better than he knows my face, but doesn't know he's never seen either until now.

I'm taking a calculated risk that Jimmy and his drones are rat-mazing through a mental health ward for a time before word of my transfer to jail catches up, and that I'm out before someone on their payroll takes a fall for a traffic warrant and pays someone to be in the same cell as me. House of cards. House of glass cards. House of razor blades in a slight breeze, and I'm standing under it all.

"Good afternoon, Mr. Edwards," he says and takes a seat, opens his briefcase. For the second time today, I'm in a secured room against my will with another state employee reading through my file that isn't my file.

I'm counting on the inefficiency, lags, paperwork that I abuse to hopscotch from one name to another to work in my favor just once more. Keep Daniel Fletcher's mental health alert a few steps behind Steven Edwards's warrants, get Steven *Edward* out before either Steven Edwards or Daniel Fletcher catches up.

"I'm going to be straight with you, Mr. Edwards," he says. "You're out of options. I have only one suggestion for you."

"Edward," I cut him off. "No *s*."

I hold my hands up to chest level, as high as the cuffs will allow and fan my left fingers.

"You've mistaken me for somebody else."

The lawyer didn't understand, saw Steven Edwards's name, stats and photo in his file. He knew Steven personally, knew with a long squint at my face and a second, then third, look at my fingers that I wasn't Steven Edwards.

"This is the strangest thing I've ever seen," he says. He could be talking about my uncanny similarity to Steve-only-slower or my fingers, but I don't ask. I don't ask what Edwards, Steven B., is wanted for, don't care.

He checks the Steven Edwards file for Distinguishing Marks, asks for my Steven Edward address and driver's license number. I give him my San Francisco address, tell him *I just moved here* and wait for him to run the check, knowing it's clean and that it will come back with my picture.

The lawyer pulls the few strings that court-appointed lawyers will pull, gets me back to a phone while he talks to the D.A., who runs a background check. Stay here as long as I can because it means I'm alone, don't have to watch my back.

No coins, I exhume Raymond O'Donnell's credit card from my memory. Picture the raised white numbers, say them out loud and remember the rhythm of the sequence. Call home, see if anyone picks up.

Hey, sweetie. I'm okay. They're letting me come home...

If they had her, they'd make her answer. She doesn't, so they don't. Call the bar, ask for Keara.

She quit today, said she was moving down to her sister's...

411, check for her name and her sister's. Greater San Diego, Leucadia, Del Mar, Oceanside, Mission Beach. Brick wall, brick wall, brick wall.

I'm sorry, sir, but there's nobody by that name in the directory listing.

Can you check under 'Wheeler?'

And the first name?

Brick wall, brick wall, brick wall.

Dressed me, moved to her sister's.

Close my eyes, see our apartment in my head, measure it out, think, think, think. Twelve-foot by fourteen-foot living room, painted the color of bleached bone with a ceramic tile fireplace on the north wall. The junkyard couch is mine, but the Mexican blanket draped over the arm is Keara's. I can't see that blanket in my head. Open my eyes. Payphone, steel table and shatterproof window. Close them, walk through the apartment but I can't see anything. In my head, our place is as empty as the day we moved in.

Sometimes I know things before I know them. Stitch my recollections together. Remember.

She hated her face. So much like her sister's, but not. Their eyes are identical, their smiles distinguish them more than any other feature. Andrea's smile is even, with the gap between her front teeth. Keara smiles more with the left side of her lips than her right, like the woman at the hospital.

You slam the car door, then remember your keys. The plane lifts off, you remember the coffeepot is still on. That wordless, bone-deep, quantum-second understanding where your whole body is shocked with cold static.

She hadn't been upset when I told her I'd fabricated my life story and my name and everything else. She'd been happy. Told me she'd lost her lease, soon after that. Brought a girlfriend home and had a party, just the three of us, and they fucked my eyes loose. Keara's name isn't on the lease or any of the utilities.

I'm cold. It's August, daylight fading but swamp-gas hot, and I'm shivering.

Job-hopping, leaving employers without notice to work somewhere else, she always had a reason. Said her driving record stank, so Sarah registered her car. Midnight phone calls and hang-ups.

Cold, cold, cold.

Someone in a pickup had been blaring a horn outside her old apartment complex. *The guy broke a window and the goddamned manager thinks it's my fault.*

Told me she rescued Rasputin as a kitten from a shelter. Healthy outdoor cat, until someone in a pickup ran him down.

Close my eyes and see the photos of Andrea and Keara. Relax, don't force the memory, let it bubble to the surface on its own. They're there, side by side in my head. Different faces, but not. I remember the woman at the hospital, and how different she's going to look when the doctors are finished. Keara's teeth looked so bright white and sculpted and perfect because they were. Cast porcelain from a custom mold. Threaded titanium mounts planted into her jaw – they won't change size with the weather, so they won't hurt – with the teeth screwed in.

I want to say *What happened?* but I know. Jesus God, baby.

She doesn't want to be found, wants to hide. Absolutely must hide, and nobody will ever find her because I taught her everything I know. She asked me to. Wanted to learn the ropes. Sometimes I can be so smart, and sometimes I can be so stupid. Can't feel my fingers. Stretch them out, make a fist.

I did some things when I was younger. Even after I stopped, I still went to jail. That lawyer, he took a set of facts and moved them around, changed their order for a whole different truth. That's what he does, what he's good at.

I've had a lifetime of practice doing the same thing. Don't know if I've got it right, but I want to because it means she's okay. It means she's gone and they can't find her. It means whoever she's hiding from can't find her, and the people she doesn't know she's hiding from can't find her, either. Neither can I. As long as I don't know, I can't tell anyone. It means she's okay. Can't describe what I'm feeling. Not that simple.

I've cultivated some bad habits, but trust isn't one of them. I'd sooner share a needle with someone than trust them. Then there's Keara. The one time I give in, I pick the most kinked, dull, rusty and blood-mottled needle of the lot.

Over the next eighty minutes, I show my fingers and non-tattooed forearm to three deputies, the warden who confirms the lawyer's call to the D.A., and, finally, the judge. Gavel, escort, holding cell, lunch – cheese sandwich and warm fruit punch, hot and turgid in my stomach – wait, wait, wait, another escort, sign for my belongings, changing under watch, three gates and I'm out into the late afternoon light of downtown. The tail end of summer as autumn approaches, thin clouds streaking the orange sky like flaming brushstrokes and the warmth feels like God's kiss on my skin and my eyes and in my lungs.

The longest non-godsplitter day I've ever had. I've lived my whole life in the last twenty-four hours:

Bedroom.

Hospital.

Psych ward.

Jail.

New name.

Crash survivor logic takes hold: *Enough of this*. I haven't seen a doctor voluntarily since I was a child, except as a scam. But maybe they have something new, some new test or treatment. I'm good with numbers, but I've lost count of my 'maybes.'

My liver can't withstand much more. Neither can my heart – drugs, electroshock, hoping someday I'll see Keara again but knowing I won't. Not wondering what's happened to Dad or Shelly, not even knowing where Mom is buried.

Drowning man's promise. Junkie-gambler's promise: I'm going to get better, find help. I'm going to find Dad and I'm going to find Keara and tell her that she's safe, that she can call me Johnny all she wants, whenever she wants, from now on. The cold fist in my stomach melts away, gone, gone, gone. One of those rare moments when I can feel every cubic inch of my own flesh, blood and bone.

My name is John Dolan Vincent. I was born April 3, 1959, to John Dolan Vincent Sr. and Shelly Marie Vincent. I have one sister, Shelly Anne. I am twenty-eight years old. I have a juvenile offender record that has been sealed, no high school diploma and no college education. I have a rare, congenital abnormality: a fully articulated, supernumerary, fourth metacarpus on my left hand. I'm good with numbers, especially spatial coordinates. I have a photographic memory and a steady hand. And I have a drug problem.

I can't go home. The Personnel Department will be waiting for me, and it's a matter of time before they figure out I'm here. Back inside the station lobby, I make a pay phone call to the only safe passage out of here.

I'm waiting by yet another vending machine in yet another plastic chair, counting the minutes and hoping Jimmy doesn't show up first.

"Daniel," Dr. Carlisle holds his hand out, eyes squinted to a hazy smile, a mixture of relief and confusion. I return the handshake.

"But it's really not 'Daniel,' is it?"

"Steve, either," I say.

"I assumed so. What should I call you, then?"

"Can we just stick with 'Daniel' for now?"

He nods.

"I don't normally do this," he says, pulling away from the station. He punches his dashboard lighter, says, "You left your cigarettes. I thought you might want them."

"I do, but they're not mine. Thanks." I light a smoke, and Carlisle slips on a pair of sunglasses in the bright afternoon light. Flashback – I'm in another passenger seat outside another jail with my entire life inside yet another brown envelope.

"I'm glad you don't own a Ranchero," I tell him.

"Why's that?"

"Long story."

"I'll bet it is," he says. "Maybe you can tell it while I drive. Where are we going, anyway?"

"I'm not sure. Just head toward downtown. Union Station." Silence, then he says, "I normally wouldn't do this unless it were an emergency."

"It is."

"I mean life or death."

"Like I said."

"Some people were looking for you at the ward," he continues. "I'd seen them earlier at the hospital."

"I know."

"They're not friends of yours, are they?"

"No, they're not."

"You're in trouble."

"Yeah."

"You owe them money?"

"Far from it."

"You in some kind of witness protection program?"

"Not even close."

"Why don't you tell the police?"

"I guess I've had a different relationship with cops than you have. Besides, they couldn't help."

"Those people are above the law?"

"Yes, they are."

"At least I know you're telling the truth this time," he says.

"And how's that?"

"Because you're evading my answers. You're not so quick."

"Finally, you get something right," I say, and he laughs. Right then, I know where I want to go. I navigate through downtown, not quite as far as the train station.

"You were really impressive back there."

"I've had a lot of practice. Here, this is where you can drop me."

We stop outside a taco stand, busy with the bustle of evening traffic, Mexican dance clubs opening their doors, taking chairs down from tables and preparing for the night to come. A man with a baseball cap and a cowboy shirt, sleeves rolled down and cuffs buttoned in the heat, pushes an ice cream cart down the sidewalk. So much going on inside my head and out.

Carlisle points to the envelope.

"I guess your stuff found you. Small miracle."

Bigger than that. The cops must have taken it all with them, stored it under "Edwards" because my transfer order to County Mental Health never caught up.

"A young woman came looking for you," he says. "Molly. Presumably your Molly."

"What did she look like?"

"I don't know. She gave the admissions nurse a message, and I gave it to the police with the rest of your things."

The cold fist hits me again, I look at the brown envelope and inhale. I'm holding a live tarantula, a sample of human skin, freshly harvested.

There's no point in trying to conceal how I'm feeling, and I'm too tired for that anyhow. I know he means well, and I can't look at him when I think that. He did try to do the right thing for me, but he's letting me make my own choices now. The equation doesn't balance, so I need to make it balance.

"What I said back there," I say, my mouth suddenly more dry and nervous than it's been since I've met him, "I just had to say something. I couldn't leave with those people, and I would have if you'd discharged me. If they hadn't shown up, then it would have been different. I needed those seventy-two hours, the protection."

"And you gave yourself a detour to jail to lose them again."

"Yeah."

"Look, this is where I'm supposed to say that you can't keep running from your past. But I'm sure that sounds pretty weak to you."

"I'm way ahead of you."

"Are you?" he says. "So I'm dropping you here?"

"Do you think I'm still bluffing?"

"After the last forty-eight hours, you want to go to a taco stand?"

"I can't go home, you know that."

"You mean you don't want me to find out where you live."

"That's not it. Though maybe it's a good idea you don't know, in case someone asks you. Anyone does, you can tell them the truth about leaving me here. It's the last place you ever saw me."

"You need money?"

"I've got money. Not here, but I've got plenty." I get out of the car, and he calls to me through the window.

"You can still reach me at my office, if you need to. I've got an emergency number, too." When I don't say anything, he says, "You going to be okay?"

"I don't know. That's not important. So long as I know Molly's okay." I start to walk.

"Hey," he stops me one last time. "What's your name? Just give me that much."

"That would be cheating," I tell him.

"How about just your first name?"

I start to smile and suddenly my breath gets caught in a coming torrent of laughter, something I haven't done in a very long time. And I give him the punch line while I can still breathe.

"My name is John," and I think I'm going to suffocate because it's so funny. "I'm in the phone book."

I walk toward the taco stand, trying to breathe, with tears coming out of my eyes because I've never laughed so hard in all my life.

TWENTY-TWO

Behind the taco stand, through the ruptured chain-link fence. Twelve acres of packed dirt and weeds buffered by Los Angeles on four sides. Homeless guy sits on the ground, back against a wall, eating scab-colored chili off waxed paper, fished from the trash of a nearby burger joint.

This has been my address when I was Paul Macintyre, with a post office forwarding to a Venice Beach mail drop. I sit down on a patch of concrete, dead center in the lot. My first word was "light." *Ite*. I'm as far from a wall or a door or window or hallway as I'll ever get. Any kind of enclosure. Boundary. She interrupted me mid-sentence, across the table, and silenced me with a kiss. When was I last more than an arm's reach away from any kind of enclosure? I was on a rooftop. My eyes dart, looking for a foothold but there is none. Nothing to measure. I miss her. I know I could assemble the facts into any shape of truth I want, but I know the first one was right. She's gone, afraid of someone for a long time before she met me. She's safe, now, even if she's not here with me. I taught her everything I know.

Inside the property envelope is a letter, sealed inside an envelope of its own, neon-blue like a giant, freeze-frame spark between my fingers. She's been practicing, switching her up strokes for down and vice-versa. It's vulture-perched in my fingers, looking back at me. Any other day, I could tell you how many pages, just from the thickness.

Ite. Ite. Ite. Memories stuttering, my brain running and screaming. I tear the blue open. A blast of her smell, my present for her. *I remember every waking second with you.* I'll be seeing her face in every woman for a long time. I breathe in and I smell her and the warmth of God sings in me and the fading day spreads out like a cold sheet of light.

Close my eyes. My name is John Dolan Vincent, after my father. My first word was *ite*. Open my eyes.

She wrote using pencil, with handwriting she's already changing, telling me the truth. Puts the facts in a row to match the row I made, one to one. My truth is the same as her truth. She begins with the word that she's only whispered to me in the dark:

Johnny,

AFTERWORD

When I was very young, I used to disappear. Not literally, but saying *figuratively disappear* doesn't sound right. But every now and again, in the midst of a group – in class; on the playground – I would feel myself spontaneously detach from the here and now and slip across to, I don't know, somewhere else.

I've spent my life at the yoke of distraction. My mind has a mind of its own, so I'm intimately familiar with how my imagination wanders (*zoning out, spacing out, drifting off*, or whatever you call it), but these moments were the absolute contrary. My entire awareness would be anchored to my surroundings; I was wholly present, yet I felt invisible. The sensation was so visceral that, were there a drug to induce it, I'd be first in line for human trials.

Imagine being in the midst of your friends and classmates, in all of your shared humanness. Your memories and ideas are contained within a mass of spongy tissue housed in a shell of thick bone, itself mounted atop a scaffold of more bone that can move and articulate as long as the blood and oxygen keep flowing. Maybe you're waiting your turn at some game or you've been tagged out, but for a few moments, you're not moving or talking. The sun is warm on your face, you catch the scent of freshly cut grass, and that scab on your knee has been torn loose but you don't really notice. Then you slip.

Poof.

Your body vanishes from the scene. You can no longer feel your own weight, your feet on the ground, or your own hands brushing against you. The distinction between *you* and *not you* is gone; your flesh and blood vanishes but your disembodied perception remains, acutely observing everything. Your awareness is present, but the settling dust passes right through you.

This feeling of spontaneously slipping out time, out of reality, would come out of nowhere and every time, I'd realize I'd forgotten about it. I'd think, *Oh, yeah, this happens, sometimes...* Whether it lasted seconds or minutes, I don't know. Time passes differently when you're peering through a keyhole from Elsewhere.

If anyone spoke to me, or if I moved slightly, I'd feel the pull of gravity on my bones, the friction of my own sheath of monkey leather distinct from my surroundings, and I'd be snapped back to the present. I'd forget about that blissful, disembodied-but-wholly-focused stretch of time, like it never happened. Until it happened again.

It came infrequently but regularly when I was a boy; less as I grew older. Whether it was an ordinary artifact of a developing brain, a synaptic test-fire in a growing prefrontal cortex, or a distant early warning of something amiss, a failure to launch of a normal (read: statistically common) neural configuration, I don't know.

This involuntary slipping is almost non-existent in my adulthood but still, throughout my twenties and thirties, I felt slightly detached, a few beats behind everyone else. Imposter Syndrome, but without the accompanying achievement or expertise. Strangers appeared to be awaiting my response to questions they didn't ask, and I felt like *the new guy* everywhere but work: stopping for gas, buying groceries, or checking my mailbox. I was always on the verge of getting caught doing exactly what I was supposed to be doing.

With more time – a lot of it – I understood this feeling was common in varying degrees. Everyone has their own level of social comfort, but they all rest on the same continuum. Gradually, I gave less weight to others' opinions of me, and lesser still to what I assumed those opinions were. I came to own my strengths and be more honest about my weaknesses (a process, still), to appreciate the long-term ripple effect of my actions and behave accordingly. Belonging became less important than being genuine. In short, I became an adult.

And after years of being an adult with an adult career, I hit a crisis point. My whole life, I'd wanted to be a writer, but that ambition had drowned in the demands of the booming tech industry. My salary back then seems like science fiction to me now, a twice monthly reward for my complicity in the culture where every little thing was the Next Big Thing, and your work hours only counted as much as they exceeded your colleagues'. After a decade on the dot.com treadmill, I quit, hid from the world for two years and wrote the novel you're now holding in your hands.

The narrator, John Vincent, represents an idea that had crystallized after years of wondering why I felt so out of step with the world: anyone who says, *I don't care what other people think*, is lying. Either that, or they've never once interviewed for a job, gone on a date, been in front of a camera, stood before a judge, or otherwise been accountable to another human being, at the mercy of a person or group whose opinion determines their future.

John Vincent doesn't have the luxury of that lie. While he's a keen observer of human behavior in all its minutiae, Vincent only sees the *what* and *how* behind people's actions. He remains utterly guileless as to the *why*.

The first hardcover edition of *The Contortionist's Handbook* was published in September of 2002 to a starred Kirkus review but little fanfare otherwise, and with negligible interest from booksellers and distributors. Like most any writer, however coldly realistic and humble my expectations, I still harbored a sliver of hope for breakout success, the kind measured in royalties and reviews. I had hope, but I wasn't delusional.

A few positive write-ups appeared in a handful noteworthy publications, but sales remained quiet. With no takers for the rights, my publisher released the trade paperback version a year later. Some very kind words from Chuck Palahniuk (to whom I'm forever grateful, along with Irvine Welsh with the U.K. version) made for a spike in sales; soon after, I was welcomed into a writing community that sprung from his original website, and I still count many of the members – some of whom have built solid, even stellar, writing careers since then – among my very good friends. But this was my debut novel – a slim one – with a small, independent press, so I kenneled my expectations of wealth and fame. But I hadn't seen the letters coming.

Social media was barely in its infancy, so they first arrived at my publisher's office or the P.O. box I'd listed on my old website. There weren't many, but they came from readers who'd connected with the story. People who suffered migraines, struggled with addiction, who'd spent time in juvenille hall, who'd been tangled in the derelict psychiatric wing of our American health care system; people who'd been undiagnosed, misdiagnosed or otherwise mislabeled by people who'd held sway over their lives. All those things in the story that I'd made up in an effort to tell the truth – or at least *a* truth – turned out to be, for a lot of readers, *their* truth.

And there were the tattoos. Very few, sure, but when someone permanently inks a line or symbol from your book into their skin, your vanity is thrown naked into the daylight and rapidly changes to humility.

I work to be a better writer – and in some ways a different writer – with each story. It's been more than twenty years since I wrote this novel, so re-visiting it was difficult, to say the least. I can think of a different (read, *better*) way I could have (read, *should have*) executed most every sentence; given free reign, I might red-line the text into non-existence. And that urge to tinker, to obsessively look for ways to improve things at such a granular level calls for me to ignore the readers who connected with the novel *as I wrote it*, however flawed I may see it in hindsight.

Beyond its core social commentary, the *Handbook* was my effort to give shape to my lifetime of feeling unconnected, out of step, or otherwise completely alien to life around me. While I know more about writing than I did two decades ago, I still know very little about being a writer. I'm adrift at conferences and out of my depth on panels; I routinely stumble over my words when I meet those I consider "real writers" because I'm always the new guy. An imposter. John Vincent introduced me to readers who felt likewise.

I wrote this novel with the goal of being read, and the hope of being read widely. I hadn't expected to be heard.

Thanks for listening.

– *Craig Clevenger*

ACKNOWLEDGMENTS

My deepest and sincerest thanks to:

The original true believers, Paul Fritz, Becky Fritz, Shannon Wright, Charlie Wright, Jill Nani, Tony Vick, Rita Suddick and Jim Matison. I'm indebted to you all for, among other things, braving the first blind, wet and screaming versions of the story.

To Mickey Clevenger, Kim Noyes, Phil Clevenger, Todd Bogdan, Scott Krinsky, Damir Zekhtser, Jerry Whiting, Susan Marshall, David Marshall, Jim Lambert, Ray Bussolari, Cori Bussolari, Michael Herf, Chris Casilli, Wendy Dale, Kai Gradert, Scott Fegette, Dennis Widmeyer, Yvonne LeCroy for their invaluable support; Jon Gonzales, Javier Roca and Dorothy Eckel for being behind me from before the beginning.

To the bookstore crew – Jeff Seibel, Melinda Reta, Kristi Gardner, Peter Conover, Katie Heimsoth, Jason Wood, and Rayshaun Grimes for the support both on the job and off, and to Dawn O'Brien and her crew at the Mercury Lounge and the Firebird – Jacob Rama Berman, Jaime Bishop, Louisa Dale, Brad Gustavson, Chuck Haines, Jim Kallaos, Lynda Martin, Sheryl Schroeder, Layla Lynn-Winkler and Anne M. Yoch for taking such good care of me for so long; to Josh Bates and Eric Shiflett for those first celebratory pints.

And finally, to Jeff Agassi, Melanie Mitchell, Amy Stoll,

John Gray, Emily McManus, Tasha Reynolds, J.P. Moriarty, Scott Allen, Kate Nitze, Avril Sande, and especially to Dorothy Smith for sticking her neck out for me.

I am grateful to you all, more than you'll ever know.

Addendum to the above: this re-issue would not have been possible without the fine folks at Datura. Caroline Lambe, Gemma Creffield, Amy Portsmouth, April Northall and Desola Coker all had a hand in putting this novel back on shelves. Most of all, I'm indebted to my editor, Daniel Culver, and my agent, Sam Chidley. Cheers, lads.